SUMMERLAND

Hannu Rajaniemi

GOLLANCZ
LONDON

First published in Great Britain in 2018 by Gollancz
an imprint of the Orion Publishing Group Ltd
Carmelite House, 50 Victoria Embankment
London EC4Y 0DZ

An Hachette UK Company

1 3 5 7 9 10 8 6 4 2

A CIP catalogue record for this book
is available from the British Library

ISBN (Trade Paperback) 978 1 473 20328 0
ISBN (eBook) 978 1 473 20330 3

Typeset by Deltatype Ltd, Birkenhead, Merseyside

Printed by Clays Ltd, St Ives plc

www.orionbooks.co.uk
www.gollancz.co.uk

SUMMERLAND

Also by Hannu Rajaniemi from Gollancz:

The Jean le Flambeur series
The Quantum Thief
The Fractal Prince
The Causal Angel

Short Story Collections
Invisible Planets

To my mother
Mirja Rajaniemi
(1948–2015)

ONE

A Duel at the Langham Hotel, 29th October 1938

Rachel White flung the cab door open, tossed the driver a banknote and dived into the rain.

She ran across the gloom of Portland Place towards the gilded mountain of light that was the Langham Hotel. The downpour tore at her hat. Her heels slipped and twisted on the wet pavement. The raindrops tasted like fear.

Fifteen minutes earlier, her ectophone had rattled out a message: KULAGIN IN A DUEL COME AT ONCE. She had imagined a .22 hole in Yakov Mikhailovich Kulagin's forehead, all the dark secrets in his brain leaking out and washing away, dragging her twenty-year career in the Secret Intelligence Service with them.

She took the stairs to the arched entranceway of the hotel two steps at a time.

Stairs, marble floors, thick carpets, Renaissance pillars, ladies in ermine and pearls, spirit-armoured mediums channelling New Dead visiting from Summerland. She collided with a waiter and toppled a tray of champagne glasses. Curses and laughter followed her. Then she was through a set of French doors at the top of a broad staircase and outside once again. She stopped and breathed in the heady smell of roses in the rain.

A small crowd in evening wear huddled beneath umbrellas in the garden, watching two men. Both were in their shirt-sleeves and completely drenched, holding silver pistols. One of them, a fair-haired youth, inspected his weapon with the calm detachment of a marksman.

The other was Kulagin. His shirt was open at the collar and stained with deep, dark red along his ribs. His pistol hung limply from one hand as if forgotten. He saw Rachel and performed a mock salute, a mad broad grin on his face.

She hurried down. The duellists were getting ready again. Kulagin's second, a thickset man in a trilby hat, was talking to him, gesturing, pleading: Major Allen, the Service officer on Watch detail tonight. The Russian defector brushed him away and walked back to the centre of the garden, swaying slightly.

Allen touched the brim of his hat when he saw Rachel. There was a look of desperation on his ruddy face.

'What are you doing?' she hissed. 'Why didn't you stop him?'

'I tried my best, Mrs White, but it was too late. He insulted Mr Shaw-Asquith's poetry and then assaulted him. It is a matter of honour now.'

'It is much worse than that. If he gets himself killed and Hill's boys in the Summer Court pick him up, Sir Stewart will have our heads!'

'We might still have a chance. Mr Kulagin's injury is not severe, it is the third shot coming up already, and Mr

Shaw-Asquith may declare satisfaction afterwards.'

The young man had to be Julian, the eldest son of Sir Patrick Shaw-Asquith, the managing director of Baring Bank. He wore an expensive, fashionable waistcoat that imitated the coppery weave of spirit armour. A dark purple bruise marred one cherubic cheekbone. The way he stared at Kulagin suggested that no satisfaction would be granted before death.

'Major, I take it you will explain to Sir Stewart how either the son of his club associate or our best NKVD source in years ended up with a bullet in the brain?'

Allen raised his bushy eyebrows. 'I did not wish to attract attention. You see, we don't want the whole world to know that the Crown has something to do with this—'

'I understand the need for discretion, Major,' Rachel interrupted. There were a lot of ex-colonials like Allen in the Service, infuriatingly dense regarding aspects of intelligence work that did not involve torpedo boats or sword canes. 'You were right to call me. I will talk to him.'

But it was too late. A red-faced maître d' stepped up and lifted a handkerchief. Kulagin and Shaw-Asquith tightened their grips on their weapons, eyes fixed on the wet white cloth. Allen rocked back and forth on his heels as if he was watching a cricket match.

'We will just have to see what happens this round. Fair play and all that, eh?'

Rachel swore under her breath. Her mouth was dry and her stomach tingled. This must be how the field operatives whose reports she pored over felt when they had to make lightning decisions. She grabbed Allen's arm.

'Fair play can wait. Delay them. I need a few minutes.'

3

'But what shall I say?'

'Anything! Inspect his wound, make sure his weapon is loaded, whatever it takes. And make sure you tell me before they start again, no matter what. Move, man!'

She used her sharpest tone. It triggered some military reflex in Allen, who nodded stiffly and waved at the maître d', making a show about inspecting Kulagin's wound. In his thick brown coat and hat, he looked like a sparrow amongst hawks. Groans and boos sounded from Shaw-Asquith's side of the audience.

In the commotion, Rachel stepped behind a large rosebush and took her ectophone from her handbag. She shook out the headphone wire and screwed a black rubber bud tight into her left ear. Then she pressed one of the four preset buttons on the Bakelite device. It hummed in her hands as it heated up. She bent over to shield it from the rain and hoped the temperamental machine had stayed dry. A hissing noise was followed by the high-pitched, familiar wailing of the newly dead – sure to gather around any transmitter – and then she had a connection.

'Registry clerk on duty,' a thin male voice said in her ear.

Beyond the rosebush, there was more booing and jeering.

'Authorisation F three six one.'

'Go ahead, Mrs White,' said the spirit clerk.

'I need whatever we have on Julian Shaw-Asquith, right now.' She spelled the name out carefully. 'Any leverage? It's urgent. And what kind of poetry does he write?'

'Searching now. Please wait.'

It would take the spirit only instants to thought-travel to the Registry in Summerland and locate the information in the aetheric stacks – something that would have taken her hours when she joined the Secret Intelligence Service as a junior clerk at the end of the war, when everything was still on paper. Even so, the wait felt like an eternity. Her gut clenched every time a raindrop bounced off a rosebush leaf.

It was a relief when the ghostly voice returned.

'We do not have much. Mr Shaw-Asquith belongs to what the magazines colourfully call the Cursed Coterie, a group of high-born and glamorous young men and ladies. He has engaged in some indiscretions, including an affair with Lady Julianna Manners—'

'That's no use. What about the poetry?'

Suddenly, she heard the voice of the maître d' again.

'Gentlemen, take your positions, please!'

What was that idiot Allen doing?

'Fashionable, Russian-influenced, depressing, traces of Pushkin, although I'm no expert. "Oh Hell of ships and cities/Hell of men like me/Fatal second Helen/Why must I follow thee?"'

Pushkin. Russian tragic romance. That would have to do. Rachel yanked the earbud out, stuffed the ectophone in her handbag and ran back towards the duelling field. Kulagin and Shaw-Asquith stood ready, eyes fixed once again on the white cloth in the maître d's hand.

She elbowed her way through the crowd, tore off her coat, tossed her drenched hat away and shook out her dark hair.

The handkerchief fell. The two pistols rose in unison. Rachel screamed and lunged forwards, into the line of fire.

The gunshots echoed in quick succession, rapid and metallic, like two keystrokes of a giant typewriter. A bullet buzzed past her cheek. Another struck a flagstone near her feet, leaving a smell of crushed rock in the air. She slipped on the wet surface and nearly fell.

'Madam! Please get out of the way!' Shaw-Asquith's voice was shrill. Rachel ignored him and ran towards Kulagin, who stared at her, eyes wide.

'Yakov! *Lyubov moya!*' she shouted, in the best Russian accent she could manage. 'Do not do this, not for me, I am not worth it, I would just follow you to Land of Summer, please let it go!'

She flung her arms around Kulagin's neck.

'Stop this nonsense right now or the deal is off,' she hissed in his ear. 'And let me do the talking.'

Amusement dawned in the Russian's dim eyes. Hesitantly, he lowered his weapon and wrapped his other arm around Rachel. She nestled close to his thick body.

Shaw-Asquith had also lowered his pistol and was staring at them, confused.

'Sir, please let matter rest,' Rachel said. 'Please forgive my poor Yakov, he was not in his right mind. We quarrelled, and he was simply mad − your beautiful words must have reminded him of how I hurt him, do not hold it against him, I beg you. And now he is wounded, my poor Yakov, poor *zvezda moya* … it is my fault, my fault!'

She poked Kulagin in the ribs on the uninjured side.

'She … she is right,' the Russian growled. 'Sir, please accept my humble apologies. I did not know what I was doing.'

'Well, then.' Shaw-Asquith flicked wet blond locks off his forehead. 'You take back your words about my mother, sir?'

'I do.'

'Then, before these witnesses, I declare that I have received satisfaction.'

Scattered murmurs rose from his side of the crowd, but Shaw-Asquith raised a hand and silenced them.

'My lady. Your intervention was most timely. Would you care to join us for a drink as a peace offering?'

'I thank you, but I must see to my Yakov's wound, and ... other injuries.'

A camera flashed and Rachel pulled Kulagin in for a deep kiss to obscure his face. His lips were cold. The liquor taste was nauseating, but she held on until the crowd cheered.

The best way to keep the real story away from the press was to give them a better one.

She took Kulagin's hand. Major Allen ploughed a path for them through the crowd, holding an umbrella above their heads, and then they were back in the glorious glow of the hotel's ballroom, warm like summer after the garden's rain.

Half-dragging, half-carrying Kulagin between them, Rachel and the major took the lift to the fourth floor and escorted the Russian to his room, number 433.

It was a business suite, small but luxurious, with dark wood-panelled walls, thick patterned carpet and a mahogany desk. Kulagin sat down heavily on the couch next to the window, leaned back and looked at Rachel.

'So, Mrs Moore, are you planning to continue where we left off?' he asked in Russian. Moore was the alias Rachel had been using during their interviews.

'In a manner of speaking,' Rachel said in the same language, then switched back to English. 'Major Allen, would you be so kind as to fetch a first-aid kit?'

'Shouldn't he see a doctor?' the major asked.

'Let me find out how bad it is first. Yakov Mikhailovich, please remove your shirt.'

7

Smirking, Kulagin unbuttoned his shirt and grunted when he pulled it off. His skin was dough-white and the fleshy folds of his paunch rolled as he moved, but his hairy arms and chest were strong, bear-like.

One of the shots had grazed Kulagin's ribs. The wound was not deep but it started bleeding again when he lifted his arm for Rachel to inspect it. Beneath the liquor, he smelled strangely fresh, of fine hotel soap and light cologne.

She fetched a small towel from the bathroom and told him to apply pressure to the wound until Allen came back. Then she poured him a glass of water. He drank it slowly, setting the glass down between sips, one crooked arm holding the bloody towel like a broken wing.

The view of Regent Street through the window was dissected into an orderly golden grid by the Faraday cage wires that kept unwanted spirits out. The heat from the radiator beneath the window made her damp clothes hot and uncomfortable.

Then it hit her.

I was nearly shot, she thought. *I could have died.* A quick flash of red pain, and then falling, that's what it was supposed to be like.

Her hands started shaking. Her heart pounded. There was no reason to be afraid, she chided herself. She wanted to go to Summerland one day, after all. But not like this, not in a messy, random, foolish way, a victim in a boys' shooting game.

Kulagin lifted his glass. 'It appears we could both use something stronger, Mrs Moore. I hope you are not unwell. A drink will warm you up. That fop Shaw-Asquith was right about that, at least! And you should get out of those wet clothes.'

Rachel folded her arms to hide her trembling hands and forced herself to smile.

'You are absolutely right, Yakov Mikhailovich. I will join you in just one moment, wearing something more comfortable.'

Rachel closed the bathroom door behind her and took off her soaked skirt and blouse. They made a dark pile on the floor. The Service was a boys' world and it helped to dress like a nun. Shivering, she wrapped herself in a heavy bathrobe that was far too big for her. Her hair was a mess. She fumbled in her handbag for a brush, focused on the mirror and straightened the thick black tresses with rapid strokes, squeezing the handle in a white-knuckled grip. After a while, the repetitive motion and the gentle pull in her scalp calmed her down.

She wiped off the rain-ruined make-up and studied her reflection with a critical eye. Shorter than she would have liked, with a desk clerk's posture. Tired grey eyes. Smooth, pale complexion that even a childhood in Bengal had not touched – her best feature. Her husband Joe said it made her look like a photograph. At least that was something. Given the way the case was going, she was unlikely to remain wrinkle-free for long.

The whole thing had been a disaster from the start. When Kulagin showed up at the gates of Wormwood Scrubs and stated that he was a Soviet illegal who wanted to defect, no one actually knew what to do with him. The only thing her superiors at the Winter Court were able to agree on was that the opportunity should be seized before the Summer Court got a whiff of it.

Her own Section F – Counter-subversion – was assigned

to formulate a debriefing strategy, led by her immediate superior, Brigadier Harker. Unsurprisingly, Vee-Vee, the head of Terrestrial Counter-intelligence Section V, and Liddell, the deputy chief, both decided to butt in and claim their share of the glory. Crowded by three senior officers, Kulagin clammed up and claimed that a sugar cube they offered for his tea was a poisoning attempt. A furious Harker left the subsequent interviews to Rachel, making it abundantly clear that he was expecting results.

The only thing she had to show for the two weeks of sullen interviews in the Langham's gilded birdcage was a short list of Russian assets in Britain, mostly code names the Winter Court already knew. All her experience told her that there had to be more. For years, she had argued that they needed direct human intelligence on the Soviets, not just the signals intelligence the Summer Court gathered, and this was her chance to prove her point.

But time was running out. Tomorrow, Rachel and the major would file their reports. Harker, Liddell and Vee-Vee would take one look at them, decide that the Russian was too volatile to be useful, trade him to the Americans for chickenfeed and send Rachel back to her desk to pore over endless files on angry Irishmen.

Unless there was a way to make Kulagin talk before dawn.

TWO

Wild Children,
29th October 1938

When Rachel returned to the room, Major Allen blushed, looked firmly away and set a small first-aid kit and a bottle of alcohol on the table, next to Kulagin's discarded duelling pistol.

'Major, could you leave us for a while and make sure we are not disturbed?' Rachel said.

The Watcher gave her a shocked look, then quickly averted his eyes again.

'This is not quite proper!' he said. 'Especially after that show you put on out there. I should call you a car, Mrs Moore. It is already late.'

Rachel sighed. Even if she could hypothetically bring herself to attempt seducing Kulagin, she was hardly Mata Hari with her wet witch-hair, sensible undergarments and thick ankle-length bathrobe that exposed no skin whatsoever.

'Major, any impropriety here is in your filthy imagination. I am sure you have done things in Her Majesty's service that are less proper than leaving a perfectly honourable man and a married woman alone in a room for an hour.'

'Please,' Kulagin said in Russian, with a pained smile. 'I am trying to keep from laughing at this oaf, but it hurts.'

Rachel returned the smile. They should have tried to get the Russian drunk sooner. She had hoped to impress Kulagin with professionalism when the opposite might have been more successful.

'What did he say?' the major asked.

'Yakov Mikhailovich is simply expressing his gratitude for your assistance and discretion,' Rachel said. 'Come now, Major, we are all professionals here. I am simply going to see to his wounds and then we will continue our interview. Nothing improper whatsoever.' She lowered her voice. 'If it makes you feel better, you can leave your sapgun with me.'

'Very well.' The major puffed out his chest. 'But any monkey business will go into my report.'

He took out his sapgun, a small shotgun-bore revolver with four rubber bullets. It was the Service's non-lethal weapon of choice. Rachel had fired one a few times but only in training. It had a terrific kick.

Rachel pocketed the weapon and narrowed her eyes. 'Thank you. Naturally, it is your duty to include every detail. But so is mine. *My* report may mention your failure to stop Mr Kulagin from insulting and assaulting a young man of high station. I would much rather focus on how you arrived too late to stop the incident, and then immediately contacted me. I wonder which set of details Vee-Vee would discover the devil in?'

Allen rubbed his moustache.

'I bid you both goodnight,' he said finally.

His back was ramrod-straight as he left the room. The moment the door closed, Kulagin started laughing.

She cleaned Kulagin's wound with alcohol, half-kneeling in front of him.

'I may have misjudged you, Mrs Moore,' Kulagin said in English. 'You are a spirited woman, ambitious. I see it now. It must be difficult in this country, especially in your Service, being surrounded by all these Etonian boy-children who – how do you say – like each other's bums?'

She pressed an alcohol-dampened cotton pad into the wound. Kulagin flinched.

'There is no need to be crude, Yakov Mikhailovich.'

'Ours is a crude profession, all shit and flies and sex, don't let the bum-boys tell you otherwise! It would have been easier for you in the Soviet Union, Mrs Moore. There we are all comrades together, men and women, in the same shit. But here? Very difficult.'

'I like difficult things. Otherwise why would I be patching up a foul-mouthed Russian who tried to get himself killed?'

'Ha!' Kulagin raised a hand. 'I did not try to get killed.' He ran his fingers along the wound. They came away covered with a thin film of blood. 'I was trying to feel alive!'

'You will not be alive much longer unless you let me clean it properly,' Rachel said dourly.

This time, she poured the alcohol directly onto the wound and Kulagin shuddered from head to toe.

'What a waste,' he said. 'We must drink together, you and I. To men and women, and being alive.'

'No, Yakov Mikhailovich, we will not drink together.'

'What?'

Kulagin's face turned dark red with fury. He struggled to get up.

Rachel grabbed his shoulders and pushed. He fell back onto the couch heavily, overcome by surprise and gravity. She doubted she could have moved the Russian's wrestler-like bulk otherwise.

'We had an agreement,' Rachel said. 'In exchange for information deemed to be of value by the Service, we will arrange new papers for you, comfortable accommodation and subsistence, or, if you prefer, a Ticket and a painless transition to Summerland. Was there anything unclear about that?'

'I was bored,' he growled. 'The young fool offended me. I acted. Nothing to do with our deal.'

'It had everything to do with our deal. The deal was with us, not with our colleagues on the Other Side. There is a reason why you have not been given a Ticket yet. If you had been shot, you would have been lost like any Ticketless ghost, Faded in a day. Is that what you wanted? Or did you have such confidence in your aim?'

She got up, poured Kulagin a brandy from the room's drinks cabinet and handed him the glass. His hand shook so badly he spilled some of the amber liquid in his lap. Then he downed the remainder in one gulp.

'See?' Rachel said. 'I cannot imagine how you expected to hit anything.'

Kulagin let out a bark-like laugh. 'Hit, miss – no difference! You just need to be the last man standing.'

Rachel returned to the drinks cabinet and refilled his glass, then took out a needle and a length of catgut thread from the first-aid kit. 'Well, right now I need you to sit still. This will hurt.'

She pinched the white folds of his skin together and started stitching the wound. Before joining the Winter Court, she had worked as a volunteer nurse and her fingers remembered the movements. Kulagin twitched and drank more, grimacing.

'You are a cruel woman, Mrs Moore,' he said between sips.

'If you say so, Yakov Mikhailovich.' Rachel knotted the last stitch, yanked the thread tight and cut it with the kit's tiny scissors. Then she put the first-aid supplies to one side and pulled out one of the desk drawers.

The recording equipment was in a false compartment installed by the Service before Kulagin moved in: an old-fashioned magnetophone in a heavy metal case. They had more modern equipment with Zöllner crystals that broadcast directly to the spirit Watchers, but the quartermaster was paranoid about using them on operations the brass did not want the Summer Court to know about.

Rachel clicked the case open and yanked out the tape. Then she sat in the leather armchair opposite Kulagin, folded her hands on top of one knee and looked at him calmly.

'Now it is just the two of us, Yakov Mikhailovich,' she said. 'No notes, no recordings, no ghosts. Just a living man and a woman, bleeding and drinking.'

Kulagin did not look drunk any more. His dark eyes burned with a cold fire.

'You have been testing us,' Rachel said, 'measuring how badly we want what you have to offer. But you have gone too far. My superiors are going to put you on a boat to America. Is that what you want? We can protect you from your former colleagues better than the Yanks can, you know that. It is why you came to us in the first place. I can help you, Yakov Mikhailovich, but only if you help me.'

Kulagin leaned forwards, hands on his knees.

'You think I am here because I am afraid, Mrs Moore? Scared that the big, bad NKVD will spank me if they catch me? I think we need to get to know each other better before we can talk. Much better.'

There it was. Rachel rolled her eyes.

'I am a married woman, Yakov Mikhailovich.'

'Aha! You are thinking of sex! Again, you misunderstand. Sex is a tool. Our Lenin School has a section, in the country-side, where women and men learn to use it. But it does not bring understanding. And I want to understand you, Mrs Moore. This thing we do, telling secrets we trained a lifetime to keep, it takes trust – on both sides.'

Kulagin got up slowly and poured more brandy, two glasses this time, and held one out to Rachel.

'I said I would not drink with you.'

'It is a small price to pay for my secrets, no? Here is what I propose. We drink. I ask questions. Not about your country, about you. You answer. If I deem your answers to be *of value*, as you said, I will tell you things in return. What do you say?'

It was another test. Did Kulagin really think she was a beginner who would open up, give him leverage?

Cautiously, she accepted the glass.

'Ha! So it is decided,' Kulagin said.

They clinked glasses and drank. The brandy was strong and made Rachel cough. It burned in her belly.

Kulagin sat back down. 'Tell me, Mrs Moore – what makes you feel alive? What gives your life meaning?'

She frowned, cupping her glass with both hands.

'Service, I suppose. Serving something greater than myself. Protecting others. Being useful.'

'Being accepted?'

'Possibly.'

'And your husband, does he understand your needs in this regard?'

Rachel hesitated. 'He understands duty.'

'And what is a wife's duty, in this country?'

Rachel bit the inside of her mouth.

'Play the game, please,' Kulagin said. 'A wife's duty is …?'

'To love her husband. To support him faithfully. To bear children.'

'Do you have children, Mrs Moore?'

'No. I do not.'

The words slipped out too quickly. As a matter of course, she had sketched a backstory for her interview alias – a former schoolteacher turned Service officer through her husband's connections. Why hadn't she given Mrs Moore children, a whole litter of them?

The Russian regarded her curiously.

'A pity. For many people, it is children who give their lives meaning. The little fallen stars. What did your great thinkers Hinton and Tait call it? The *ana* dimension, all light, where the souls come from, fall into our crude matter and take root. Some say children retain that light for a while, before it fades and they become us. And then we seek our light elsewhere. Where is your light?'

'I told you. I have no children. My work keeps other people's children safe.'

'I am not sure I believe you, Mrs Moore.'

Rachel hesitated. Kulagin was a professional. He could smell a half-baked cover story. A modicum of truth was her only option.

'I had a child, Yakov Mikhailovich,' she said slowly. 'It died.'

'I am very sorry to hear that. Do you still talk to the little one, through the ectophone?'

'No. It was never born.'

'Ah. Better that way than going to the afterlife motherless.'

Rachel said nothing. Kulagin sat quietly for a while. Then he nodded to himself, got up, poured them more brandy from the cabinet and sat down again.

'I saw many motherless children in Russia, after the Revolution. *Bezprizornii*, we called them, wild children. They hunted rats and other small animals for food. Remarkable creatures. So innocent, so cruel. In a way, we were all like them, little boys and girls whose dream of a world without parents had come true. There were no rules except tearing down what was and building something new. Nothing existed except our own wills. It was glorious. Even death was an instrument to make a new Soviet Man.

'One day, I sat in a cafe in Petrograd, signing death warrants by the dozen, finding different ways to choose the names. Letters in an alphabet. All the first names I could remember from school. Eventually, I just picked sheets at random. Then, a poet – a real poet, not like the young man tonight – came to interrupt me, accused me of tyranny. I took my revolver and shot him.'

Kulagin flexed his thick fingers. There was a look of dark pleasure on his face. Suddenly, Rachel was grateful for the sapgun in her pocket.

'Later, I regretted it. His poems were actually good. I think that was why I did not shoot young Shaw-Asquith today. Even bad poets touch something we cannot, with our games and lies. But no one dared to stop me in that cafe. Do you understand? There was no one to judge. No mother. No morality. No God. Until we built Him, in nineteen twenty-five.'

Rachel felt a chill. In spite of all their efforts, the SIS knew relatively little about the genesis of the Soviet Union's mighty guiding intellect that ran its economy with machine precision and uncovered every agent they tried to get inside OGPU with ruthless efficiency.

'The God-Builders,' Rachel said.

'Krasin, Termin, Malevich and Bogdanov, those fools,' Kulagin continued. 'Ha! They thought that the Soviet people needed a God, and so they made an electric one. And now we have little Tombs everywhere, his eyes, watching everything. He is a sterner father than the Tsar ever was. And when we die, we become Him.

'That was to be my reward, you see. I have served our radiant Father too well. I was chosen by the Immortalisation Commission to return home and to undergo the Termin Procedure, to merge my meagre soul with that of Vladimir Ilyich Lenin. An honour beyond measure.'

Kulagin sighed. 'What was I to do, Mrs Moore? I preferred to remain a wild child, fatherless, motherless. And so here I am.'

Rachel stared at Kulagin. She imagined losing her identity, joining the Soviet overmind like a raindrop falling into a dark sea, and shuddered.

'Why the tantrums and the games, then?' she asked. 'Why

not tell my superiors what you just told me? Why risk dying in a duel without a Ticket?'

'I wanted to see if your Service could protect me. It became clear that they could not. They are a bunch of schoolboys. I decided to let Shaw-Asquith kill me and take my leave. I thought it would be ... how do you say? Poetic justice. Oh, do not look so shocked. I know what you people are told about the Ticketless dead. Only a few ever return to speak to family or lovers, and Fade quickly even then. I think you are too quick to believe your Dimensionists. What if your Tickets lead the souls astray? I prefer to see where my death takes me. If there is a land without mothers and fathers, I will find it.'

'Then what are you still doing here?' Rachel asked. It was best to humour him. The man was obviously mad. She regretted sending Allen away. Slowly, she pushed her hand into the bathrobe's pocket, feeling for the sapgun.

'You, Mrs Moore, you stepped in front of a bullet for me. It may be that I can trust you with a gift before I leave. But I have to be sure.'

Kulagin got up, set down his glass and walked over to Rachel, looming in front of her. The black stitches on his side and his pale nipples made his chest and stomach look like an obscene face with a lopsided grin. Rachel fumbled for the sapgun, but the barrel caught in the pocket's edge.

Kulagin slapped her. Black dots danced in her eyes. He caught her right wrist and bent her arm back painfully. Her elbow screamed and she had to drop the weapon.

Kulagin's hands closed around her neck, crushing her windpipe.

'In Tashkent, I strangled a woman once,' Kulagin said.

'She clawed at my arms, fought to the very end. She had a child, you see.'

Rachel grabbed his wrists, tried to prise his fingers open, but the Russian's grip was like iron. Her throat was on fire.

'I want to know what you are really fighting for, Mrs Moore.'

Rachel struggled to get the words out, mouthed them. Her fingers brushed Kulagin's side. The thread and the stitches were rough.

'What is it? Tell me.'

He loosened his grip, just enough to let her pull in one ragged breath.

'For freedom, you bastard,' Rachel said.

He squeezed harder again. Black dots filled her vision.

'Whose freedom?'

Her fingers found the knotted end of the stitches.

'Mine.'

As the word escaped her lips, she pulled as hard as she could. The catgut bit into her fingers and tore a flap of skin from Kulagin's side. Droplets of blood stung her face like fat from a burst sausage.

Kulagin roared with pain. She pushed herself up, ramming her shoulder into Kulagin's belly. He stumbled against the coffee table and crashed to the floor. Rachel reached for the duelling pistol on the table but a black tunnel swallowed her vision. When it cleared, the weapon was in Kulagin's hand, pointed at her.

'Very well done,' Kulagin said. He was laughing, half-sitting, half-lying on the floor. He pressed his left hand against the torn wound in his side. Blood flowed freely between his fingers. 'Oh, but that hurts. Very well done indeed!'

His laugh was interrupted by a coughing fit. His aim wavered, but before Rachel could move, he regained his composure.

'I apologise for any discomfort I caused you, but I had to be sure. I recognise truth when I hear it. And so I am going to give you a gift, Mrs Moore, a double-edged gift. For the last two years, I have been running an agent called FELIX – a Section head in your Summer Court. He is a good lad, a little naive, a believer in the cause – more so than I, bless his soul.'

Rachel struggled to speak but her throat seized up.

'I see you don't believe me. Well, more detail may convince you. FELIX is called Peter Bloom.'

'Bloom,' Rachel said, her voice hoarse. She had served with him for a time, before he passed over. One of the Young Turks, although less dashing than the others: short, pudgy, with intense eyes and a sensual mouth. Quiet, polite, a little aloof. Promoted past her, of course, in spite of the fact that she had a decade of experience on him.

Kulagin coughed again. He lay in a spreading pool of dark crimson now.

'My darling Peter was the golden goose I was going to be rewarded for. He belongs to you now.'

Rachel's head spun. It was if all the reason in the world was leaking out together with Kulagin's blood.

'Even if I believed you,' she whispered, 'what do you expect me to do?'

'You weren't listening,' Kulagin said. 'There is no one telling you what to do. Goodbye, Mrs Moore.'

In one smooth movement, as if downing a drink, he pushed the barrel of the pistol into his mouth and pulled the trigger.

The shot felt like a slap, blinding and deafening. When her vision cleared, Rachel could not bear to look at Kulagin's ruined face.

She fled the room and slammed the door shut behind her.

'We need a – we need a doctor here!' she shouted at the top of her lungs, tearing the words from her battered throat. 'Someone get a doctor!'

Then she sank to the floor. The name pulsed in her mind, crimson and vile and impossible like Kulagin's blood on the carpet.

Peter Bloom.

THREE

Small Wars,
8th November 1938

Peter Bloom found himself haunting an ammunition truck while Madrid burned.

He could not see the flames. To a ghost, the material world was invisible, except for electricity and the soul-sparks of the living. Buildings and streets were skeletons of luminescent wiring. Human brains glowed like paper lanterns. Everything else was a pale grey mist. He would have been hopelessly lost if not for the beacon in his agent Inez Giral's ectophone that had guided him here from Summerland for their meeting.

Now he hung on to the bright coils of the phone's circuitry like a small boy gripping the hem of his mother's dress, and listened to Inez describe the world of the living.

'The Gran Vía rooftops are on fire,' she said. 'And the bombs, they fall like black pears. Big ones first, to knock buildings down. Incendiaries to light them. Shrapnel to keep the firemen away. Same thing every night. Soon there will be nothing left to burn.'

For a woman driving a truck loaded with high explosives

through a city being firebombed at night, her voice was remarkably calm.

'During the day, when we try to sleep, the planes drop leaflets on us, like seagulls shitting. Propaganda and Tickets to Franco's fake paradise. The Fascists are losing, so they try to kill us all and lure our souls into their false Heaven.'

Peter heard distant thunderclaps.

'What is that noise?' he asked.

'They are firing at the Telefónica again.'

'A reporter told me the Fascists are using it for target practice.'

The Telefónica was a solidly built skyscraper standing on the highest spot in Madrid. To Peter's hypersight, it was a stick figure, all wire and gossamer. He could imagine an artillery officer's delight in knocking it down, like he used to demolish the card fortifications he built for his war games as a child.

'Let them,' Inez said. 'It shrugs off shells.'

She might have been talking about the Spanish Republic itself. Two years ago, a mining rebellion and anger against a Church no longer able to offer answers about death had created a strange, Utopian state on the Iberian Peninsula. A coalition of generals led by Francisco Franco had decided to restore the natural order of things. Reluctantly, Britain had supported Franco. In turn, the Soviet Union had thrown its weight behind the Republic's Communist factions. And so Spain had become a Petri dish of war, a miniature of greater conflicts to come.

That was why Peter was here. Franco was losing. The SIS needed to understand why. They needed more Republic intelligence assets like Inez.

The problem was that he had no idea what she needed.

They drove through the ghost city in silence. He tried to picture what she looked like. BRIAR, the local SIS recruiter she knew as Comrade Eric, had wired him a photograph. A fierce young woman in neat blue coveralls, with pencil-line eyebrows and a striking wide mouth. She did not look like she suffered fools gladly.

He cleared his immaterial throat – the habits of the living were hard to break.

'*Señorita*—'

'Just comrade, like everybody else. Although we are not really comrades, are we?'

'I hope we can be,' Peter said. 'It's a very brave thing you are doing.'

Inez laughed a short, bitter laugh. 'You flatter me, Comrade Ghost. Bravery is for mortals. I have a Ticket to our Republic's Heaven, to the Heaven of the people. Every night I memorise it, all the weird little shapes that tickle my brain, like I'm saying paternoster. If I get hit by a shell, the Ticket will take me where all the good revolutionaries go.'

Her voice was flat. Peter considered her soul-spark, itself a miniature city of flame: a glowing flower the size of his hand, with intertwined petals of blue and red. He wished he had more experience in soul-reading. The only hues he recognised in Inez's mind were anger and frustration.

'That was not what I meant,' he said. 'Just talking to me could get you in worse trouble than being killed. It is a brave thing to risk your soul for peace.'

Inez spat. Through the microphone, it sounded like a muffled gunshot. Her soul-spark flashed cherry-red.

'Who says I want peace? Let the Fascists light the city. The fire will make us pure, and they will burn in hotter flames in Hell. When Comrade Eric says to talk to you and gave me the phone, I say why not, I get bored when I drive, I can talk and drive at the same time, no? But I don't like listening to lies. So don't talk to me about peace. Maybe I will decide I prefer the sound of guns to your voice.'

Peter swore. Clearly, BRIAR had misjudged Inez and failed to develop her properly. His report had described her frustration with how the Republic treated the Church, but that was not enough. She was not ready to be handled yet.

'Inez,' he said, 'please listen to me. Comrade Eric was right. We can just talk, about anything you want. Just—'

She hung up on him. The circuit anchoring Peter to the phone disappeared and he was ejected back into the cold grey mist.

He spun, disorientated. Inez's beacon receded into the distance. For a ghost, movement and thought were the same thing. Peter concentrated on the shape of the beacon and dashed after it in effortless, bodiless flight.

He could return to the Summer Court and blame the whole thing on BRIAR. It was tempting, if not for the fact that the Iberian Section, which Peter headed, could not afford to make yet another blunder without attracting scrutiny from C, the SIS chief.

Especially when Peter himself was the ultimate cause of their blunders. They *were* comrades, even if his job was to persuade her to betray the cause they both served.

He had to get something report-worthy out of her, but how?

The beacon was lost in the labyrinth of wires and soul-sparks. To get a better view, Peter descended in the *kata* direction – the fourth dimension where only the dead could move.

Madrid expanded into a tracery of light and flame above him, and he felt like a bird flying beneath a strange, inverted firmament. Radio waves pulsed from the Telefónica. The front was close, and he glimpsed a death – the red flash of a soul-spark leaving its body, like a rocket fired into the sky.

Then he saw the ectotank.

It looked innocent enough at first, a slowly growing white vortex in the gloom, like milk poured into tea. Closer, he saw the white was not white, but made up of countless shimmering colours. Peter felt a sudden compulsion to dive right into it, even though he knew it meant certain doom.

The ectotank ploughed through a cluster of little human lights that had to be a Republic barricade. Crimson firecrackers of dead souls bloomed in its wake, then looped back around and dived into the white whirlpool, unable to resist its allure. As the souls disappeared into the white, the ectotank vortex grew and advanced down the street like a hungry amoeba.

Inez's beacon was headed straight towards it.

Peter launched himself at the ectophone. He gripped the phone's bell circuit with aethereal fingers and shook it frantically. Nothing. The milky whirlwind of the ectotank loomed to the right. Clearly, Inez could not see it – a building invisible to Peter blocked her view.

Then he glimpsed the ectotank's eye, a tiny round window in the midst of the whiteness. Within, he saw flames and street lights and broken buildings in full vivid colour, as if he had living eyes again. He was overwhelmed by an irrational need to dive through the eye. Surely he would be alive again on the Other Side?

Far away, some distant part of him kept clawing at the circuit, three long rings, three short, three long.

'I am trying to drive, Comrade Ghost,' Inez said. 'Why don't you—'

Her voice broke the spell. 'Turn around!' Peter cried. 'There is an ectotank ahead!'

'*Jesú*,' Inez whispered. Then she let out a wordless scream.

There was static on the phone, and then the sound of screeching brakes.

The truck swerved right just as the ectotank rolled along Gran Vía like an avalanche. Inez raced down a side street like a madwoman, and even at the speed of thought, Peter had trouble keeping up. A Republic battery in the Telefónica opened fire at the ectotank with Soviet-made aetherguns. It let out a high-pitched keening that sounded like a thousand children screaming.

Finally, the truck came to a halt. Peter waited for a moment and rang again. Inez picked up, but said nothing. Her breathing was laboured and quick.

'Are you hurt?' Peter asked.

'No.'

'Why did you stop?'

'There is a hole in the road ahead. A crater where the Metro used to be, black like a gate to Hell. Maybe it is where that thing crawled out from. *Madre de Dios*, it was the size of a house, like a ... a—' Her voice broke. For a moment, Peter thought she had hung up again, and sighed with relief when she continued. 'I have never seen anything like it. How can Pope Teilhard bless the Fascists when they send devils to attack us?'

'That was no devil. There was a human being inside, a medium. What you saw was ectoplasm, spirit essence stolen from the dead, shaped by his thoughts.'

'Then his thoughts are full of devils.'

A perversion of Lodge's and Marconi's original inventions, the ectotanks were created to break the deadlock of the trenches in the Great War: weapons that grew more powerful the more they killed. He had not realised the tanks Britain had supplied Franco with were already being deployed. That would make the Soviets respond in kind, escalating the conflict. It made his mission all the more urgent.

'War brings out the devils inside us,' Peter said.

Inez exhaled, a long sigh that turned into a sob.

'What is it?'

'There are devils inside me, too, Comrade Ghost. If I was truly brave, like you say, I would put my rifle in my mouth and fire, and let God judge them.'

'And go to the Republic's Heaven?'

She laughed mirthlessly. 'Everyone knows it is not ready. Those who die are lost and Fade, unless they use the Fascists' Tickets. No, it is like Father Miaja from my village said. Confession and prayer are the only ways to Heaven. When I was a child, I imagined it. A white place, with trees of candyfloss. But it is not for me, not any more.'

How had he missed it? There was a knot in Inez's soulspark. Her thoughts kept winding around it, over and over. That was why she had agreed to speak to a disembodied voice on the phone. It had nothing to do with betraying the Republic.

She simply needed a confessor.

'Why is that?' Peter asked gently.

'Because I was in Getafe to execute the statue of Christ.'

Far away, the screams of the ectotank faded.

'Mateo gathered a squad that day,' Inez said. 'He said they were going to execute a Fascist prisoner. I wanted revenge for what they did to my mother and brother in Guernica, so I took my rifle and went along.

'We drove to Getafe in a truck. The men laughed and boasted all the way. We climbed the hill, Cerro de los Ángeles. It was hot and dry beneath the carrascos pines. The air was clear and we could see Madrid in the distance. Only when Mateo took out a scrap of cloth and blindfolded the great statue standing there did I understand.

'I took aim with the others. I could not fire, but I did not stop them. I watched the bullets shatter His face, and wept.'

Inez started the truck.

'I have said enough now. The comrades at the front need my bullets and shells. Thank you for warning me about the devil machine. Perhaps we will speak again.'

At last, Peter recognised the knotted emotion in her soul. It was paradox. She was trying to believe in a contradiction.

'Wait,' he said. 'Inez, I don't think God is done with you yet.'

Inez paused. Anger flickered in her soul-spark.

'And what do you know of God, Comrade Ghost?'

'I know what it's like to be tested. I saw a burning city, too, when I was a child.'

Inez said nothing, but her soul-spark softened, with hues of purple and green. Peter continued.

'During the Great War, there were German air raids in

London. I was five. The sirens scared me, and I would hide in the basement even after a raid was over.

'One time, when they started, my father picked me up and took me to the window in his study. I struggled, started crying, but he held me tight. My mother begged him to come to the shelter. He would not hear of it, and made me look. There was a silver cigar in the sky. Spotlight beams danced around it. Flames bloomed beneath it, bright as the sun. The windows rattled from distant booms.

'I nearly wet myself. I wanted to hide in my mother's lap. But my father told me to be brave.

'The ectoflyers came. Each man had wings like a moth, white and shimmering. They brought the airship down. They swarmed around it and fired at it and cut its belly open. Burning gas spilled out. It was the most exhilarating thing I had ever seen.

'All the while, my father held me. The airship fell, and then it was just an empty sack, floating in the Thames. I was never afraid of air raids after that.'

'It is a nice story, Comrade Ghost,' Inez said. 'But I am not a frightened child any more.' Her voice was harsh, but her soul-spark glowed gently.

'Aren't we all children, in the eyes of God? I may not share your faith, Inez. But I do believe that there is something greater than us, holding us in its arms, even while the city burns. And whoever He is, Pope Teilhard's God or your Father Miaja's or your own, He has a plan for us. He tests us, but it is only to make us face our fears. And He always forgives.'

Inez stopped the truck again. The ectophone circuit died. Without it, Peter felt the pull of Summerland in the *kata* direction and had to keep himself still with sheer will, like a swimmer treading water.

He watched her thought-forms. They fragmented into a swarm of fireflies and then merged together into one glowing green orb of certainty.

Then the circuit was back and Inez picked up the ecto-phone again. Through the static, it sounded like she had been crying. Yet there was a steely edge to her voice.

'Comrade Ghost,' she said, 'I am not stupid. You are no friend of the Republic. But maybe you are God's final test for me. So, I am going to test you in turn.

'The Soviets give us weapons, but they come with a blood price. Their spies are in all the parties now. They say they hunt for Fifth Columnists but take everyone who is not Communist.

'Answer me this: would your masters tolerate a Republic without Russians? Could we truly have peace in Spain?'

Peter hesitated.

'Yes,' he said finally. 'You have my word.'

It was *almost* true, like his story about the air raid. Only the way he had told it made it a lie. And deep in the core of his immortal being, Peter Bloom hated lies.

But just this once, it was worth it. Inez's soul-spark grew bright with hope and its echo filled Peter with joy. This was the temptation the souls who Faded fell prey to. They spent all their *vim* huddling close to the living, until Summerland's relentless pull washed away their memories and thoughts and only the bare, mindless *luz*, the soul-stone, remained.

'Then there is something you should know,' Inez said. 'Two days ago, my Mateo comes to our flat, excited. It is like a fever. He has met with a man, a Georgian, and cannot stop talking about it. This man leads a network of underground Leftist dissidents, Russians, French, Germans, Poles, all over Europe. The Soviets hunt him everywhere he goes. He claims to have come to Spain to stop the war.'

'And how is he planning to do that?'

'He takes over the Government, rejects the Soviets and makes a deal with the British instead. Without British support, Franco will be defeated overnight. And this man has many supporters amongst the Anarchists, our POUM and the other parties already.'

'Did Mateo say what the man's name was?'

'Iosif Vissarionovich Dzhugashvili.' She paused. 'Although he prefers to be called Stalin.'

Peter betrayed nothing of his surprise and delight to Inez. They talked a little more on the roadside. Inez gave him a few other names: Dzhugashvili's supporters in the Government parties, people her lover Mateo had influence with.

They arranged another meeting in a week's time and said goodbye. Peter watched Inez's soul-spark and the whirring light-wheel of the truck's engine recede towards the fireworks of the front. Then he let go of the world of the living and its illusions and sank beneath their plane.

All of Earth became visible to his hypersight. Cities were dense constellations, joined by the spiderweb of telegraph cables. Births were blue confetti. Each death was a falling star of red. They traced crimson maps of war: the Spanish fronts and the campaigns in Africa. The sight brought back another childhood memory, the game called Small Wars he used to play with Mr West, toy armies arrayed against each other on the living room floor. Wasteful deaths, he reminded himself, all unnecessary, feeding a system just as meaningless as a child's game and needing to be put away like all childish things.

And the name Inez had given him would help him to do just that.

He summoned the image of the SIS headquarters and held it in his mind. At the speed of thought, the aether carried him *kata*-wards, to Summerland.

FOUR

Natural Limitations,
30th October 1938

The rest of the night was a blur. Rachel huddled in exhaustion in an adjoining suite. The hotel doctor, a small bald man with a reassuring manner, inspected Kulagin and proclaimed him dead.

Then he checked Rachel's injuries while a sheepish-looking Allen stood nearby, nervously running his fingers through his thin, combed-over hair.

The final shot kept echoing in Rachel's head. Could she have said something to stop him? She cursed herself for being clumsy with the sapgun, and for not insisting on having spirit Watchers around. Maybe they could have caught Kulagin before he Faded ... But no, Harker would never have agreed to putting any Summer Court operatives on the case.

Special Branch showed up, two polite but hard-faced officers in bowler hats. Rachel nursed a whisky the major brought her and gave them a statement. The Branch men were confused by the absence of the victim's spirit to interview, but after a call from the SIS liaison officer, they became much more polite.

Rachel was in a daze when the major draped his coat over her bathrobe and put her in a cab.

The streets of midnight London were blue-tinged and quiet. The rain had stopped and puddles gleamed in the street lights. Rachel drifted off to fitful sleep to the soft whirr of the car's electric motor, cheek pressed against the cold glass of the window. The driver's voice startled her awake.

''Ere we are, ma'am. Have a good night now.'

The cab stopped in front of the red-brick house she shared with Joe in St John's Wood, near Regent's Park. There was frost on the ground, and Rachel was shivering when she made it to the door. Their German maid Gertrude started fussing over her before she made it past the entrance hall, where Joe's old spirit armour stood like a metallic guardsman.

'Are you all right, Mrs White? You are looking terrible, if you don't mind that I say.'

Rachel nodded. It hurt too much to talk.

Then Joe was there, in the purple Turkish-style smoking jacket she had always found ridiculous; short and rugby-solid Joe, with his weather-beaten face and thick, close-cropped chestnut hair and the permanent marks on his temples from an RAF spirit armour's Crookes crown. He said nothing, just took her in his arms and held her tight.

For a moment, she was ready to love him all over again, just for that, and for his smell, for all his comforting imperfections, the lantern jaw that pressed against her shoulder, the tiny unkempt hairs in his ears. Then her breath grew short, his arms felt heavy around her and her heart started fluttering like a bird caught inside a house.

'Joe, it is perfectly all right,' she whispered, pulling away. 'It was a dreadful night. But I am fine, really.'

'I know you are,' he said, taking her hand and squeezing it gently. 'Come on, love. Let's get you to bed.'

Allen would have called him, she knew. Until his recent leave of absence, Joe had been the Winter Court liaison officer for the Royal Aetheric Force. That was how they had met, at a staff meeting in Blenheim Palace. He had less Etonian polish and was less eager to impress than the Court spies. He did not drink, which in Court terms made him something like a fish without gills. The smile and a kinship born out of not quite belonging had led to a dinner, a dance and, two years ago, marriage.

'I think I will have a bath first, if you don't mind, dear.'

'Of course.' He gave her a familiar shy smile, quick like a wingbeat, and kissed her forehead. 'I will wait up with some tea.'

'Yes, dear. Tea would be lovely.'

He stood watching as she went up the stairs to the master bathroom. She closed the door behind her and sat down, back against the door, and let the tears come.

Later, she awoke in their bed, shaking. The warmth of the tea and the bath had faded. Chills of bone-deep exhaustion ran down her spine, but she could not get back to sleep. She looked at Joe next to her and wanted to embrace him again, bury the image of Kulagin's face in his broad back.

Instead, she sat up and hugged her knees. She did not want to wake him. He had trouble sleeping. At night, the soul-fragments he carried from the war spilled out and made cold spots in the bedroom. When it got really bad, tendrils of ectoplasm sneaked out from his mouth and nose like the roots of a dead white plant. He was calm now, for once, asleep on his belly in a half-crawl, clutching his pillow.

Besides, holding him too tight would feel like grinding the ends of a fractured bone together, wrong and cruel, and she was not ready for that, not yet.

She sneaked out of the bed, wrapped herself in a dressing gown and went into the hallway. The house was quiet. It was four in the morning. She stopped at the door of the empty nursery and thought of Kulagin's wild children. Then she went into her study, sat down in front of the electric typewriter and started writing her report.

'And exactly why was it, Major, that you felt the need to leave the room at that juncture?'

Brigadier Oswald 'Jasper' Harker, Director of Section B of the SIS – Counter-subversion – leaned over his desk and pushed his tanned, angular face forward until it looked like he was about to launch himself at Major Allen's throat. It was five thirty in the afternoon, and both Rachel and Allen had been summoned to the director's office for a debriefing.

'Well, the thing is, sir, Mrs White was, uh …'

Allen squirmed. He was holding the sweat-blotted remains of his report in his thick-fingered hands like a talisman. Rachel sat quietly next to him, glad that Harker's fierce scowl – accentuated by the brigadier's coal-black eyebrows – was not directed at her for the time being.

'Come on, man, spit it out!'

'Well, sir, she asked me to leave. And she was not entirely decent when I reluctantly complied.'

'Bloody hell, White! The Soviets may resort to honeytrap tricks, but we have to stick to fair play or we are no better than they are. What did you think you were doing?'

Rachel cleared her throat and flinched. It still hurt to talk, and she was wearing a scarf to hide the bruises.

'Sir, the major's version of events is—'

'White, I do not care whose version is correct.' The brigadier sat down heavily. 'The fact is that Kulagin played us for fools. Look around you, both of you. What do you see? Where are we?'

Harker waved at the rough, whitewashed walls of his tiny office. The single small window high up on one wall showed a dismal glimpse of the Wormwood Scrubs green, gently furred by frost. A rusty electric heater in a corner struggled to keep the room at Harker's preferred Bombay temperature.

Rachel and Allen glanced at each other and stayed silent.

'Exactly! The bloody Spooks get Blenheim Palace and crystal castles in Summerland, but where does Her Majesty's real Secret Intelligence Service end up? In a prison. Miraculously, we get a chance – one chance! – to catch the Spooks with their spectral pants down, and what happens? One of you lets our source fight a duel and the other, the other—' Harker's face was red as his fury almost choked him. 'The *other* first saves him and then lets him blow his brains out! And gets her picture taken for the blasted Sunday paper.'

The brigadier slammed his palm on an open page of *The Times* on his desk. It showed a blurry photograph of the scene in the Langham, a surprised-looking Kulagin with

Rachel's arms wrapped around him. Thankfully, her face was not visible.

'The last time I checked, we still had the word "Secret" in our job description, for God's sake.'

Harker took a deep breath. 'You are dismissed. But make no mistake, we are not done. I will confer with Vivian and the deputy chief regarding the ultimate fate of Mr Kulagin. If I can use your hides to patch the holes in this sinking ship, I will. Is that understood?'

'Yes, sir,' Allen said. The major slunk out of the room, head bowed, the tattered remains of his report in one hand, trying to make his hulking form as small as possible. Rachel waited until he closed the door behind him.

'What is it, White?'

Rachel could barely get a whisper out.

'There is one item I ... omitted from my report, sir. For your ears only.'

'And what would that be?'

'Mr Kulagin did volunteer some information, sir. The identity of a mole within the SIS. Code name FELIX. In the Summer Court.'

Harker blinked. 'Well, well, well. Now that *would* be interesting, wouldn't it?' he said.

'I thought so, sir.'

'Perhaps God is not a Communist after all. So who is this FELIX, then?'

'Peter Bloom.'

The brigadier raised his eyebrows in a furry wave of astonishment. Then his eyes brightened.

'I see what is happening here, White. I see what is

happening. I should have seen it from the start.' He paused and massaged his forehead.

Rachel seized the opening. 'Sir, it is my recommendation that we act upon this information with all possible speed and inform Noel Symonds's Section in the Summer Court. With respect, sir, it might go down better if it came from Deputy Director Liddell.'

Harker clicked his tongue. 'No. Absolutely not.'

'Sir, I know how strongly you feel about us making the collar here, but the Russians are not stupid – they will assume that Kulagin has told us everything he knows. They might extract Bloom, dismantle his network. And as Bloom's in the Summer City, sir, surely the Summer Court is better placed to—'

The brigadier held up a hand. 'White, you have been here longer than I have, yes?'

Rachel nodded. *Yes, and you are on that side of the desk only because you went to Eton with Sir Stewart and are able to pee standing up*, she thought to herself, keeping her face neutral.

'Joined in nineteen seventeen, sir, just before the war ended.'

'All that experience and you still don't see it, do you? Well, let me break it down for you.' He held up a finger. 'A rambunctious Russian turns up, causes all manner of trouble, claims he wants to defect, but clams up when senior officers are present. Why?'

Rachel stared at Harker blankly.

The brigadier continued, 'Because he thinks he has a better chance of fooling the female officer assigned to interview him, of course! He pretends to open up, makes her feel special, then gifts her with information, claiming that there is a mole

42

in a sister Service. He gives her a sound trashing just to make sure he looks serious. And finally, he blows his brains out, so we can't question him further.

'We take his "information" at face value, make complete fools of ourselves in front of the Spooks, and while we squabble, the Russians have a field day with those bloody Luddites and other idiots who think the dead are taking their jobs. How does that sound to you, White?'

Like the stupidest thing I have ever heard in my life, Rachel thought. The rage flowed into her, icy and potent like vodka. It filled her to the brim until it felt like any motion or word could disrupt its delicate surface tension and spill it out, all at once.

She sat still and breathed deeply until the tide of her ire receded. The brigadier leaned back.

'Well, White?'

'With respect, sir,' Rachel said slowly, 'I interviewed Kulagin for two weeks. He was not an agent provocateur. I stake my professional reputation as an interrogator on that. Yes, I believe it was not his intention to cooperate fully with us, but if there is even a chance that the intelligence he shared is genuine, we must act upon it.'

'Well, there you have it. It cannot be possibly be genuine.'

'Why is that?'

'Bloom was vetted. We know his people. I *personally* know his people. It simply isn't possible that he is a traitor.'

'As I have been saying for years, sir, this is exactly our problem – discounting the potential depth and breadth of Soviet penetration of the Service. Counter-subversion is all well and good, we can follow the money trails of the British

Communist Party or the Luddites all we want, but if you are denying even the possibility of a real threat—'

'White. Stop. Please.'

Rachel swallowed. Her throat felt like a raw wound.

'If you are denying it, well, that is just … incompetence.' As she spat out the last word, her voice died.

'You have just proven my point, White,' Harker said. He smiled faintly, and his voice was warm and understanding. 'You know, when I was in India, I once had an officer whipped for speaking to me much the same way you just did. Good practice, that. Would do a world of good here, make no mistake. But I would not be a gentleman if I did not appreciate your limitations.

'Kulagin chose you as his target since he was able to play your pet obsessions, you see. All these hysterics—' The brigadier tutted. 'That has always been my concern with you, White. This is difficult, nerve-wracking work, and I will say you have done well with the odd Irishman and Luddite and the like. Remarkable, really, given your natural limitations. But when I last reviewed your record, it looked to me like you did your best work in the Registry. A supporting role would be better suited for your sensibilities, at least temporarily. Shorter hours, less of a strain on your nerves. I am sure Joe would agree, don't you think?'

Rachel was speechless. The world spun around her.

'I believe there is an opening in the Finance Section. Miss Scaplehorn could really use a person of your calibre.'

'I would rather resign,' she croaked.

'You have that option, of course. However, in that instance we would have issues with your pension and Ticket. That would be extremely regrettable.'

'I – I—'

'No need to say anything, White, you have to allow yourself time to heal. Why don't you take a few days off and then report to Building F on Thursday? Dismissed. And give my best to dear old Joe, will you?'

Rachel strode along the main corridor of Wormwood Scrubs. Voices, footsteps and metallic ectophone ringtones echoed constantly from the walls of brick and concrete, drowning out the confused chorus of her thoughts. She could not face her tiny cell of an office – hers not much longer – and so she grabbed her coat and made her way to a side exit that opened into a small square, formerly the prison's exercise yard.

The cold air cleared her head. The early evening sky was overcast. She could not see past the high red-brick walls, but the capital's lights turned the clouds into sheets of amber and purple. She imagined that was how London looked from Summerland. What was it like to be Peter Bloom, to see the celestial city above and know that he was weakening its foundations with every action, every thought?

Her career was one thing, but a mole in the Summer Court – it was a wound in the very heart of the Service. Maybe that was why Harker refused to believe it. It defied his conception of natural order. And yet it made sense. The recent operations in Spain had been minor disasters. They still had no good assets in Russia itself, and a mole was a simpler explanation for that than an omnipotent Presence.

'Hullo, Rachel.'

Roger Hollis stood at the yard entrance, wearing a dapper charcoal-grey raincoat and carrying a small bouquet of flowers. He had what one could charitably call a dour face, wavy brown hair and a boyish complexion in spite of his thirty-two years of age.

'Roger? What are you doing here? Aren't you supposed to be making tea for your new chief in Blenheim?'

For all her resentment of Harker, Rachel had to admit that there was something unfair about the fact that the Domestic Sections – F, V, A and others – were squeezed into the Scrubs whereas the Foreign Intelligence and Summer Court Liaison Sections had the resplendent Blenheim Palace in Oxfordshire to themselves.

'Oh, I drop in from time to time – to see old friends.'

Rachel smiled. It was an open secret that Roger's former secretary Kathleen Wiltshire in Section V was his mistress.

'Anyway, I came by and heard that you were in the lion's den today, didn't find you in your office and remembered this was your escape. How did it go?'

'Did Allen say something? I swear that man gossips more than the secretaries.' Rachel sighed. 'I came away with a face-ful of lion dung. It looks like I am to assist Finance with their sums from now on.'

'You are not serious.'

Rachel smiled wryly. Roger tended to have a calming effect on her. They had been friends since a tennis match that Laura, one of her school friends, arranged a few years ago in an attempt to integrate her into the society of her peers, and – Rachel suspected – in a poorly hidden attempt at matchmaking. Nothing ever happened between them, but she recognised something familiar in him. Beneath the arrogance and boyish charm, there was a void that needed to be filled, and that had drawn him to the Service.

46

'There was an incident with a source,' she said. 'Somebody had to take the blame.'

'Well, that seems unusually thick, even for old Jasper.' Roger cleared his throat and the sound turned into a hacky cough that had persisted since a bout of tuberculosis in Hong Kong. It was worse than Rachel remembered.

He wiped his lips with a handkerchief. 'Why don't you come in from the cold and tell me all about it?'

Rachel's office had been converted from a two-person cell. It was windowless and she tried to spend as little time in it as possible, preferring to work in the senior staff room or the library. As a result, her small desk was mainly a parking lot for memos and copies of files, covered in yellowing piles of paper with a musty smell. She sat on the edge of her desk, offering Roger her chair.

Without naming Kulagin or going into the details of the operation, she explained the situation.

'Basically, my worry is this: if we do not do something quickly, this mole is going to disappear deep into its hole and take our vegetables with it. I am positive that as we speak, the NKVD is thinking about how to get their man out and do as much damage as they can in the process. I won't be able to prevent that while filing expense forms for Miss Scaplehorn.'

'What do you have in mind?' Roger asked.

'Well, we both know a few Young Turks in the Summer Court – Burgess, Pickering, Symonds, that lot – and some of them still attend the Harrises' soirées. I could simply drop a hint that there is a cuckoo in their nest.'

Roger leaned back in the chair. 'Did our misbehaving defector provide a name?'

A terrible, paranoid thought struck her with the chill of the night air. Roger could go to Harker, tell him that she was planning to go over his head. It would be the logical thing to do. She looked at him, considering. His eyes glinted black in the flickering light of the unadorned light bulb in the ceiling. Then he coughed and was her friend Roger again.

Much as she loathed the old boys' network that allowed men like Harker to attain high positions without any real qualifications or competence, Roger was the one case where she had used her own rank to help a friend. He had applied to the Service twice and been rejected. The argument against him was that he had associated with dubious characters during his time as a journalist in Hong Kong. To Rachel, that only meant he had been doing his job properly.

She had gone to Sir Vernon, the head of the Service at the time, and suggested that Roger be allowed to apply one more time, and that she would vet him informally and take responsibility for him. As a result, he became her assistant. He had never given her cause to regret her decision – he was a conscientious researcher with occasional flashes of brilliance, and she had been happy for him when Blenheim snapped him up. Still, it did not hurt to be cautious.

'No,' she said finally. 'Just a codename. FELIX.'

'I see. To be honest, Rachel, I don't think that would be enough. Death has made those reprobates cautious like old women. They all want to preen their feathers in front of C. You need something more solid to convince them. Besides, Jasper may not know his arse from his elbow, but he has a point. Maybe this Russian chap *was* sent here to cause havoc.

48

You know I have tremendous respect for your judgment, Rachel, but—'

'But what?' She could not keep the edge from her voice. She was cranky and exhausted after the sleepless night and the meeting with Harker, and the last thing she wanted to hear was Roger agreeing with the brigadier.

'Steady on, now.'

He held up his hands placatingly, then took out a packet of cigarettes from his jacket pocket, offered her one, took one himself and lit both with an ornate gold-plated lighter decorated with a dragon.

'What I am saying, Rachel, is that maybe you should wait this one out. I know Liddell and Vivian respect you. They might go to Sir Stewart. I would put good money on this backfiring on Jasper.'

'Liddell and Vivian need a scapegoat for this mess just as much as Jasper does.'

Rachel took a hasty drag on the cigarette.

'Well, I may be in a position to do more for you, in a little while,' Roger said.

She stared at him.

'They say it does not hurt too much, especially with barbiturates. Trying to memorise the Ticket gives me headaches, though. I think they put extra twists and turns for the Court especially.'

'That is splendid, Roger. I am happy for you,' Rachel said, her voice flat.

'I am not ungrateful,' he said quietly. 'I owe it all to you, Rachel. Just lie low and I will spread the word that it was all Jasper's fault. People will believe that. A few months with

Miss Scaplehorn, what is that? You can handle it. Do some busywork and relax with Joe in the meantime.'

'The stakes are too high! I may have issues with Harker, but what if the Summer Court *is* compromised? If there is the faintest chance that the source was telling the truth, I have to do something.'

'But we do not know that. We do not know who the mole is, or what they have access to. It's not as bad as you think. You are overreacting because this brute hurt you, I can see how shaken you are. Think – think rationally for a minute—'

'Oh, is *that* it? Jasper just finished telling me that my *natural limitations* make me unsuitable for this work. You think I am upset because the big, bad Russian hurt me? Thank you very much, Roger. I am so very glad that you explained it to me.'

'For God's sake, Rachel, I know you have nerves of steel. I just do not think you understand the Winter Court at all.'

'I have been here half my life. I think I understand it well enough.'

'With all due respect, perhaps you don't allow yourself to understand. You don't want to believe that incompetents like Harker get all the glory while we do all the work. But they are also petty and fight amongst themselves. That is something we can use to beat them at their own game. '

'Sounds like it worked out for you, at least.'

What was wrong with her? She should have been pleased for Roger, but when she opened her mouth, only bitter words came out.

Roger sighed. 'It's all because you trusted me, once, Rachel. I am just trying to return the favour and protect you.'

'I don't need to be protected.'

'Only from yourself. Do you remember what we talked about, after that tennis game?'

Rachel's cigarette was a flaking cylinder of ash. She dropped it into the wastepaper basket. She felt numb and tired and empty and said nothing.

'You asked me about Hong Kong, what it was like in a different country with a different language. I told you it was hard, how even after a long time you could never tell what people really thought, there was always this invisible wall of glass between you and them. That it was lonely. I think you have to decide which country you want to live in, Rachel. I'll be here if you need me.'

His cough echoed hollowly down the corridor as he went.

Rachel sat alone for a while, looking at the faded pencil lines on the wall she used as an impromptu blackboard. Roger was right, she knew. Keep your head down, seek allies, cash in favours, bide your time. That was how it worked. And that was exactly what Bloom was exploiting.

Kulagin's face rose up in her mind again, and behind it, another being loomed like a malevolent planet, a broad forehead, a neatly trimmed, sharp-tipped spade of a beard, larger than life, made of darkness and the souls of the dying. She thought of the agents lost in Spain. She thought of her mother in Summerland and her memory garden, her voice on the ectophone. The Empire had conquered what was once the most terrifying frontier of all, and the SIS were the Empire's guardians. When she joined the Service during the Great War, all those years ago, everyone had understood that. They were so young, so alive. No one minded that a

Registry clerk like her had stepped up and started analysing radio transcripts when they were a man short.

If you had something more solid, Roger said. And then Harker's voice: *We know his people.*

Who knew Peter Bloom's people? Who had vetted him?

It was late, and she still had access to the Registry. She sat down at her desk, excavated her ectoterminal from beneath dusty papers and typed in a query. Half an hour later she was on her way home, a brown Manila folder in her handbag.

FIVE

A Day at the Summer Court, 9th November 1938

When Peter Bloom awoke the next day, his house in Under-may in the Summer City had forgotten what it was supposed to be.

When he opened his eyes, he lay naked on the floor of a bare, twilit room with rough sandstone walls covered in chalk symbols and dark rusty stains. It looked like a torture chamber. The air smelled of sharp sooty smoke.

Peter swore. He must have fallen asleep, and the house had taken advantage of his slumber to revert to its previous existence.

Like everything permanent in Summerland, the house was made of souls. Each one of its bricks was a *luz* stone, an adamantine kernel that remained when a soul fully Faded and thought and memory were gone. Millennia ago, the Old Dead – the eschatologists' name for the lost civilisation pre-ceding the modern era – had gathered them and used them to create the Summer City. Then the ancient builders had disappeared. After the invention of the ectophone opened the afterlife for exploration at the turn of the century, England's dead had arrived. Aethertects had reshaped the city, including Peter's house, which had become a Victorian residence fit for a gentleman. But the bricks retained other memories, too, and if you didn't show them who was the master, they leaked out.

Peter felt hollow and weak. He had been so depleted of *vim* that he had fallen into a brief torpor, allowing the house to run out of control. But why? With sudden horror, he realised his memories of the previous day were sparse, the first sign of Fading. He knew he had gone to Madrid. But had he learned key information he had already forgotten?

Fortunately, the Fountain was still in its place: a lamp-like stand with a brass nozzle surrounded by dials, connected to the wall by a tube. He turned a dial. Bright *vim* poured out, expanding into a sphere the size of a candle flame that lit up the room and radiated warmth.

Peter cupped his hands and a tendril of the liquid light flowed out of the bright sphere and into them. He drank it, and his thoughts turned its un-taste into honeyed porridge. As the distilled life essence filled him, his memory gradually returned, like photographs being developed. He ran through the previous day in his mind, and was relieved to find there were no gaps.

Tired from meeting Inez, nevertheless he had forced himself to write his usual two reports, one to his handler George in cipher, and one to C, the Chief, at the Summer Court. Usually, the two documents were identical, but Dzhugashvili's presence in Spain warranted consulting with George before sending the report C.

Peter had tried to thought-travel to one of their dead drops – a battery-powered ectophone for recording messages – but had found the beacon inactive. That was not unusual: the ectophone batteries lasted less than a week and had to be manually replaced. However, the beacons for the two fallback phones were dark as well. George had to be out of the country, and his operatives had neglected to maintain the dead drops. Completely drained by the thought-travel attempts, Peter had no choice but to ectomail his report to C uncensored. A reply arrived almost immediately by spirit courier, requesting his presence at 9 a.m. sharp. In death, the old spymaster never slept – unlike Peter, who had been overcome by his exertions.

Fully awake and filled with the luminescent power of the *vim*, Peter hurled a thought at the rough-hewn walls. The torture chamber wavered as if giving an embarrassed shrug and was replaced by a pleasant room with white wallpaper, a soft tan carpet and a curtained window. It was small and bare, modelled after his old rooms at Cambridge, with little in the way of personal items except for his ledger-sized diary on a writing desk, closed with a soul lock that only his own *luz* could open.

In a way, he felt sorry for the house, forced to wear a mask. What did it really matter what it looked like, when ultimately all was aether and souls? For decades, physicists had known that even what the living thought of as solid matter was only knotted vortices in the aether. In the four dimensions of Summerland, any knot could be undone, and thus a spirit could reshape reality with a thought – but maintaining any given configuration took energy.

The small aetheric clock on the desk showed 8.10 a.m. Greenwich Mean Time. He could still make it to the Summer Court by 9 a.m.

He glanced at the hypermirror, a tall, silver-framed prism of polished *luz* that was his only other piece of furniture. A hyperlight reflection provided a three-dimensional image that could be studied from all sides. Inside the prism, there was a serious-looking naked boy of perhaps eleven years old, dark-haired, round-faced, with striking silver-grey eyes.

He stared at the image and concentrated. The boy grew up in an instant and became a young man with a more rounded paunch than he would have liked, a widow's peak in his dark hair, and a thoughtful expression. Peter shaped himself clothes from the aether, a charcoal pinstriped suit, Oxford shoes, a tie in Trinity colours and a golden watch chain. With a flick of his wrist, he completed his wardrobe with a hat and a raincoat. Satisfied, he headed for the door and stepped on something hard and angular.

Thought-chaff had accumulated on the floor during his sleep. It could be dangerous to dream in Summerland, where the pliable aether might give your nightmares form. This time, the things his subconscious mind had birthed looked harmless enough: an abstract, spiralling ribbon, a few dead white-winged moths and a toy soldier.

On impulse, he picked the soldier up. It was crudely cast tin but lovingly painted in khaki and green. He put it in his pocket. It could sit on his desk at work, until it Faded away.

Rows of marble facades blushed pink in Summerland's unchanging twilight glow as Peter walked down Ear Street.

The aethertects had done their jobs well. The Summer City housed millions of New Dead with Tickets in surroundings designed to evoke the best of what the British Empire had to offer, spun from aether and made solid by collective belief. When Peter first moved to Undermay, he could have mistaken the borough for Mayfair, if not for the lack of birdsong and the absence of nights and days.

Yet the longer you lived in Summerland, the stranger things became. Your hypersight grew more acute, and little by little, you developed an awareness of two additional directions that were invisible to the living.

One was the *ana* direction, or four-up. Towards *ana* lay the world of the living, in its own thin slice of the aether. It was the direction of the Unseen, the mysterious source of hyperlight and souls. *Luz* stones fell from *ana*, lodged themselves in dense aetheric configurations like brains at birth.

Upon death, the *luz* detached and fell below the plane of the living world in the *kata* direction – the equivalent of down in the fourth dimension. The soul-stone took the person's memories with it to Summerland like mud stuck in the roots of an uprooted tree. It was only Fading that shed them away until only the *luz* remained.

Peter often wondered how most spirits were able to simply ignore the infinite *kata* beneath them. Even now, as he walked through the small but perfectly groomed Adelphi Park towards the fourtube station at the corner of Fortress Road and Echoes, he felt as if he were crossing a theatre set made of papier mâché, something he could rupture with one sharp poke.

Much like what would happen to his entire existence, if he made a single misstep with C.

It was peak commuting time. The fourtube stop was crowded, mostly affluent New Dead who worked in the *ana*-higher levels of the city. Some of the besuited men had been deceased long enough to have given up walking, moving instead in a peculiar gliding motion, polished shoes barely touching the cobblestones.

Peter took the steps down to the station and joined the orderly queue on the circular platform encircling the dome-shaped tunnel head. The fourtube car arrived – a large crystal hemisphere that shimmered into existence. Peter filed in with the rest of the commuters, grasped a bar fixed to the ceiling and held on tight as the vessel shot in the *ana* direction.

Thought-travel would have been faster, but public transport was a good way to conserve *vim*, and the hypersight views through the crystal gave you a glimpse of the four-dimensional nature of the city. In the fourth direction, buildings were stacked on top of each other like layers in a wedding cake. The attics and purely decorative chimneys merged with the basements of the adjacent *ana* or *kata* level, or kissed each other's walls or roofs in Escherian angles. Not for the first time, Peter thought it resembled a honeycomb.

He glanced at the impassive faces of the commuters, who opened their newspapers with the rustle of dead insect wings. What would Inez think of this bourgeois afterlife, where the dead still repeated the routines of life like reanimated worker bees? Perhaps she would realise that her very struggle for something greater than herself was itself a kind of Heaven. As the train climbed *ana*-wards and the light of the Unseen brightened, Peter found himself fervently wishing that he would not have to take that away from her.

Peter got off at the Albert Park stop on the *ana* end of Fortress Road, a short walk from his destination.

The Summer Court headquarters was modelled after Blenheim Palace, its counterpart in the living world – a sprawling baroque-style building with severe towering stone belvederes ornamenting the skyline. It housed thousands of spirits whose tasks ranged from agent-running, logistics and archiving to compiling and analysing signals intelligence, as well as providing secure communications for Her Majesty's armed forces. Walking briskly towards it, Peter ran through the report in his mind one more time.

A Russian dissident wanting to take over the Spanish Republic. A source close to him. A likely aggressive response from the Soviets to the ectotank deployment. He could not escape the feeling that he had made a mistake, that C suspected something.

Peter ascended the broad stairs of the main entrance, and suddenly the distinctly Summerland character of the Summer Court became clear. It had too many walls and corners at impossible angles, and occasionally the entire building bent and wavered, mirage-like. The Court was a hypercube, with soul-stone walls protecting its secrets from all sides, even in *ana* and *kata*.

He signed the entrance book with an imprint of his *luz* and waited until an attendant spirit arrived to lead him to C's office on the sixth *ana* floor. Even a Section head like Peter needed a guide. The building's aethertecture was constantly changed to eliminate any fixed points that could be used for unauthorised thought-travel, resulting in a warren of corridors, passageways and mezzanines, hypermirrors and blind corners. It was like wandering through an optical illusion.

Peter's anxiety grew as they approached C's office. He tried to cling to the fact that none of the security measures were enough to protect the Court from within. But as he ascended the kaleidoscopic flights of stairs that occasionally took one sideways, *kata-* or *ana*-wards, his usual sense of superiority eluded him.

When Peter entered C's office, at first he saw only the man's silhouette, dominated by the jutting chin outlined against the blinding light of the Unseen from the window.

'Bloom. Come in.'

Peter sat in the chair in front of the large desk. It took a few seconds to adjust to the light and he kept his face impassive. The Chief liked to have a moment to assess each visitor.

C turned and bent his round head with its thinning coppery hair over the paperwork on the desk and proceeded to ignore Peter for several minutes. Occasionally, his fine bow of a mouth twitched slightly, but whether in pleasure or displeasure, Peter could not tell. Soul-reading was only possible with the living or newly deceased spirits who had not yet mastered aether-weaving.

Finally, C leaned back in his chair and lifted a horn-rimmed monocle to his right eye, which was then magnified to ridiculous proportions. Yet the cyclopean stare was so piercing that an involuntary laugh died on Peter's lips.

'Well?' C said.

'Sir?'

C said nothing. Peter cleared his throat.

'Sir, I thought you asked me here to discuss my report.'

'No.' C shook his head sharply and the monocle fell from his eye. Somehow, the pinched stare of his normal-sized eyes was even more intense.

'No?'

'No, I asked you here because I am going to need a new head of the Iberian Section.' C's mouth twitched again. 'What do you have to say for yourself?'

Peter's *luz* became a cold, dead lump in his chest. In the back of his mind, George's voice whispered the litany for the moment of being exposed. Admit nothing. Deny everything. Make counter-allegations.

He straightened his back and looked at the Chief.

'Sir, I am aware that the Section has faced some challenges recently and I take full responsibility. However, I do believe that the recruitment of CARRASCOS' – the code name Peter had assigned to Inez – 'was a breakthrough, and—'

'Yes, I agree.'

'You agree with what, sir?'

'That it was a breakthrough. That is why I need your recommendation for a new Section head.'

'I don't understand.'

'My dear boy, it is very simple. Starting from now, you will be too busy to manage your Section. Your new job is in the recently formed Special Committee for the Iberian Problem. You are going to help me convince the prime minister that we need this Dzhugashvili chap to take over Spain.'

Convince the prime minister.

This time, Peter nearly lost control over his aetheric self. Suddenly, the hands resting on his pinstriped knees were a small boy's, sticking out from oversized sleeves. He closed his eyes and tried to concentrate on his self-image. Something pressed painfully against his thigh in his pocket, and he remembered the toy soldier with its broken bayonet.

'Bloom? Are you all right?'

He took a deep breath. 'I'm quite all right, sir. Just …
surprised.'

'I can send for some *vim* if you want.'

Peter shook his head. C steepled his fingers and looked at
him.

'Bloom, I was expecting a slightly different reaction from
you.'

'Sir … I am honoured. Truly, I am. It's just that … Sir,
as you saw from my report, BRIAR moved too quickly with
CARRASCOS, and it was through pure luck that I was able
to find something that resonated with her. My recommendation would be to spend more time developing her before
involving her in a major operation. And with all due respect,
sir, right now I am best qualified to do that.'

Besides the overflowing paperwork, there were a number
of small glass vials containing coloured liquids in a wooden
rack on the edge of C's desk. Supposedly, they were memen-
tos of the invisible inks that the SIS had relied upon in the
living world, in the days before the Summer Court. C picked
one up and examined it carefully.

'Do you know,' he said, 'that one of the best inks we had
early on was semen?' The Chief smiled wryly. 'No, really. It
worked quite well, and the operator had, ah, a reliable supply. One of our lads in Russia tried to store it up in advance,
and his letters stank to high heaven. We had to tell him that
a fresh supply was needed for each communication. You
may laugh, but I always thought it was rather poetic. Our
soldiers bleed, but how many times are we asked to give that
particular bodily fluid for Her Majesty? You never served,
did you, Bloom?'

'No, sir.'

'Then you may not fully understand the sacrifices we are sometimes asked to make.'

C leaned back and massaged his left leg absently. The Chief had passed over in a horrific car accident that also cost the life of his son – who hadn't possessed a Ticket. C's mangled leg had been stuck in the wreckage. He sawed it off with a penknife and crawled to the boy. Their bodies were found together, the father holding the son.

C had been back at work a month later.

'I will be candid with you, Bloom. Your Section could have done its job more effectively, and we have a bloody mess in our hands. The Admiralty is baying for war. This is going to get worse before it gets better. The PM explicitly said he wants first-hand information, so your number's up. We have some very difficult things to tell him. If hearing them from you makes it easier to stop a war, you will show up and talk until your face turns blue. BRIAR can handle your new source. Is that understood?'

Peter swallowed. 'Yes, sir.'

C's gruff voice was gentler this time. 'You'll do, Bloom,' he said. 'You'll do.'

Peter left C's office in a daze. His own office was on the fourth *ana* floor. He made his way through the Polish and Italian Sections and past the entrance to the Chimney – a *luz* tower that reached all the way to the aether of the living world and allowed you to make secure ectophone calls to Whitehall and Blenheim without leaving the confines of the Summer Court.

He closed the door, sat down at his desk and leaned back.

Notes and diagrams for the Spanish operation, written in aether itself with a thought, floated everywhere like cobwebs. Inez's picture from BRIAR was at the centre of it all, and if possible, her gaze looked even fiercer than he remembered. In frustration, Peter waved a hand. The rows of neat white writing, lines and boxes wavered and evaporated like smoke.

In theory, he should have been delighted. He would have unprecedented access to the highest levels of power in the Empire at a critical time when he could be extremely valuable to the Presence's cause. George would be overjoyed.

So why was he utterly and completely terrified?

Peter took the tin soldier from his pocket and set it on his desk. It looked at him expectantly, rough, fingerless hands gripping the rifle. He remembered a game played on his parents' living room floor a long time ago, a round-bellied man setting up armies of tiny troops, crawling on all fours, a red-faced Gulliver hovering over a Lilliputian nation.

The prime minister.

Suddenly, he felt the tight *luz* grip of the Summer Court's walls all around him like a vice. He was supposed to work – C had told him to prepare an overview for the PM in two days' time – but it was impossible to concentrate.

George. He had to see George. His handler must be told about Dzhugashvili and the opportunity. It was more than enough grounds for a face-to-face meeting in the world of the living.

For a moment, he even managed to convince himself that was the real reason he wanted to see George.

Peter took his coat and hat and headed back out.

*

Once he was safely outside the Court and headed down the wide walking avenue through the resplendent green of Albert Park, amber-tinted in the unchanging Unseen light, he considered his options. It was nearly a month before their next meeting was due. He would have to use the protocol for an emergency meeting, something he had never done before. George had emphasised that it was to be employed only for the gravest of reasons.

Peter concentrated, pictured a statue of a lion at the end of Fortress Road and thought-travelled.

Albert Park blurred into an orange haze as the image of the lion pulled him through the aether. Or perhaps he stayed still and the aether flowed around him and through him like cold water, taking *vim* with it until the distinction between the vision and reality disappeared.

Peter stood between the forepaws of a marble lion statue. He turned around, and in front of him loomed the enormous black half-pearl of the Fortress, the oldest structure in the city. The Fortress dwarfed all the fanciful aethertect creations near Albert Park. Its dark, hemispherical mass was present in all the levels of the city. There had been proposals to dismantle the ancient structure and use its uncountable *luz* stones elsewhere, but so far the Empire's scientists had been unable to unravel the lost aetheric arts used to build it millennia ago.

A small crowd was gathered in the square. The Fortress attracted visitors, especially the newly dead taking in the sights of the city. Peter passed groups of deceased children whose undisciplined soul-sparks blazed with wonder and terror, and raucous soldiers whose aetheric bodies openly flaunted the horrific injuries that had ended their lives. He followed the rim of the Fortress until he found the Listener.

The Listener was a pale man who had Faded to the point where his *luz* was a bright star in his chest and his face was barely visible. He ran grey, smokelike fingers along the black tiles of the curving wall and whispered faintly to himself, echoing the inaudible whispers of the ancient soul-stones. His hat lay on the ground. A handful of *luz* shillings and pence gleamed inside it.

Peter gave him a look of genuine pity. Although in theory the National Death Service guaranteed a minimum supply of *vim* and accommodation in the ever-expanding Summer City to anyone with a Ticket, occasionally premature Fading meant that a spirit simply forgot to be a part of the system any longer. It was an unpredictable process. Many Faded retained a single memory or an obsession that defined their entire existence.

'The old soul-stones speak,' the Listener said in a reed-thin voice. 'They tell your past and your future. One *vim* shilling to find out.'

Peter smiled and shook his head. 'No, thank you. I prefer to find out the old-fashioned way.'

Peter wondered if the man truly served the Presence, or if he was an intermediary for another agent. Was the Listening simply an act, or had he sacrificed his memories, his very self, for the cause? Yet there was something familiar in the Listener's utter dedication to things others could not see or hear.

Using a simple code agreed with George, Peter measured out the desired date of their meeting – tomorrow – in *luz* coins. As the bright discs clinked into the hat, the weight on his shoulders vanished.

His handler would know what to do.

The Listener ignored him and returned to his work. Peter walked on until he found a section of the wall with no one nearby. Then he pressed his ear against the smooth, cold surface, closed his eyes and listened.

SIX

How to Tame an Elephant,
5th November 1938

On Saturday, Rachel White was on her way to meet the dead spymaster when she realised she was being followed.

It was little more than instinct at first, a glimpse of a familiar gait, face or hat. The crowd in Charing Cross was thick, drawn out by the sunny autumn afternoon. She stopped at a booth that sold old records, pretended to study the cover of a Schubert music sheet, and watched the passers-by.

Newsboys carried advert placards on their backs: THE TRUTH HURTS – THIS AWFUL TRUTH WILL MAKE YOU SCREAM. Workmen pasted down steaming, pungent asphalt. Sleek electric cars and tottering old buses huddled shoulder to shoulder in a traffic jam and blared their horns. A young man in a sweater gave her an appreciative look. Ectofactory workers wearing dishevelled coats and pasty complexions shuffled past. A cabbie union man offered her a leaflet on the evils of spirit cabs and unemployment.

Nothing. No familiar faces, hats or gaits. Her street tradecraft – a spy's art of clandestine encounters and surveillance evasion – was rusty but she still knew how to execute a surveillance-detection route: a logical path through the city that was designed to force any observers to reveal themselves. In the past three hours, she had criss-crossed the city on the Tube, taken several cabs and wandered through Harrods. Foyles bookstore was going to serve as her final choke point.

Of course, it was possible for a team of agents to shadow a suspect without being spotted. More than four were practically undetectable. In addition, she had no way of sensing aetheric surveillance, although spirit Watchers were nearly useless in the daytime.

Was she being overcautious? As far as anyone in the Winter Court knew, she was now happily working as a clerk in the Finance Section, doing exactly what Roger had advised. She shuffled dull paperwork any office girl could have handled, except for the high clearance required, approved bank wires to fund overseas operations and reconciled accounts with deliberately obscure line items. She lunched with the junior staff in the canteen, away from her former colleagues. On the rare occasions when she interacted with Liddell, Vee-Vee or other senior personnel, she gracefully accepted empty promises of support and hinted that she might want to retire early, as soon as her pension and Ticket were secure.

Rachel might almost have believed it herself if not for the contents of the Manila folder she had taken from Wormwood Scrubs, and the response to the anonymous ectomail she had sent to the folder's subject two days earlier.

She crossed the road, navigated the puddles of last night's rain and entered Foyles. She made sure to spend time in the bird section, looking for a book on feeding finches. That would come in handy for the cover story she was working on.

Over breakfast, she had told Joe she was going shopping. He had suffered another bad night. A cold spot had appeared in the bedroom and Rachel had slept in the guest room. When she woke, she had found Joe lying down on the couch in the drawing room with curtains closed, Gertrude fussing over him.

'Maybe you can bring me a new head, dear,' he said. 'I heard they are on sale at Harrods.'

She felt guilty at the easy lie. 'I like this one just fine,' she said and kissed his forehead.

Now, as she breathed in the smell of new books and made her way through the labyrinth of shelves, she wondered if actually getting birds would be a bad idea.

Then she recognised the young blond man in the camel-hair coat, leafing through a book barely thirty feet away.

Memory matched his features to other impressions from her route, like light glinting off facets of a jewel. A sandy brown coat glimpsed in Harrods. The face of a man bent over a newspaper on the Oxford Court Line. Thin blond hair, combed back from a high forehead, and improbably chiselled features.

Rachel made sure to walk across his field of vision and then proceeded further into the bookstore's depths. When he turned a corner into the history section, she was waiting.

The man froze when he saw her standing there, only a few steps away.

Of *course* the Service was watching. She had been an idiot to think otherwise. Someone – probably Harker or Roger – had already passed her information to C in the Summer Court, and they were keeping an eye on her just in case she planned to do something foolish. The feeling was both reassuring and embarrassing at the same time, like when her mother had caught her as a child after she ran away with her wet nurse's daughter in Bombay to make chapattis in the local bakery.

The man pretended to ignore her, studied the shelves and touched the spine of a book with a gloved hand. He was remarkably handsome, too much so for the field, where the real heroes were faceless, average-looking men.

Rachel herself, on the other hand, belonged exactly where she was. Behind a desk. On the shelf. She just refused to admit it. That was why she had saved Kulagin from the duel. She had wanted something more than the empty nursery and the haunted man in her bedroom.

No matter. There was no arguing with tradecraft: no rendezvous under surveillance. Harker was probably laughing behind her back, but she was not going to give him the satisfaction of acknowledging that she had been caught. She headed back to the bird section and bought a book on the care and breeding of Gouldian finches. There was a hollow feeling in her stomach when she walked back towards the Tube station.

'Excuse me, Mrs White?' said a voice with an impeccable public-school accent.

The young man in the camel-hair coat stood in front of her.

Rachel sighed. 'Tell Harker to send you back to Brickendomby Hall for more training,' she said.

'You misunderstand me, madam. I am not a Watcher.'

'Enlighten me, then.'

'My name is Henry. I am merely a messenger. Would you be so kind as to step inside for a moment?' He gestured at the entrance to a wax museum that advertised THE HORRORS OF THE TRENCHES — OVER 100 FIGURES.

She stared at him.

'It will only take a minute,' the man said reassuringly. 'Allow me, please.' He offered her his arm. 'This is supposed to be a splendid show. Our mutual friend you worked with in Wolverhampton thinks so, too.'

Rachel raised her eyebrows, accepted the man's arm and allowed herself to be led inside.

The wax museum was crowded, hot and smelled of burning dust. The exhibits were in small, low rooms filled with sandbags to make them look like trenches. In the dim light, stiff wax figures in their broad-rimmed helmets and uniforms enacted scenes from the war.

A medic offered a wounded soldier with a bloody bandage around his head a Ticket and a vial of cyanide. A group of Tommies huddled behind barbed wire while an old rattling newsreel played on the wall – hulking forms of ectotanks over charging soldiers, striding forward and growing bigger with every death, picking up field guns with ectoplasm tentacles. A group of doctors and technicians, white coats stained by dust and grime, doing final checks on a spirit-armoured soldier before his transformation. The metal plates and heavy coiled wire evoked a medieval knight. Rachel stared at that tableau for a long time. Was this what Joe's nightmares were like?

'Here, Mrs White,' Henry said. He ducked under a piece of tape blocking a corridor, indicating an unfinished part of the exhibit. She followed him into a pitch-black dead end. He fumbled with a light switch. A bulb flickered into a half-hearted glow and revealed a group of naked wax dolls standing at attention.

Henry removed his hat. Underneath, he was wearing a Crookes aetheric resonator, or a spirit crown as it was colloquially known. It was an expensive model, too: the filigreed silver net practically vanished into his hair, and it was only now that she noticed the skin-coloured power cord that ran into the pocket of his coat. That explained the good looks: Henry was a high-class medium who rented his body to affluent spirits. He smiled a little sadly and reached into his pocket. There was a small click and his features contorted unnaturally, his eyes flickering from side to side and then rolling back in his head. No wonder mediums usually wore masks.

'Mrs White,' he said in a new voice. It was gentle and mellifluous, lower than Henry's own, and made her think of a kindly old uncle. Children across Britain loved that voice, the voice of Max Chevalier, the famous naturalist and author whose radio shows were a part of many a family's Sunday ritual even after his passage to Summerland. What most people did not know was that Chevalier had been the head of his own Section in the Winter Court and the most successful agent runner in the Service.

Until he was assigned to vet Peter Bloom.

'You passed the test, Mrs White,' Chevalier said. 'I hope you will forgive my little ruse. It is always good to observe wild animals from afar for a while before approaching.'

Rachel stared into the medium's white, empty eyes. Henry's handsome features were contorted into something resembling a mischievous grin, but exaggerated, like a Mr Punch figure in a street booth.

'Do you mind if I smoke a pipe while we talk? It's a pleasure I rarely experience – thought-forms simply are not the same – so I asked Henry to bring it especially.'

Rachel nodded and waited while the medium took a curved pipe from an inside pocket and filled it. His movements were jerky and a lot of the tobacco spilled to the floor. Then he lit it, filling the corridor with pungent smoke.

'Ah, that is better. Now, I have made some enquiries about you, Mrs White. I understand you had something of a career setback recently. A pity. A real pity.' He blew out a cloud of smoke that obscured his unnatural face.

'I do not want your pity, Mr Chevalier. I want answers.'

'Please call me Max. And I can assure you that it is not pity making me spend my meagre savings on Henry's services to meet with you like this. It's curiosity. Tell me, do you actually plan to breed finches?'

'I might. As you say, I have suffered a career setback and have more spare time on my hands.'

'Intelligent creatures, more so than they get credit for. But very fragile, Mrs White. A sudden cold, shock or unhappiness can kill them. Prone to tumours, as well. You need to keep them warm. Feed them fennel seeds.'

'With all due respect, I did not seek you out to discuss birds.'

'Oh? A good intelligence officer needs to be a naturalist. I myself am currently raising a cuckoo – with the help of my lovely Susi, of course, my living pair of hands – and it is most instructive.'

'Tell me about Peter Bloom.'

'Ah. Now there is a rare and interesting bird.'

'You had your own Section, practically your own miniature Service. Then you vetted Peter Bloom. Suddenly there were rumours about you being a deranged witch-hunter. You passed away very suddenly. There was talk of suicide. The

Summer Court did not want you. What happened?'

Max Chevalier's spirit puffed on the pipe. Tendrils of smoke swirled around the medium's face like ectoplasm.

'You have already answered your question, Mrs White. You see, I raised a fox once. It was a sweet creature as a cub, like a cross between a cat and a dog. As it grew older, it became troublesome: very good at sneaking into henhouses while still allowing itself to be cuddled. One day, it tore up my favourite pair of slippers. I took it to the back yard and shot it in the head. It looked surprised when I pulled the trigger.'

Rachel frowned. 'So you grew too bold and Bloom was merely an excuse to put you down?'

'Yes. In this case by planting documents on one of my agents to make it look like we had framed an innocent man, a public outcry, et cetera, et cetera.'

'What did you find out about Bloom that was so dangerous?'

'Sir Stewart asked me to vet Bloom, and I did some digging, not realising it was a trap. It turned out that Bloom's father, Charles, was an MP for an anti-Dimensionist Labour group before he died without a Ticket. His mother, Ann Veronica née Reeve, had radical leanings in her youth and took up the struggle. And then Peter engaged in some adolescent indiscretions at Cambridge. Burned his own Ticket, if you can believe that. But that could be disregarded – rebellion is a prerogative of the young, after all. Still, I advised against hiring him. I was overruled.'

'By whom?'

'I believe the final decision was made during dinner at White's, with Sir Stewart in attendance and a certain author of some renown – a Mr Herbert Blanco West.'

Rachel stared at him. 'The prime minister?'

Max nodded. 'I made a very bad error, then. Fortunes can turn quickly in the Service, as you know.'

'But why was the PM involved?'

'If you had the patience to dig up old gossip pages like I did, Mrs White, you would have discovered that Mr West engaged in an affair with a young Miss Reeve – whose subsequent marriage to Charles Bloom was very sudden indeed.'

Rachel drew a sharp breath. 'You mean to say that—'

'Peter Bloom is untouchable, Mrs White. Whatever your grievance with him may be, your superiors will do anything to keep him safe in order to secure favours from the highest level. The windmill you are tilting at is very high and ancient and English: privilege.'

Rachel looked at the cartoon horrors of the Great War around them and felt sick. She thought about what it felt like to share a cigarette in the trenches and then see a comrade blown apart into red mist, see green fields transformed into landscapes of death and nightmare. She remembered her first night as a volunteer nurse, the first burn victim of a Zeppelin bombing, his peeling flesh and pustules and charred skin.

And then the memory of lying sprawled on the bathroom floor, touching the spongy, seedlike thing that came out of her.

There are wounds in the world, she thought.

'No,' Rachel said quietly.

Max said nothing. For a moment, there was just the noise of the crowd a corridor's length away and the eyes of the dead man looking at her, unblinking.

'No one is untouchable. Not if we can find evidence.'

'You are far too idealistic, Mrs White.'

'You thought you were untouchable, once.'

'Ah, but I was just a peasant reaching above my station. Bloom belongs in all the right clubs.'

'There has to be a way to find proof. Locate his handler.'

'That would present considerable difficulties. For one thing, you are still alive, Mrs White.'

'But you are not.'

'Mrs White, I am content with my afterlife. I have my loyal listeners, my books. The next one is going to be called *How to Tame an Elephant*. Fascinating creatures. Did you know that they may have souls? Edison has been testing a kind of spirit armour for pachyderms. And I have my cuckoo Goo and other creatures in Sloane Square. Why should I help you?'

It was difficult to read someone wearing another person's body, but there was something familiar in the way Max cocked his head.

'Revenge would be enough for most people: your enemies used Bloom to destroy you, why not use him to destroy them? Only I do not think you care about that. You are a naturalist. You like to understand creatures like Bloom. He had everything, so why did he turn, like a well-treated dog that bites its master? I think, deep down, you want to know.'

The medium's thin lips curled in a devilish parody of a kindly uncle's grin.

'Ah, Mrs White, you do not disappoint.'

At five in the afternoon, two hours later, Rachel returned home to St John's Wood, carrying a covered birdcage.

Gertrude took the cage and rolled her eyes when it chirped,

but said nothing. Joe came down the stairs to meet her. He was still unshaven and dishevelled, but his eyes were brighter.

'What do you have there, dear?'

'Finches.' Rachel felt playful and strangely free. Her mind tingled with ideas. She and Max had scheduled a planning session on Tuesday in a flat that he maintained on Sloane Square. In the meantime, she was going to investigate opening a credit line for their illicit operation. A part of her – the part that had been Head Girl at Princess Helena College – recoiled from the very idea of misuse of government funds. Another part found it inexplicably thrilling.

'I thought my old bird could use some company,' she said.

'You know very well that I could never even keep a house plant alive.'

'You always liked a challenge. Don't worry, I can help. Now that I have more time on my hands.'

Joe took her hand. That was the closest she had come to acknowledging that she had trouble at work.

'Gertrude, would you do the honours, please?' Rachel asked.

Gertrude drew the heavy cloth aside. There was a storm of feathers inside. Two frantic, brightly coloured birds bounced from one perch to another.

'*Scheisse*,' she swore. 'Begging your pardon, madam.'

Eventually the birds settled down. One was bright yellow-green with a red head, the other blue and grey with a bonnet of pale silver. Their beadlike eyes were alert. The yellow-green one cocked its head to one side and stared at them.

'Aren't they really difficult to keep?' Joe asked.

'I met an old colleague who keeps birds. Max Chevalier.'

The bird she knew to be the male started bouncing up

and down at a furious pace and sang a continuous, trilling, complex song. The other bird – a female – raised her head slightly, listening.

'What on Earth is it doing?' Joe asked.

The male was like a wound-up toy. It continued the joyous bouncing until Rachel was sure its tiny brain would be addled. She giggled a little, then laughed. Once she started it was hard to stop, and then Joe joined her.

Finally, they both had to wipe tears from her eyes.

'Very well,' Joe said. 'I suppose I can look after these silly creatures for a while. And here I was thinking that I could go to the club later tonight.'

Rachel looked at him. 'I think I would like it if you stayed at home, dear,' she said quietly.

Joe blinked.

'Oh.'

'Don't look so surprised. It is not like you have to jump up and down to impress me any more.'

'Indeed, but it is just that since—'

Rachel was dimly aware of Gertrude making a discreet retreat in the background.

'I know,' she said, then took Joe's hand and led him upstairs to the bedroom.

They had not made love for six months. It was long enough to make it clumsy at first. Joe alternated between being too rough and too gentle, first squeezing and biting and grunting, then barely daring to touch her, caressing her thighs and belly with spidery fingers, a sensation she hated.

Eventually, they found an old rhythm, half-sitting, him

inside her. He had the sweaty smell of a day spent in bed and his mouth tasted of tobacco. She did not care, breathed it in, lapped at his lips teasingly, tore at his greying chest fuzz with her fingers. Joe groaned. He was skinnier than she remembered. Old burn scars were prominent on his chest and wiry arms. His hands were cold.

She was close to her climax when it happened.

Joe's eyes became white pools. Tendrils of ectoplasm poured out of his mouth and onto her skin, milky and cold. He made mumbling, chattering sounds, his voice shifting registers as if many people were trying to speak through him at once. Then the coldness was inside her, swelling.

Rachel screamed. She beat at Joe's frigid, sweaty chest. Then she bit his shoulder as hard as she could, tasting blood.

He jolted and toppled. She rolled to the side and out of the bed.

'Joe! Joe, come back!'

The ectoplasm floated around him for a moment like a white halo and then evaporated. She stood up, breathing heavily. Then Joe's eyes were his own again. He stared at her and then at his hands in horror.

'I am so sorry, Rachel. Are you all right? I am so sorry.'

She nodded. It was cold in the room and the sweat chilled on her skin. Gingerly, she climbed back into the bed and drew most of the blanket to her. Joe sat up but kept himself away from her.

'I shouldn't have,' he said. 'After ... after I was decommissioned, they said most of the ... ability would be gone. I'm so sorry, Rachel. It has been getting worse. I didn't want to worry you. Especially after—' He paused.

'After the baby,' Rachel said.

Joe nodded. The old guilt rose up in Rachel, colder than ectoplasm.

'Maybe I should sleep in the guest bedroom,' Joe said.

'No,' she said quietly. 'Lie down with me.' She pulled him next to her and pressed her face against his neck. His skin was still like ice, but she forced herself to bear it, holding him tight. After a while, his breathing grew steady and he slept.

Rachel lay awake and pulled away from the chill of him, into a warm place, her India, imagined the humid heat, the smell of spices, and when the image was firm in her mind, she started making plans.

SEVEN

The Termin Procedure, 10th November 1938

The November wind whipped up leaves in the nondescriptly opulent Chelsea Square. Peter Bloom shivered in his borrowed flesh and nervously rubbed his numb hands together. It had been a while since he last walked amongst the living and it had not occurred to him to bring an overcoat. But the autumn air was not the only thing that chilled him.

The windows of the safe house were dark. That meant George was late, and he was never late.

There were times when George had shown up drunk, or decided to lecture on avant-garde poetry instead of debriefing Peter. But the Russian never strayed from the best practices of tradecraft. Was it possible that he had not received the message in time? Or perhaps the Listener had proved to be as erratic a messenger as his appearance had promised.

The steady ticking of the spirit crown's control unit over his heart reminded Peter that he had less than six hours left. The device's aetheric field anchored his soul into the medium's rented skull, but at midnight the timer would switch the circuit off and banish him to Summerland.

It sounded like a fairy tale, but the transaction with the medium, a licensed charter-body named Pendlebury whom Peter favoured due to a slight resemblance, had been extremely prosaic. For an hourly fee equivalent to that of a high-class barrister, the medium quieted the vibrations of his own soul-spark and allowed a deceased visitor to take control. It was not quite the same as being alive again – fine motor control was difficult, for example – but more than worth the price. Naturally, the use of an amnesia-inducing anaesthetic that ensured the medium retained no memories of the spirit's actions cost extra.

Peter entered the small, barren garden in the centre of the square. Mud squelched under his polished Oxford shoes. The key was hidden under a rock, and as he picked it up he was overcome by the tang of dead leaves and earth. It took him back to the first time he met George, three years ago.

It had been autumn then, too, and Peter was still alive. He had little idea of what to expect: a fanatic, perhaps, or an unforgiving taskmaster. When George opened the door, he embraced Peter like an affectionate bear. They sat by the fireplace, in a small circle of warm light in the empty house, with its scarred wallpaper where the electric wiring had been removed, and got drunk on cheap red wine.

Towards the end of the evening, the Russian asked Peter why he'd turned. Flustered, Peter muttered platitudes about inequality and war and world peace. George seized him by the shoulders and told him to pull his head out of his backside. George's job was to help Peter, to safeguard him, to defend him from both the British and George's own masters who sometimes did not see clearly. He could not do that if Peter was not honest. Did Peter understand?

After that, Peter did his best to explain what had happened to him at Cambridge. George laughed so hard he started coughing, and Peter had to pound him on the back to make it stop.

Peter realised he was now kneeling in the mud. His memories always became more intense while re-embodied. In Summerland, one's senses were muted, especially smell – not surprising since all sensory impressions there were memories imprinted in the aether. Maybe that, in part, led to Fading: losing the keys that unlocked one's past.

He stood up, brushed off his wet knees and went to the door. Before opening it, he ran his fingers along the hinges.

The pencil lead George always placed there when leaving was missing. The safe house was compromised.

Panic washed over Peter. His rented heart missed a beat. Pendlebury's sedated soul stirred and clawed at the inside of his skull like a trapped rat.

His leg muscles spasmed. He leaned on the door and fumbled for the spirit crown's control unit in his pocket. His hands felt like oversized mittens, but he managed to twist the crown's tuning dial. Feedback screamed in his head, and then he was in control again.

He tried to breathe the chilly air steadily as he replaced the key in its hiding place. He risked one last glance at the safe house. Its curtainless, blank windows had a haunted look. Turning his back on it felt like a betrayal.

Peter tried a brisk walking pace but managed only a wretched limp, his leg muscles still twitching. He cursed himself for not following a more rigorous surveillance-detection route from Pendlebury's flat in Marylebone. For all he knew, the house was under observation and he had just blown his cover.

Briefly, he considered going directly to the Soviet Embassy, simply walking in and asking for asylum. It was tempting in the manner of the strange compulsion to leap one felt when standing near a cliff's edge. But it meant abandoning all the progress he had made so far.

No, the thing to do was assume he was under observation and calmly act according to his cover story – which meant attending the soirée at the Harrises', a couple who hosted a regular social event for the intelligence community. Later, he would check George's dead drops for messages.

Absurdly, he wondered how to explain his muddy knees to Hildy Harris.

Just as he was about to hail a cab, a black electric car slid quietly from a cul-de-sac and swerved in front of him. The back door swung open.

'FELIX,' said a woman sitting in the back, using Peter's Soviet code name and motioning with a gloved hand. 'Get in.'

Peter hesitated, heart pounding. Was this some kind of Winter Court sting? But the woman did not look like any SIS agent he had ever seen. She had round cheeks and wore pink lipstick. Her hair cascaded in cherubic ringlets under a flowered hat. The dark green overcoat strained against a generous figure. The overall impression was that of a voluptuous tulip and he nearly laughed – until he saw her blue eyes.

Her pupils were pinpoints, and the utter lack of doubt and fear in her gaze belonged to someone who had spoken to God.

Gingerly, Peter climbed into the car and closed the door.

A man in a raincoat sat behind the steering wheel. He was young, perhaps twenty-five, with a long, sad face, protruding ears and dark, slicked-back hair. Apart from the rakish angle of his bowler hat, he looked thoroughly unremarkable.

'I am sorry about this,' he said as he manoeuvred the car back into the flow of traffic. Like the woman, he had a faint accent that might have been Dutch. 'We received your message, but we had to make sure you were not followed.'

'Who are you?' Peter asked.

'My name is Otto. This – this is my associate—'

'Shut up, dear,' the woman said. 'I am his wife. You can call me Nora.' Street lights flickered on her face and gave it a porcelain-like pallor. 'Now, let's have a look at you.'

With a nurse's impersonal touch, she patted Peter down and, before he could protest, pulled the spirit crown's control unit from his pocket. She cradled it in her hands and smiled.

'I will hold on to this for a while. We have a lot to talk about, and we would not want you to leave us too soon.'

'Nora. Show some respect,' Otto said.

'He understands, dear. He is a professional. Aren't you, FELIX?'

Peter said nothing. The thought of escaping to Summerland had crossed his mind, but leaving Pendlebury with these two was hardly an option. Besides, they were likely to be armed.

'Please excuse my wife,' Otto said. 'We were instructed to take precautions.'

'Instructed? By whom?'

'Your new case officer,' Nora said, smiling. 'And speaking of precautions, take off your mask and tie this around your eyes.' She held up a piece of black cloth.

'No. I want to know what this is about. Who is this new officer? What happened to George?'

Nora's smile vanished. She exchanged a look with Otto via the rear-view mirror.

'His name his Shpiegelglass,' she said quietly. 'He will explain everything. Now do as I say.'

She took his wrist in an iron grip and pressed the cloth in his hand.

Peter removed his mask. It was a custom for the New Dead to wear them when using mediums, both to separate the medium's identity from the customer's, and to hide the unavoidable 'possessed' look that resulted from the spirit's inability to control their facial muscles. Pendlebury's face was reflected in the window, slack-jawed and dead-eyed. Tufts of dark hair stuck out from the spirit crown's silver net.

Quickly, Peter tied the blindfold over his eyes.

'That's better,' Nora said.

Peter's throat was dry. They drove in silence for a while.

When the car came to a halt, Nora took Peter's hand. He could feel the cord of the spirit crown in her grip like a leash.

'Now, let's go and see Shpiegelglass,' she said.

Nora led Peter out of the car, through a door and into a cold, empty space that smelled musty. Glass shards crunched beneath his shoes. They descended a narrow spiral staircase for several minutes, the air growing thick and oppressive. They had to be deep underground.

Ahead, somebody – Otto? – opened a heavy door. Peter smelled the mixture of antiseptic and poorly washed humanity he associated with hospitals.

Then Nora took Peter's shoulders and gently eased him into a chair. She removed the blindfold, and he blinked at dim fluorescent lights in a high, arched ceiling. They were in a small space partitioned off from something big and cavernous with green hospital curtains.

A small, stout, blond man with protruding eyes sat on a folding chair in front of Peter, leaning forward, elbows on his knees, the tips of his thick fingers pressed together. There was a heavy leather suitcase on the floor next to him.

'Good evening, FELIX,' the man said. 'It is a pleasure to meet you. I am Shpiegelglass. I am sure you have many questions, but if you don't mind, I am going to start with a few of my own.'

He motioned to Nora, who handed the spirit crown control box to Otto and took a step forward.

'Is this really necessary?' Otto asked, his voice reedy and thin. 'We made sure he was not followed—'

'Comrade Otto,' Shpiegelglass said, 'would you prefer to answer a few questions instead?'

Peter heard Otto shuffling his feet.

Nora was holding a hammer and a very sharp, needle-like chisel. Shpiegelglass nodded to her. She stood behind Peter and pressed the chisel's tip against one of the thick vertebrae in his neck.

'What are you doing?' Peter hissed.

'I am sorry about this, Comrade,' Otto said.

The small smile on Shpiegelglass's face did not waver.

'Our Nora is not only beautiful but also talented. She is an accomplished sculptress who has exhibited bold work in Rotterdam. She is a student of anatomy, and is able to sever your spinal cord with one blow, just at the right spot to paralyse but not kill. I do apologise for the discomfort. This is merely a precaution, you understand, in case your answers do not prove satisfactory. We have other guests who have failed to be helpful. I am sure you have no desire to join them.'

There was a faint moan somewhere beyond the green curtains. Peter imagined lying in a hospital bed, trapped in Pendlebury's paralysed body until the medium's brain started to reject the foreign spirit and developed the inevitable tumours.

'Why are you doing this?' he whispered. 'What have I done?'

Shpiegelglass pulled his chair closer and leaned forward until Peter could smell his faint aftershave and meaty breath. He gave Peter's knee a fatherly pat.

'Why, that is precisely what we are trying to find out. Tell me, why did you request an in-person meeting?'

Shpiegelglass's voice was gentle, yet Peter hesitated. Telling him about Inez felt like sharing something intimate with a stranger. The tip of Nora's chisel was a tingling point against his neck. He could feel its slight rise and fall in rhythm with her breathing.

'FELIX. I understand you are upset. You are not sure why I am asking these questions, why I am treating you like an enemy. All will be made clear. I am here to help you, just like George was. But I cannot do it blindfolded. Please. Why did you ask for the meeting?'

'There is a couple, the Harrises, who work for the SIS,' Peter said. 'They are hosting a soirée tonight. It offered me an opportunity to give my regular report to George.'

'I am sure you know that an ectophone recording or an

encrypted ectomail would have been much safer. I take it you had something very important to share? I want to believe you are not here to betray us, FELIX. I know Nora does, too.'

'For the love of God, I am not here to betray anyone! Why can't you tell me where George is?'

Tears rose into Peter's eyes. He wished he still had his mask to conceal the hideousness of a crying man with a dead, empty face.

Shpiegelglass leaned back in his chair and stroked his upper lip with a crooked finger.

'I cannot tell you because I do not know,' he said slowly. 'A month ago, I came to London with a very pleasant task. I was to perform the Termin Procedure on George. He was to receive his reward for long service and join the Presence.' Shpiegelglass's smile vanished. 'Imagine my surprise when he was nowhere to be found. We had to reconsolidate his network – not an easy task, as it turned out that many of his reports had been incomplete. Finally, a source inside the SIS informed us that a senior Russian intelligence officer had defected. A bear of a man, bald, with a fondness for drink.'

The words were a punch in Peter's gut. Pendlebury's soul felt his pain and squirmed inside him. He was half a ghost again, half a living man, a contradiction.

Like George being a defector.

In mathematics, if you started with a contradiction, you could prove anything to be true. One could be made to equal two. Black could be turned white.

Was it the Termin Procedure? George had often talked about the Presence in an irascible manner, like describing an overbearing relative. Maybe George was afraid. Maybe if Peter had explained to him what the Presence was, if he had only tried harder that night they first met, George would have understood—

'Why?' Peter whispered.

'The why no longer matters,' Shpiegelglass said quietly. 'Now you see why we took precautions. You could have been followed, or used as a decoy duck. George could have turned you as well. Observing your reaction, I do not believe he did. However, it is possible that the SIS knows about you. It is prudent to assume they do. Therefore, it is imperative that you tell us what you were going to tell George, since that is the one thing left about this operation that is not compromised.'

'No,' Peter said. 'This has to be some kind of misinformation operation, he is under instructions from the Presence—'

Shpiegelglass shook his head and touched Peter's shoulder.

'Betrayal feels sharper than Nora's chisel, I know.' He motioned to the woman and the metallic pressure against Peter's neck disappeared.

Peter massaged the sore point. The words rolled out easily now.

'I asked for a meeting because I have a new source in Madrid,' he said. 'A Republican fighter. She told me that Iosif Dzhugashvili, Stalin, is in Spain. The SIS wants to put him in charge of the Republic so Britain can stop supporting Franco. I am supposed to present to a special committee tomorrow, including the prime minister. I wanted to talk to George because I did not know what to do.'

Nora started to take notes as Shpiegelglass asked more questions.

Peter told him about Inez's recruitment process, BRIAR and what he had gleaned about the uneasy alliance of parties that formed the Republican Government. It took the better part of an hour, and when the spirit crown's timer chimed, he realised it was seven in the evening.

'I am nearly due at the Harrises',' he said. 'I will be missed if I don't attend.'

Abruptly, Shpiegelglass stood up. He folded his hands behind his back and paced around in tight circles. Then he picked up the suitcase, placed it on top of a small surgical instrument trolley and opened it.

'I am afraid you will not be attending, FELIX.'

The case contained a Fialka Terminal, easily recognisable by its ten wired rotors, typewriter keyboard, silver-grey sheen and a Ouija-style alphabet disc for displaying answers. Only a few illegals – NKVD operatives living in foreign countries with a false identity – possessed a Terminal, a direct line to the Presence. The last time Peter had seen one was in Cambridge.

'There is a high likelihood that you have been compromised,' Shpiegelglass said. He punched a long sequence of letters and numbers into the machine. The rotors spun and sparked, and spun again.

Peter's new handler opened a second compartment and took out a contraption that resembled a spirit crown but was larger and of distinctly utilitarian Soviet make. It had a thick frame that went over the skull and a halo-like arc with two porcelain-tipped electrodes. Curly copper wire connected them to the terminal.

'If your cover is blown, it is safer if you do not go back. And the fastest way to convey your findings to the Presence,' Shpiegelglass said, 'is to perform the Termin Procedure on you.'

Peter stared at the device. A sense of relief washed over

him. He would not have to face West tomorrow. He would never have to lie again.

He was going to join the Presence.

Peter smiled as Shpiegelglass placed the device on his head. It was heavy and barely fitted over the spirit crown. Its function was exactly the opposite: to push the soul out, to transmit it directly to the Presence. The body he occupied would not survive.

For a moment, Peter felt a twinge of regret for Pendlebury. But at least in death the man would be free from having his body used as a receptacle for the pleasures of wealthy dead.

Shpiegelglass's fingers danced deftly on the Fialka's keyboard. The electrodes pressing against Peter's head warmed up. The air smelled of ozone.

He tensed, but there was no pain. The world began to warp into a sphere, like a fisheye lens. Then everything went dark, except for a white pinpoint in the distance. It rushed towards him and grew. It was a face, made of light. Its benevolent smile was framed by a perfect, triangular beard. Its radiant vastness filled Peter's vision.

The song of the Presence washed over him. The voices of the countless souls that made up the Being rose in praise. Longing to join the chorus, he tried to dive into the smiling god-star's corona.

He was denied. The will of the Presence held him suspended before its all-seeing gaze.

Let me in, he screamed silently. *I want to be you.*

The Being swallowed him.

It was like drowning in an ocean of light. Suddenly, he knew that – like the mind of the ectotank – the white around him was the sum of many colours, many souls.

The brightness poured in through his eyes like a liquid and filled his skull. It left no room for fear or doubt. For an instant, Peter Bloom ceased to be.

And then the Presence withdrew.

Its absence was worse than death. Peter could not bear it. He heard a terrible sound and realised it was his own voice, screaming. In a mad hope he clawed at the spirit crown's cable. If he escaped Pendlebury's body, maybe he could still follow the Presence.

Then Otto and Nora grabbed his arms and held him tight. The only light he could see was the cold, greenish fluorescence of the underground hospital.

`Send me back!' Peter cried, tears flowing from his eyes. His mind throbbed like an open wound. 'Please. Try again. Send me back.'

Shpiegelglass frowned and punched a string of letters into the still-humming Fialka. The arrow on the alphabet disc moved instantly and spelled out a sentence, twitching from one letter to the next. The Soviet agent let out a surprised, musical chuckle. Then he flipped a switch. The Fialka sparked one more time and died.

'Well, FELIX,' he said, 'our task is not yet finished. The Presence thinks having access to the Iberian Commission is more important than the risk of exposing you. And if I know George, he will play the SIS for a while, bargain and cajole. You will be his last card. So there is still a little time.'

Shpiegelglass closed the suitcase with a snap.

'I have been instructed to go to Spain immediately. Otto and Nora will be your case officers in my absence. As for you, young man – it looks like you are going to make it to your soirée of spies after all.'

EIGHT

An Evening at the Harrises', 10th November 1938

The following Thursday evening, Rachel had butterflies in her stomach when the cab left her at 6 Chesterfield Gardens in Mayfair. She was there to attend a social function hosted by Tommy and Hildy Harris, and potentially to betray her country.

In contrast to the nondescript middle-class flats of most spies, the Harrises lived in a magnificent, sprawling house Tommy Harris's father, a prominent art dealer, had bought with his fortune. The brisk night air carried down notes of cello music from the well-lit salon on the second floor, mixed with a faint hubbub of conversation and clinking glasses. It sounded like the Group – as the spies who informally gathered at the Harrises were called – was present in full force.

Tommy and his wife Hildy were endlessly gracious hosts. At one point, they had even worked as de facto caretakers and cooks for the Service's operations school at Brickendomby Hall. They had an apparently bottomless wine cellar and a Latin passion for cooking and entertainment.

They instinctively understood that the people of the secret world needed a safe place where tongues could be let loose and guards lowered with no regard for rank or secrecy, and were utterly dedicated to making their home a safe haven for spies.

Yet, for the first time, Rachel felt apprehensive when she rang the doorbell beneath the marble arch of the main entrance. The wine-red evening dress, high-heeled shoes and thick layer of make-up felt uncomfortable, and there was a touch of cold sweat at the small of her back.

Hildy herself opened the door. She was a small woman, pretty like a doll, with rounded cheeks, a tiny nub of a nose and a ready smile – a stark contrast to the dark and enigmatic Tommy. She stood up on her tiptoes to kiss Rachel's cheeks, then gripped her forearms firmly.

'I heard,' Hildy said in a low voice. There were few women in the secret world, but they had never been close. Rachel had always appreciated that Hildy treated her as one of the boys, keeping her distance and playing the host. But now her tone was warm. 'It is lovely to see you, regardless.'

'I wouldn't have missed it for the *world*!' The last word was a squeal. Rachel giggled. 'Excuse me,' she said. 'I may have started with a couple of large glasses of Merlot at home. Please don't tell anyone. I'll behave myself, I promise.'

Hildy frowned. 'Of course,' she said. 'Please do come in. Everybody is here!'

Rachel took a deep breath and followed her inside, desperately hoping that *everybody* included Peter Bloom.

*

She had been against Max's scheme from the start.

'This is ridiculous,' she had protested two days earlier, after their planning session. 'I have no training in this.'

In response, the large blue-breasted Amazon parrot sitting on a perch screamed an obscenity in Portuguese. They were in the dead spymaster's jungle-like conservatory in his flat on Sloane Square. Rachel sat on a rickety wooden chair in the shade of a palm tree, balancing a saucer and a teacup on her knee.

'Ssh,' Max said in a rattling, gramophone-like voice. 'Goo is finally sleeping.'

His spirit presently inhabited a life-sized Edison doll, with nyctoscope camera eyes and an amplified ectophone in its belly. It wore an expensive smoking jacket covered in bird droppings. Rachel missed Henry the medium. While the doll was a good likeness, with its saturnine, hawk-nosed face and bushy eyebrows, its black pinpoint eyes and complete stillness were unsettling. Some of the newer models had small electric motors the spirit could control to make basic movements, but to Rachel that was even worse. Still, it did not appear to bother Goo, the baby cuckoo resting peacefully between the Max doll's folded wooden arms.

'My apologies to Goo,' Rachel said. 'But I really do not think this is a good idea.'

'Can you come closer? I can't hear you very well.'

That was hardly surprising given the cacophony of animal noises that filled the place. Every room in the small flat apart from the bedroom of Susi the maid was a veritable zoo. At the door, Rachel had been received by a white bull terrier and a large, lumbering black dog – which turned out to be a bear cub called Jasper, considerably more affectionate than his namesake at the Winter Court. When she used the bathroom, she barely suppressed a scream when she spotted a tangle of live bullfinch snakes in the bathtub.

Sighing, Rachel pulled her chair over next to the Max doll and angled its head to improve the pickup of its microphone ears.

'That's better,' Max said. 'Now, as to training, none of my agents ever had any. That was what made them so effective. They were ordinary women, secretaries, clerks. Utterly without guile, yet possessing extraordinary courage—'

'I must say that when it comes to Mata Hari tactics, I am with Harker.'

'Ah! The sex drive does not come into it, not at all! And in this case, I doubt it would work on Bloom in the first place, even if he was still alive, all due respect to your charms, Mrs White. No, I am guessing that with him it will be about ideology.'

'So how do I approach him?'

'You don't. You make him come to you. We will turn you into a desirable candidate for recruitment. That will require surprisingly little effort, wouldn't you agree?'

Rachel opened her mouth to protest. Then she imagined reading her own file, as she might have done in the old Registry's reading room. *An outstanding officer, one of the first women in the Service, but demoted for insubordination. Considered resigning. Financially dependent on her husband. Marital troubles?*

'All right. On paper, I am a promising target. But is it going to be enough?'

'Not quite. We need something else, an ... incident. The Harris soirée should do fine.' The doll's fixed smile appeared to widen. 'Remember that I can quite literally see into your soul, Mrs White. Just have a few drinks and it will all happen quite naturally.'

Goo the cuckoo moved in the doll's lap and stretched its wings.

'Now the poor thing is awake,' Max said. 'And we haven't even started on the breeding and care of finches.'

With a spring in her step, Hildy led Rachel up a long, narrow staircase, past a priceless red-and-gold tapestry and precious Spanish furniture of dark wood, and into a large salon on the second floor where the Group was holding court.

Guy Liddell was playing the cello, more for his own pleasure than as formal entertainment. Tommy Harris was seated next to him, tapping his foot. He was darkly handsome, with black hair and intense Mediterranean eyes.

There were perhaps two dozen guests, enough to make the L-shaped room a little crowded. Rachel recognised several faces: Anthony Blunt, Tim Milne, Victor Rothschild, Richard Brooman-White – all younger Winter Court officers, all drinking red wine or something stronger, engaged in lively conversation.

A smaller contingent from the Summer Court hovered near the grand piano by the window, all in charter-bodies – no Edison dolls for Group meetings. The New Dead often chose mediums who resembled their past selves, but Rachel had only ever met Bloom briefly when he was alive and wasn't sure if she would recognise him by the medium he had chosen. In any case, these particular charter-bodies all looked identical, like exotic birds in their evening wear and white or black Venetian masks and metal-crested spirit crowns.

When Rachel and Hildy entered, there was the briefest hush in the conversation. Rachel tensed. The furtive glances cast towards her felt like splashes of cold water.

Hildy took her arm. 'Kim is playing barman as usual,' she said. 'I have to abandon you to these beasts and check up on a few things in the kitchen.'

A large, ancient oak table beneath a gold-framed landscape painting served as the bar, displaying a small cityscape of alcohol. Tommy had once said that no good table could be spoiled by wine stains. Kim Philby stood behind it, busy pouring drinks, improvising cocktails and refilling glasses.

'Look after this one, Kim,' Hildy told him. 'She had a bit of a head start at home, so go easy on her. We want to make sure she gets to the finish line.'

Kim gave Rachel a dimpled grin. He had a friendly, boyishly chubby face with a heavy drinker's complexion, and one of those voices that tickled your belly, no matter what he said. He was an up-and-coming young officer, close to Sir Stewart, who worked at Blenheim Palace liaising with the Summer Court. Rachel reckoned he was the perfect target for Max's scene. The dance of her gastric butterflies became a brisk waltz.

'Have we finally broken through your defences, Mrs White?' he asked. 'I have never known you to drink anything stronger than tea.'

'Perhaps that was my problem all along,' Rachel said, swaying slightly. 'I never quite appreciated that drinking was the best part of the job. Can you make me a short one, please?'

'Nothing would give me greater pleasure, madam.'

Kim poured her a Pimm's and laced it with absinthe. She

downed the concoction in one go. It went straight into her stomach and sent up a fountain of warmth that left her dizzy.

'Thank you. I think this one was a tad too short. Could you make the next one longer?'

Laughing, Kim mixed her another drink. As she sipped it, his expression grew serious.

'Listen, I could not help hearing about what happened. A terrible shame, really. Those old colonials can be dreadful. My former Section V chief Cowgill was the same, paranoid and frankly quite dim. So chin up. There's nothing that time and unfeasible quantities of drink won't cure. Bottoms up, what?'

'Bottoms up,' Rachel said and lifted her glass.

They gossiped for a short while. Apparently all the secretaries at Blenheim had already been warned about Roger Hollis and his philandering ways, and no one would go out with him. Rachel laughed loudly at that, for appearances' sake, and said that Roger's reputation was exaggerated. To her knowledge, he was hopelessly smitten with one secretary in particular.

Defending Roger reminded her that she had been unfair to him. He was one of the good ones, like Kim. And now she would have to be unfair to Kim, too, for England.

Halfway through her fourth drink, she decided it was time.

Rachel closed her eyes and leaned on the table, exaggerating her state of inebriation just a little.

'Thank you for all the sympathy, Kim. I appreciate it. Really. I am sure it is well meant. It's just that I can't drink my way to the Summer Court like you. I wish I could, but the only thing I will get for my troubles is cirrhosis, and they don't give out Tickets for that.'

'Steady on, now—' Kim started.

'You know, I have been at the Court for nearly twenty years. Where were you twenty years ago, Kim? I started as a clerk. How did you start?'

'Look, Rachel—'

'Tell me. How did you start at the Court?'

'Well, I think it was Guy Burgess who talked his way in first and put in a good word for me,' Kim said. 'Listen, I understand that you are upset, but you must know that you are amongst friends here.'

'Easy for you to say. I get blamed for something I could do nothing about and now I am doing sums for Miss Scaplehorn.' She let out a small sob. 'No one put in a good word for me. No one.'

She leaned on the table heavily now. Kim started to come around to her side but she shook a finger at him.

'No touching! No fraternising with colleagues, now. I am just one of the boys to you, aren't I? Or is that what you prefer, like with Nick Elliott?'

She hated herself for saying it. But the bitterness had to ring true, and so she forced the words out. Philby's face darkened.

'Only I am not one of the boys, Kim. I am the girl. I will always be the girl. If I make a mistake, it is because I have a nervous temperament, not because I am following orders from an incompetent nincompoop. If I get upset, maybe it's that time of the month.'

'Rachel—'

'Mrs White to you! I am a married woman. I should not be here on my own, with all these dis-disreputable people.' She managed slur the words convincingly and raised her voice.

'Good girls don't get to go to Summerland. Good girls don't get to be spies.' A tear ran down her face. Max had made her rehearse the outburst several times, but she had never managed to cry before. People were watching her now. Tommy Harris stood up. She hoped that Bloom was amongst the crowd, but if not, the story would get to him soon enough.

'So maybe it's time I stopped pretending to be one.'

She wiped her nose. Her elbow brushed against her glass. It plummeted to the floor and shattered into glittering fragments.

At least I did not get any more stains on Tommy's table, Rachel thought. Then she cried a mixture of fake and real tears, and allowed Tommy and Philby to lead her away.

'No, really, Tommy, I am absolutely fine. I don't need a taxi.'

Tommy Harris refilled her water glass from a crystal carafe and handed it back to Rachel. She drank gratefully. They were in his studio – Tommy was an amateur painter – a brightly lit, high-ceilinged room with an unvarnished wooden floor and covered canvases. It smelled of paint and pipe tobacco.

'Are you sure? It's no trouble.'

'I am so sorry about making a scene. It was stupid. I want to stay.'

'Of course. You are always welcome here, Rachel, no matter what happens.'

There was a knock on the door.

'Hullo there.' Guy Liddell, the deputy chief of the Winter Court, gave them a jowly, apologetic smile. His banker's suit was even more rumpled than usual. 'Would you mind if I have a quick word with our patient, Tommy?'

'Of course. Make sure you stay for food, Rachel. We went an extra mile, this time.' He vanished through the door, and after a moment they heard the grand piano.

Liddell sat down on Tommy's painter's stool.

'I want you to know that nobody blames you for Kulagin,' he said. 'I spoke to Harker. He overreacted, of course. But you overstepped. And I do agree with him, for once. It was a misinformation gambit. You could not have known.'

'I should have known.'

'Nonsense. None of us saw it. It was a mess, with me pulling one way, Harker and Vee-Vee the other. You got caught in the middle. I am truly sorry, and I will do everything I can to help.'

Rachel squirmed mentally. She had not expected Liddell's support. It made her feel warm.

'Like I told Tommy, it is perfectly all right,' she said. 'I might take some time off. Travel with Joe. There is a nice place in France we haven't been to for a while.'

Liddell patted her arm with a stubby-fingered hand.

'That's good. That's good. When the fuss dies down, there might be an opening in the Irish Section, if you are interested.'

It *would* be a sensible thing to do. She had the experience. She could be leading the Section in a couple of years. But her rant at Philby had not been entirely fabricated. Was that Max's trick? Maybe he saw what was inside his agents and used them in just the right way to bring it out?

Rachel forced a smile. 'I will think about it.'

'That's all I ask. And, Rachel? I am sure I don't have to tell you this, but whatever nonsense Kulagin told you – do keep it to yourself. We have enough trouble with the Summer Court as it is.'

Not Liddell, too, Rachel thought.

Your superiors will do anything to keep him safe in order to secure favours from the highest level, Max had said.

'Of course,' she said aloud. 'I completely understand.'

'Now, shall we go and face the music?'

Liddell offered his arm. Rachel took it, and together they walked back towards the piano music and conversation. She tried not to hear the barely perceptible dip in the murmur of voices when they entered the ballroom.

Food was served around eight, an exquisite spread of tapas and cheeses. It was delicious enough that Rachel forgot her worries and simply enjoyed the stuffed peppers, small sausages and Spanish omelette. She had not eaten a proper meal for days.

As the evening wore on, Rachel drifted from one small group to another, light-headed and fatigued from making small talk. There was a jarring shift in the conversation whenever she tried to join, like a gramophone needle jumping over a record's grooves. People became polite and distant and talked of inconsequential things. It was the mask one adopted with people who were not a part of the secret world, the uninitiated.

Ironically, the only person who stuck with her for a while was Guy Burgess, Kim Philby's original gateway into the Service. Burgess was one of the more openly flamboyant Summer Court officers. He was unmasked, stank of liquor and cigarettes, and his open-collared shirt was covered in wine stains. He inhabited the body of a dark-haired, rakish medium with olive skin whose slack face was a stark contrast to his spirit rider's sharp wit.

'I applaud you for coming here, Mrs White,' he said. 'But I think you were right. You ought to go home to your husband and find something to do other than spying. It shouldn't be difficult, and I would know: I only got into it because it was the most useless thing I could think of.'

'Well, Mr Burgess,' said Rachel, 'looking at you, I can assure you that it is not the most useless thing *I* can think of.'

Burgess laughed. 'I see we met too late. Sad. I am going to miss you now. Please don't leave.' He tossed his hand-rolled cigarette stub onto the Harrises' thick burgundy carpet. 'Actually, there is a host of little angels in the Summer Court more useless than me. That bounder Bloom, for example. We were supposed to meet for a drink but he is not even here yet.'

Rachel smiled, but inside, she was furious. Had she made a fool of herself for nothing? It might be months before Bloom visited the living world again, and by then it would be too late.

Burgess noticed her pause and looked at her, swaying slightly in his odd, pigeon-toed stance.

'I don't suppose I can entice you along on a secret mission to Tommy's wine cellar, hmm? I am guessing he had new locks installed after my last visit.'

'It is tempting,' Rachel said, 'but I think I will try my luck with Kim again.'

'Suit yourself.' He looked at Rachel. 'I know it feels like you were not picked for the polo team, Mrs White. But imagine what a stupid game that is, sitting on top of smelly animals and trying to hit balls with long sticks.'

'Yes. Only men could invent such a game,' Rachel said.

*

Around ten o'clock, she found herself standing alone, drinking dark Spanish wine from a glass Kim had poured for her after making a show of arguing that the best way to sober her up was to push her through drunkenness and to the other side. Kim's grin had been the same as ever, but his eyes were flinty.

At the other end of the room, Hildy and Tommy Harris held forth on one of the subjects they were both experts in – art, sculpture, music, cuisine or treachery. She considered joining the circle of listeners but could not bear another moment of hushed awkwardness.

Drinking more was not a good idea, but she continued anyway, in the faint hope that imbibing the Harrises' *grand vin* would revive her connection to the secret world. Or failing that, magically summon Peter Bloom.

To distract herself, she studied a large Velázquez painting of the Madonna. The Mother of God floated in the air, surrounded by a bright halo. There were dirty, dark-haired people below her, reaching up, while she lifted two fingers in a serene but uncaring benediction.

Rachel was sceptical of religion like any intelligence officer faced with a poor cover story. The Anglican Church had adapted its doctrine to argue that Heaven and the Kingdom of God lay in the *ana* direction, where souls came from. Summerland was merely where the souls of the dead resided until Judgment Day, when they would return to their bodies on Earth and the chosen would be taken up to the true Heaven above.

The view was opposite to that of Pope Teilhard, who argued that the spirits evolved towards Godhead, and that the fourth dimension wrapped around itself in a circle. Summerland was the purgatory; the process of Fading – one's memories being stripped away from the *luz*, the soul-stone – was a cleansing. Heaven waited in the infinite abyss of *kata*. It was heresy to cling to the world of the living for too long.

She finished her wine and cradled the empty glass against her collarbone, staring at the Madonna's beatific face. Maybe Teilhard was right. Maybe she should just let it go.

'Excuse me.'

A New Dead guest stood next to her. He was shorter than her, with dark, thinning hair, hands clasped behind his back. He wore a full face mask, a white, featureless oval with a thin golden net over the eyeholes. There appeared to be something wrong with his spirit crown: it made an audible humming sound.

'Yes?'

'I wanted to thank you. For creating a little scandal. I was worried it was going to be dreadfully dull and took my time getting here. Instead, everybody has been talking about you.'

Rachel's heart jumped.

'To be honest, sir, I could use a little more dull myself. But you are welcome. Have we met?'

'I'm so sorry – where are my manners? We met only briefly, before my transition. Peter Bloom. Peter. I'm with the Iberian Section.' His hand had a charter-body's chill, but the grip was practised and firm.

'Rachel White.'

'Guy Burgess told me what you said,' Peter said. He twitched, put a hand in his pocket, adjusted something and then shrugged. 'Excuse me. Poor connection. I had a bit of a tumble earlier. I expect the medium will charge me an arm and a leg for it.'

That explained Bloom's slightly dishevelled look. There were fresh mud stains on his trousers.

'Are you going to offer me your sympathies as well, Peter? I'm afraid I've had enough of that for one evening.'

'Not at all. In fact, I agree with you. Both branches of the Service have their problems, and nepotism is one of them. Section heads fighting turf wars is another. And then there is interservice rivalry. We wine and dine together here, but your people resent mine, and the Summer Court has a tendency to feel a bit ...' Bloom trailed off.

'Superior? Arrogant? Stuck-up?'

'Your words, not mine. In any case, you are not the only one who has been treated unjustly. It is a shame, isn't it? We join the Service to experience something bigger than ourselves. Something holy, even.' Bloom looked up at the painting, head cocked to one side.

'Well, not asking questions or rebelling worked out for Mary,' Rachel said. 'She did what she was told and we still honour her. Perhaps I should follow her example.' Her tone was bitter.

'You are in a very cynical mood.'

'I am a cynical sort of person. An occupational hazard, I suppose.'

She had not rehearsed this with Max. He had simply urged her to say what came naturally. She studied Bloom, but it was hard to read him with his full mask.

'So why did *you* join the Service, then, Rachel?'

'Well, I was born in Bengal. I was seven when my family moved back here, so I grew up thinking of England as this mythical place. My *ayah*, my nurse, made up all kinds of stories about the Queen and her court of spirits and I ate them up. I suppose I never quite stopped believing in them, in the *idea* of the Empire. At Princess Helena College, when the other girls picked on me for sounding different, I would tell them I was just as British as they were, and that one day I was going to work for the Queen.

'When the war started, I handed out white lilies as symbols of cowardice to young men who would not join up. I volunteered as a nurse for a while. My father was horrified and got me a desk job at the Registry instead. Fortunately, I was very good at it – and no one there cared that I was a wisp of a girl as long as I pulled my weight.

'Of course, real life turned out to be more complex than my *ayah*'s stories. But it felt good to be able to make a difference.'

'And the Finance Section does not fill you with that feeling?'

'I am not a snob. In a war, every soldier is important. But I have more to offer than rubber-stamping classified purchase orders. I like to think so, anyway.' She frowned. 'Why do you care about any of this, Peter?'

'Well, first, I know a few things about being unappreciated.' Bloom's voice wavered, suddenly. He paused and made a show of adjusting his spirit crown. Rachel realised that in spite of his calm manner, something had upset him very recently. She wondered exactly where those mud stains had come from.

'Excuse me. It is not my night with aetheric connections,' Bloom said after a moment. 'Second, you may be aware of the issues we have been experiencing in Spain, many of which are the result of a lack of cooperation between Winter and Summer. Your lot recruits assets on the ground, we run them, but we don't coordinate well enough.'

'Maybe you should take that up with liaison officers like Kim.'

'Well, that's the thing. Many of the young, capable officers in the Winter Court are distracted by ambition. They would rather advance their careers than facilitate cooperation. So some of us have been talking to people like you who do not lack passion but whose future paths are less clear.'

'Go on.'

'There might be a few things you could do for us, unofficially. If that is of interest to you, I am happy to discuss further.'

Rachel hesitated. Listening to Bloom, it was much easier to believe that Kulagin's claims had been misinformation. There *was* interservice rivalry, and the Harrises' was exactly the place to try to build ties to address it. Or to trap insubordinate officers like her before the Soviets could recruit them.

Ultimately, it did come down to faith.

'I would like that,' Rachel said.

'Very well. I will arrange an ectophone call. Perhaps next week?'

'That would be perfect.'

Bloom shook her hand again. 'It was a pleasure to meet you, Rachel.'

'Enjoy the rest of your evening. Guy Burgess told me you had plans.'

He stiffened a little, but Rachel could not tell if he blushed under the mask.

'I always have plans,' he said after a moment's pause. 'Can't be a spy without them.'

*

A little later, Rachel said her goodbyes to Hildy and Tommy. The gathering was likely to go on until the small hours, with more than one guest staying over in the bedrooms on the third floor. Tommy held her hand tight between his and said she was always welcome, but Rachel saw the closed door in his eyes.

She waited for her cab outside, breath steaming in the chill. The cold air cleared her head. She felt a mixture of terror and exhilaration, rubbing her hands against the cold.

A street light flickered and the ectophone in her handbag rattled.

WELL DONE, the brass letters said.

WE'LL SEE, she replied to the ghost of Max Chevalier.

NINE

Special Committee on the Iberian Problem, 11th November 1938

The Special Committee on the Iberian Problem met the following evening, and Peter Bloom arrived late.

He signed the Summer Court entrance book hastily, violated protocol by not waiting for the attendant and nearly got lost on his way to the Chimney.

He had spent the last few hours in intense preparation that had left him feeling transparent and thin, a warning sign of Fading. His work had been interrupted by a furious Pendlebury, who sent him a tart ectomail complaining about soiled clothes, and a headache from a poorly tuned spirit crown. Placating him required an ectophone call – another *vim*-costly journey to listen to the medium's nasal voice listing his grievances.

But exhaustion and an irate medium were minor worries compared to what waited for him at the top of the tower. Standing in the Chimney's aethervator, which was propelled to Whitehall by a massive *luz* counterweight, he wondered if this was what Fascist prisoners in Spain felt like when the firing squad raised their rifles.

He tried to stay calm. The Presence had a plan for him. And surely he would not be permitted in the PM's presence if the SIS knew about his true loyalties? Unless this was all elaborate theatre to feed the Presence misinformation. And maybe the god-mind knew that, and was playing a deeper game.

He remembered the chill of its rejection, and shuddered.

The journey *ana*-wards took only a minute. The top of the Chimney overlapped with an electromagnetically shielded room in Whitehall. Peter stepped out of the aethervator into a glowing cylindrical Faraday cage, where C and his stone-faced deputy chief George Hill were already standing around an ectophone's prismatic circuit. It was strange to see their usual impeccable self-images, nearly identical to the way they had looked in life, superimposed against the stark electrical geometry of the living world.

C frowned at Peter. 'Kind of you to join us, Bloom,' he said. 'Fortunately, His Nibs is running behind as well.'

Peter took his place next to the two older spies. Hill was a lantern-jawed old soldier, a veteran of pre-Revolutionary Russian operations. Rumour had it he was there on the night Rasputin died. Although his face was impassive, hostility radiated from him in chilly waves. Peter gave him a smile and arranged his notes in mid-air into a floating wall of imprinted aether between them.

Then Prime Minister Herbert Blanco West entered the room.

His soul-spark was one of the largest Peter had ever seen and took up nearly half of the Faraday cage. It was a kaleidoscope of thought-forms so vivid you could almost glimpse actual images of what the great man thought and saw. Peter spotted a ship made of blue light, and faces, but they changed too quickly for him to recognise, like flames.

Another living soul accompanied him. This had to be Sir Stewart Menzies, the head of the Winter Court, the terrestrial branch of the SIS. Next to the PM, his mind was a tiny moon orbiting a huge primordial planet.

'Gentlemen,' West said. His voice was in sharp contrast to the soul-spark, a little wheezy, an old man's voice. 'Apologies for my tardiness. Parliament was murder today. I understand you have found a sword to cut through this Gordian tangle of ours. Let us find out how sharp it is.'

As C started laying out the facts of the Spanish situation, Peter could not help staring at the blaze of the prime minister's thoughts. They reminded him of another fire, and of the night he first heard Herbert West's name.

It was 1916, towards the end of the war. Peter was five years old.

His family sat in front of the fireplace in the cosy drawing room, one of the few in the huge Palace Gardens Terrace house they actually used. Peter's father had just returned from the Office of Communications where he worked. His mother had spent the evening writing poetry. There were stacks of small notebooks at her feet. Peter lay on his special flying carpet – the old velvety rug behind his mother's chair – almost asleep in the comforting murmur of his parents' voices.

Later, he picked their actual words from his memory like

shards of glass and dissected the details of the scene. The auburn sweep of his mother's hair, his father's round face, made apple-like by the soft light from the fire, and the plumpness that would stay with him until the illness and the end.

'West came by the Office today.' His father's smell was overpowering and sweet, but that evening it was still as safe and familiar as his baritone voice.

'Oh,' Peter's mother said.

'He wants to do some war work. War work! Can you believe him? After everything his Dimensionists have done to get us into that mess in the first place.'

'What did you say to him?'

'Well, no matter what I think about the old boy's politics, he is Herbert Blanco West. I could hardly refuse him.' Peter's father leaned back. 'I said that if he was not too busy with campaigning, we would be happy to have a few morale pieces from him. He was very enthusiastic, kept saying how he wants to do his part. I wanted to tell him, HB, you did your part already by persuading Marconi to give us those ghastly ectotanks, but I bit my tongue. Just tried to play it like it was the good old days.'

'It is a bit unfair to hold that against him, Charles. You know what I think about the Dimensionists, but it is wartime. We need all the weapons we can get.'

'Well, that is exactly what they want us to think, isn't it?'

'Charles, we are both tired, let us not argue politics, please. How was HB otherwise?'

'Looked a bit fatigued, but hale as a horse otherwise. Would not shut up about his new book. Another history thing. A "joint symphony of the living and the dead", he called it. A bit grandiose, if you ask me.'

'Well, if there is anyone who can succeed in something like that, it's him. Did he say anything else?'

'He did hint at some new affair, if that is what you want to know. But I think he has to be more careful now that he is planning to run for office.'

Peter's mother closed her book slowly and put away her pen.

'In fact, I did not want to know that, Charles. But thank you.'

'I am sorry. It was unkind of me. It's just that whenever I see him, I wonder—'

'Well, you have nothing to wonder about,' Peter's mother said gently. She stood up, walked over to the other chair and stroked the man's cheek.

'It has been a while,' she said.

'Not in front of the boy, Ann.'

'The poor boy is fast asleep. Perhaps we could—'

The electric lamp in the corner flickered and went out. A thunder-like rumble woke Peter up fully.

'Who is Mr West?' he asked.

'So, who is this Dzhugashvili chap, then?' the prime minister asked.

His voice brought Peter back to the present, and he blinked owlishly at his notes.

C rolled his eyes at him. 'I believe that is your cue, Bloom.'

'Dzhugahsvili, Iosif, also known as Josif Stalin,' Peter read from his notes. 'Born in Georgia. Instrumental in obtaining early funds for the Revolution, often via criminal means. One of the contenders to succeed Lenin until the God-Builders drove him into exile.' Peter recited Dzhugashvili's biography while pondering the question that had troubled him since the meeting with C.

Why had West requested him, after all these years?

Even though the PM could not see spirits, Peter felt the soul-spark's attention directed at him. It was like standing next to a bonfire.

'Over the last decade, Dzhugashvili has been creating a network of agents and counter-revolutionary cells all over Europe, notably in Paris, Prague and Rotterdam. However, Spain is the first region where he has operated this openly. Given extensive NKVD penetration of the Communist parties of the Republic, he is taking a considerable risk. He may be genuinely trying to establish a power base in the Iberian Peninsula. It could well be in our interest to aid him.'

'I think I met this Dzhugashvili once, in Petrograd,' the prime minister said wistfully. 'Back then, he wrote poetry. Not bad, if I recall correctly.'

'Begging your pardon, sir,' Sir Stewart said, 'but poets rarely make the best statesmen. Present company excepted, of course.'

The PM chuckled. 'I was never much of a poet.'

'That just proves my point, eh? Our aetheric colleagues have obviously discovered something interesting – with the help of our own BRIAR, of course. But they lack the perspective to understand the bigger picture. They just dance around Communists. We hunt down agitators infiltrating the unions.

'I say that a Communist is a Communist, and this Dzhugashvili is no different. If he fails, we have the same situation as before – a Soviet puppet state on our doorstep.

If he succeeds, it is conceivably even worse: an ideologue strongman setting an example to both our workers and the rest of Europe.

'No, gentlemen, I propose we stick to the devil we know and support Franco. Maybe your chap can create pandemonium on the Republic side, but there is no need to get our own hands dirty. Besides, that did not work out too well last time, as Mr Hill well knows.'

Hill's self-image grew pale with rage, but C raised a hand to silence him.

'Sir Stewart is droll, as always,' he said. 'Perhaps he was too busy chasing agitators to read Mr Bloom's report? Or maybe the subtle implications simply eluded him.'

It did not take an experienced soul-reader to interpret the forest of red crystal spikes that appeared in Sir Stewart's soul-spark.

'Look here—' Sir Stewart started.

'My apologies,' C said. 'I spoke out of turn. But I would do Her Majesty's government a disservice if I failed to emphasise the seriousness of the matter. Previously, I also agreed to support the Fascists, but now the Soviets have upped the game twofold. First, their agents are rapidly infiltrating the Republic's government. Second, they are providing the Republic with aetherguns to counter Franco's ectotanks. That means sending Russian officers to train the Spanish forces. We are one escalation step away from actual war.

'Prime Minister, sir, let us do this. We have an opportunity to turn the tables on the Soviets. We make Dzhugashvili our man, and he will cut out the NKVD cancer from Spain's flesh. We can set conditions, install observers, steer things in the right direction. And remember, the Republic will need someone to build an afterlife. Why not Marconi? Once that is in place, Dzhugashvili may find it difficult not to embrace the virtues of ectocapitalism.'

The intelligence chiefs paused and waited for the prime minister's response. West's thought-forms were darker now, with hues of green and deep red. The more Peter studied them, the clearer they became. He was certain he could see dark, multi-legged shapes moving through green clouds, and a burning city.

Peter thought of Madrid, of the lie he had told Inez, and the truth that lay behind it.

That evening in 1916, after Peter asked his question, Mr Bloom frowned.

'Peter, it is not polite to listen in to grown-up conversations. You should—'

'Let me take care of this, Charles.'

Peter's mother took his face between her small, warm hands and looked at him seriously.

'Mr West is a writer, like Mummy. It means he tells stories. Except that his stories are a lot sillier than Mummy's. And he is a very silly little man, and we are not going to talk about him any more.'

The glass in the windows tinkled and sirens started howling in the distance.

'Oh, bloody hell, not again,' Peter's father said. He stood up with a jerk, walked to the window and pulled the curtain aside. A pale green light played on his features as the rumbling and the siren howls continued.

'A Zeppelin,' he said darkly. 'The ectoflyers are already up there. I think they are going to bring it down.'

'I want to see!' Peter ran to his father and held his arms out. Mr Bloom picked him up and for a moment Peter was lost in his smell and the feeling of flying. But his father's face was not playful at all.

'Charles,' Peter's mother said, with a hint of danger in her tone.

'The boy needs to see this. Look, Peter. This is what Mr West and his friends have brought to us.'

A silvery, cigar-shaped craft drifted slowly above the jagged skyline in the distance, scissored by pale spotlight beams. Orange and golden flames bloomed beneath its bulk, and every fiery burst was followed by a delayed thunderclap that made the windows jingle. A small whimper escaped Peter's lips.

'Come on, now, Peter, be a brave boy, there is nothing to be afraid of. Just watch.'

A cloud of pale, fluttering things rose up around the airship, casting shadows on its gleaming hull. It was hard to see the details, but they had wings made from a translucent white substance that glowed faintly in the dark. They reminded Peter of the moths that had scared him one time when he hid in the cupboard beneath the stairs. But these were much larger, and man-shaped. Long, flexible tendrils trailed behind them.

'Charles, you are being an ass,' Peter's mother said. 'Give him to me. We are going to the basement right now.'

'In a minute.'

As Peter watched, a moth-man swooped along the belly of the enemy vessel. One of his tendrils snaked out, hook-like, and traced a fiery wound on the silver surface. Fire poured out like blood and the nose of the airship dipped suddenly. The white moth-things swarmed around it. The pop and crackle of the distant fireworks reached a crescendo. Several of the flyers fell from the sky, their ghostly substance evaporating into nothingness as they plummeted towards the ground. Peter gasped, hot pressure in his bladder.

'Those are ectoflyers, Peter,' his father said. 'The men with wings. That sounds wonderful, doesn't it? Only they can't fly unless they eat dead people. Their wings are made from the soul-stuff, which they push out through their mouths and eyes. Would you want wings like that, Peter?'

'Charles, that is enough!' Peter's mother snatched Peter from his father's arms.

'I just wanted to make him understand how silly Mr West's stories really are, Ann. Especially when they come true.'

Peter started crying. A warmth spread through his trousers and the shame made him cry louder. His mother carried him away, and the last thing he saw before she ran down the stairs to the basement was his father, standing at the window alone, lost in thought.

'And what do you think about all this, Mr Bloom?' the prime minister asked. His soul-spark had folded up like a flower closing, with only a glimmer of gold within.

'I am not sure it is my place to say, sir,' Peter said.

C's monocle dropped from his eye and he gave Peter a long look.

'Well, I am glad to hear at least one Spook has a modicum of modesty,' Sir Stewart said.

'Nonsense. Of course it is your place,' West said. 'I would not have asked you here if I did not want your opinion. There is more to the situation on the ground than the things you can capture in writing. I remember reading Colonel Bedford's first transmissions, trying to make sense of it all—'

His soul-spark fluttered suddenly, like a candle flame in a current of air.

'Where was I?' the prime minister muttered.

'You wanted to hear what Bloom thinks about the situation in Spain,' C said.

'Ah yes. So I did. What shall we do with this Dzhugashvili of yours, then? What would the Spaniards have us do?'

Peter hesitated. *What does he want me to say?* he wondered. But the magic lantern of the old man's soul was now dim and shrunken, and offered no hints. C was looking at Peter impatiently. There was no time for anything but the truth.

'The Spaniards want the war to end,' he said. 'In places like Barcelona, the class society is already reasserting itself. Many, like CARRASCOS, are having a crisis of religious faith. There is constant infighting between the parties, much of it fed by the NKVD. The economy is in tatters.

'Yet the Spanish are a proud people, and they hate Franco and his Moorish butchers. They will force the Fascists to turn every city into a Guernica before they give up. A quick Franco victory is only possible if we throw our full weight behind him. That means ground troops in Spain – and a Soviet response in kind.'

And there it was again, the familiar sting of a contradiction. To serve the Presence, he had to convince C of his loyalty and thus argue against the Presence's interests in Spain. At the same time, there was a truth to the argument he could not ignore, bright like Inez's soul-spark in the burning city.

If you started with a contradiction, you could prove anything, just like his mother taught him, long ago.

They did not sit in the drawing room again for a long time. After the war, Mrs Bloom started working for the Labour Ministry and spent all her evenings in her study. Peter's father won a seat for the Liberal Party and was consumed by politics. Every night, he arrived home late, dishevelled and worn, and stayed up even later writing speeches with manic energy.

One bleak winter afternoon when he was ten years old, Peter returned from school and found his mother sitting in the drawing room. The crystal set he thought was safely hidden amongst his toys under his bed lay in her lap. It was the size of a cigarette box, with a frayed cardboard casing, a Bakelite tuning dial and a tinny speaker that you had to hold up against your ear. Peter had bought it from Neville, an older boy at school.

'Nanny Schmidt found this while cleaning,' she said, tapping the set. 'Tell me, Pete – what do the dead say when you talk to them?'

'You ... you can't talk to them with the basic kit, you can only listen,' Peter said. 'There is a lot of static. Mostly you only get the recent dead. They don't make much sense.'

'I see.'

'I just wanted to understand how it worked.'

'And do you?'

'Of course I do, Mother, it's all in *Powell's Aetheric Mechanics for Boys*. The Zöllner crystal has a tiny four-dimensional extent and the spirits can touch it and make it vibrate, and the amplifier translates it into sound, and—'

'I believe you, Peter. But do you understand how the *world* works?'

She stood up and leaned on the mantelpiece. She looked tiny, suddenly, birdlike.

'Of course you don't, you are too young. Do you remember Doctor Cummings who treated you when you had measles? Well, soon there will be no doctors. If you get sick, you will just pass over.'

'If you have a Ticket,' Peter said.

'That's right. And soon, having a Ticket will be the only thing anyone cares about. Not studying, not working, not doing the right thing. Nothing real.'

'But Tickets are real!' Peter protested. 'Mr Hinton showed that if you imagine a four-dimensional object, it really exists in the aether. The spirits can see it, or thought-travel to it. That's how Tickets and ectophone beacons work.'

Mrs Bloom sighed. 'Peter, you are a very clever boy, so I know you will understand what I am going to say. Your father and I want you to grow up in a world where it matters to be alive. We want you to learn to care about *this* world, about sunshine, about other people. And that is why I never want to see one of these things in this house again.'

She lifted the crystal set high and smashed it against the mantelpiece. The casing crumpled and glittering fragments of the Zöllner crystal rained on the carpet.

'Mother!'

She knelt and started gathering the shards into a coal shovel.

'You don't know how lucky you are that Nanny came to

me first. Your father has a temper. He would have done something he would have regretted.'

Peter made a face. But he knew his mother was right. He felt a cold flush of fear in his belly, remembering the night of the airship, his father's unyielding grip and the anger in his voice.

'Now, we will tidy up,' Mrs Bloom said. 'Then you will sit with me and do your homework. And not a word about crystal sets, is that understood?'

'Yes, madam,' Peter said quietly.

His father came home two hours later. When he saw Peter and his mother by the fire, his exhausted smile was like a light shining through buttered paper.

'What have we here?'

'My study was very cold today,' Peter's mother said. 'I asked Nanny to bring supper here instead.'

Mr Bloom sank to his chair. 'That sounds lovely. We had a rally in the Warringdon Pump House and it was dreadfully cold.'

A coughing fit made him double over. Peter's mother got up and covered him with a blanket.

'What about you, Peter?' he asked, when the fit had passed. 'What have you been doing today?' He leaned back in his chair, eyes already half-closed.

Peter opened his mouth, trying to think of what to say. The truth was a leaden weight in his chest. But before he could speak, a gentle snore escaped Mr Bloom's lips.

Mrs Bloom looked at Peter, and then back at his father. She smiled sadly.

'He tries so hard,' she whispered. 'Do you understand now?'

Peter did not, but nodded anyway. Suddenly, he was furious at his father. How could he spoil everything, even when he was asleep? Oblivious to Peter's rage, his mother smiled.

After he finished his homework and supper, he excused himself. He got ready for bed and took out the book he kept in the small space between his night table and the wall. The hiding place had been too narrow for the crystal set.

The Science of Death by Herbert Blanco West, said the title page.

Peter opened the chapter he had started the previous night, the one about William Crookes's experiment showing that *luz* particles had an affinity with structures of higher complexity like brains. But it was difficult to concentrate.

It was not that he did not care about being alive, of course he did. But from everything he read, in Summerland things simply made much more sense. You could fly, for one thing, or thought-travel, which was even better. You were not trapped in a pudgy body that ensured you got picked on at school. And you could see other people's thoughts.

In Summerland, his mother would not have broken the crystal set. Peter would have understood why she was so angry. And there would have been no need to keep secrets from his father.

Or maybe he had it the wrong way around. Maybe it was his father who would be better off in Summerland, without Peter and his mother.

After a while, he heard his parents coming up the stairs together. His mother stifled a giggle. Peter ignored the sounds and lay awake in the dim glow of his night light, imagining what it would be like if his father was dead.

*

127

'So, Mr Bloom, what is your recommendation?' the prime minister asked.

'Sir, I am with the Chief. Dzhugashvili is our best option to calm things down and avoid an all-out war.'

The prime minister paced the room. His soul-spark brightened again and bopped to the rhythm of his footsteps like some exotic sea creature in a current.

'Sir, I do urge you to consider the alternative,' Sir Stewart said. 'The Admiralty considers a military victory in Spain eminently achievable. There is a need to test new weapons in the field, against a modern enemy, and in our estimation it is doubtful that the Soviets would fully commit to an armed response. The logistical challenges alone—'

'Would be challenging to a human intellect, I agree,' the prime minister interrupted. 'But that is not what we are dealing with here. To the Presence, such challenges may be trivial. Naturally, many of the claims about its capabilities are propaganda, but we should not dismiss them entirely. Indeed, if we truly appreciated the possibility that we are dealing with something more than human, we would not choose such an obvious course as using Dzhugashvili. Have you factored that into your analysis, Mr Bloom?'

The Chief butted in before Peter could respond. 'So far, the Presence's direct contribution to intelligence matters has been limited to vetting operatives in Russia, which is the primary reason why we have not been able to infiltrate the Kremlin. In practice, it is the NKVD old guard and the God-Builders' inner circle who make the actual operational decisions. In fact, we have reason to believe that the Soviet intelligence apparatus is currently distracted by internal purges, so it is the perfect time for decisive action.'

West's soul-spark formed into a glowing Platonic solid of clarity.

'As Bloom has pointed out, there is the human element to consider here as well,' he said slowly. 'Franco may have been the wrong horse to back in this race from the start. I was never very fond of the little general. We shall try our luck with Dzhugashvili.'

'Thank you, sir,' C said. 'You will not regret it.'

'However, I want the Winter Court to take the lead in this one. It is clear that terrestrial assets, BRIAR and CARRASCOS, were the key elements here. Sir Stewart will create a team that will assume operational control of them both. I will also instruct the Admiralty to investigate the worst-case scenario.'

Peter could hardly believe his ears. C's monocle came loose again and floated in front of his face like the lure of a deep-sea fish.

'I must protest,' Peter said. 'I have been developing CARRASCOS so far, and it would be extremely detrimental from an operational standpoint to change handlers so abruptly. Not to mention the risk in arranging physical meetings—'

'Your protest is noted, Mr Bloom,' West said. He sounded tired. 'Nevertheless, my decision is made, based on all the available information. Sir Stewart, I want a meeting with our man within the week, if possible. That will be all, gentlemen.'

C's mouth was set in a grim line. Sir Stewart's soul-spark was like a full moon, round and golden.

'This is it, Bloom,' the Chief hissed, not touching the ecto-phone circuit so that the PM and Sir Stewart could not hear him. 'This whole set-up was that bastard Menzies making his move. The old man seems to listen to you. Try to see if you can make him change his mind, via any means necessary. Otherwise we are all in the shit.'

Before the ectophone circuit vanished, Peter spoke.

'Prime Minister, sir, I would like to have a word with you in private.'

West's voice sounded surprised, but his soul-spark shrank into solid, angular inscrutability.

'And why is that, Mr Bloom?'

'It concerns a conversation we had a long time ago. I feel it may shed some light on the Spanish situation.'

'I see. And where did we have that conversation?'

'In Palace Gardens Terrace, sir.'

The prime minister chuckled. 'I suppose I did ask you here for your perspective. It is only fair that I give you another minute to share it. The rest of you, carry on. England needs you, and so does Spain.'

Three months after Mr Bloom's death, in 1921, Mr West came to visit Palace Terrace Gardens, late at night.

Peter hid at the top of the stairs and watched him enter. Nanny Schmidt, their housekeeper, took Mr West's coat and hat. Next to burly Nanny, he looked tiny and round, a bit like Humpty Dumpty. Even in the dim light, his eyes had a silver sheen. Mrs Bloom came to greet him, and they went into the drawing room together.

Peter tiptoed to the salon. The furniture there was covered in white bedsheets that made the cavernous room look like a snowy landscape. He crawled beneath the sheet thrown over a billiard table and huddled there. The musty cloth muffled the sound a bit, but he could still make out the conversation in the next room.

'My sweet Gorgon, I am so very sorry,' Mr West told Peter's mother.

'Please don't call me that,' she said in a small voice.

'A thousand pardons. Also for not attending the funeral. You know how it is, right now. But I wanted to come and pay my respects.'

'It's fine, HB, it really is.'

'I hoped he would have taken a Ticket.'

'That was never an option, you know that.'

'I suppose so. Still.'

'HB,' Mrs Bloom said, 'I loved him, in the end. He worked so hard. I tried to help, but it wasn't enough. He was trying to be you.' She let out a sob. 'In a way, we killed him, you and I.'

'Don't say that. He was a good man, but he chose his fate. I respected that. We have to respect that now.'

'Oh, I do, more than you know. I have decided to run for his seat.'

'I see. I did think there was something familiar in his essays. It was you all along, wasn't it? Well, I could not wish for a worthier opponent.'

'I know you would rather have sent him to your Summerland,' Peter's mother said. 'But this way, his life means something. He will not be gone, as long as I remember him. As long as Peter does.'

'And how is the boy?'

'Oh, HB.' Mrs Bloom's voice broke. 'He will not speak to me. I broke his crystal set, a few months before Charles passed. He thought he could have spoken to Charles, before he Faded.'

Mr West said nothing.

'Now he sits in his room and won't go outside. I don't know what to do.'

'He is young. Time heals. Let me talk to him.'

'Do you think that is wise?'

'Why not? I am nothing but an old friend of yours, here to pay my respects. And Charles and I were friends, too, once. What's the harm? Besides, I brought him a gift.'

'It's one of your games, isn't it?'

'I am telling you, my dear, my games are what they will remember me for, a century hence.'

Mrs Bloom laughed. 'I will let him decide that. Peter!'

Peter sprang up, bumped his head on the billiard table's bottom and ran back towards his room. He made it to the top of the stairs just as Mr West and his mother appeared in the hallway.

'There is someone I want you to meet,' Mrs Bloom said.

Mr West's hands were plump and soft but his handshake was firm. He smelled faintly of honey.

Peter sat upright in his chair. Nanny brought them tea, but he was too nervous to touch it. Mrs Bloom wished them a good evening and retired to her study.

'I read your book,' Peter said.

'Oh? Which one?'

'*The Science of Death*. I liked it.'

'Ah. Thank you. That is not the one most younger readers mention,' Mr West said. 'Perhaps we will not discuss it to-night, for your mother's sake. But tell me, Peter – have you ever played at war?'

Peter shook his head. 'I don't feel like playing much. And that sort of thing is for little boys.'

'Oh, I beg to differ!'

Mr West held up the brown paper bag he had brought with him and took out a large cardboard box. The cover showed a khaki-uniformed army on a battlefield, and the words SMALL WARS in large, elaborate letters.

'If I am not too old, you are not too old. It is only logical. Let me show you.'

The little man opened the box. It contained painted tin soldiers and spring-loaded cannons, cardboard terrain that folded out into hills and trees, dice and sheets of paper with tables. Mr West got down on all fours and crawled around, arraying his little armies against each other on the drawing room floor. Peter watched, a tangled knot in his chest.

Still, Mr West's enthusiasm was infectious, and the game was sort of interesting. You rolled dice to determine the outcomes of cannon shots and encounters between units. Mr West had created it based on the Prussian *Kriegspielen* used to train officers in the old days.

'It should not be random,' Peter said, after one of his cavalry units had been annihilated by a lucky cannon shot.

'How so?'

'Like in your book, you say that if you have a solution to the Maxwell–Kelvin equations, you know what the aether is going to do, for all time. There is nothing random. Why should a battle be any different?'

'Well, in theory it is the same – if we knew all the variables and the equations governing them, and their initial values. Unfortunately, we are not intelligent enough to construct such equations, and thus nothing in war – or love, for that matter – is ever certain.'

'So you can never be certain about anything?'

'Well, you can in pure mathematics, I suppose. You start with axioms, and you prove that certain things follow logically. In number theory, you can prove that there are an infinite number of primes, for example. Sadly, most of these true things have little practical use. It's better to live with uncertainty and roll the dice, even if we don't always like the outcome.'

Peter looked at the battlefield and his fallen cavalry unit.

Nanny Schmidt had found Mr Bloom in the morning after his last rally. He had stumbled home late, fallen, hit his head and then suffocated in his own vomit. The doctor explained it all cheerfully, until he learned that Mr Bloom did not have a Ticket.

Peter knew that only the strongest Ticketless spirits, one in a thousand, survived more than a day after passing over – the others got lost in their own thoughts, pursuing dreams or nightmares in the infinite aether until they Faded. His mother refused to get an ectophone to even try, adamant that it was what Mr Bloom would have wanted.

'Peter,' Mr West said quietly, 'you mustn't blame your mother for not being able to calculate the future. She did what she believed to be right. She loves you, and right now she needs you.'

'I am not angry with Mother.'

'Well, she certainly seems to think you are.'

'I wished he were dead,' Peter said. The words came out like the ball from a spring-loaded cannon. 'I wished Father were dead and I never meant it and I never got to tell him I'm sorry.'

'Peter,' Mr West said in a throaty voice, 'he knew. Of

course he knew. And if I ever knew my friend Charles Bloom at all, he forgave you.'

Clumsily, he stretched out a hand and squeezed Peter's shoulder.

'Let me tell you a secret, Peter. Charles and I had this one big disagreement. In the end, I think he was right and I was wrong, but I just could not bring myself to admit it. And now I'll never get to tell him. But that's the thing about those we love. Sometimes they don't have to be told the important things.' Mr West's silver eyes shimmered. 'Now, shall we continue playing a bit? I do believe you were winning.'

Peter wiped his eyes. They finished the game, which ended in Mr West's defeat. Peter helped him put the soldiers away.

'Could you come and visit us again?' he asked.

Mr West looked down and stroked his moustache.

'I'm afraid that will not be possible, Peter.'

'Why not?'

'It is difficult to explain. You will understand when you are older. It is not a very good answer, I know. But I will be thinking of you, and your mother. You can keep the game.'

There was another world, Peter suddenly knew, where things were very different. Not Summerland, but a land that lay sideways in time. As Mr West put on his coat and hat and said goodbye to his mother, Peter very much wished he could travel there, no matter how far away it was.

Once, George asked Peter if he hated Herbert West. It had been Peter's turn to laugh. Whatever West's faults, he was there for Peter on that evening. After that, Peter had been able to speak to his mother again. And West's words had convinced him to read mathematics at Cambridge.

No, Peter did not hate West. Sometimes he wished he did.

Although they were alone now, the prime minister's manner was tense. 'Mr Bloom, I know you mean well, and no doubt my old friend Mansfeld Cumming' – he used C's real name – 'has been pressuring you to influence me. I am afraid my decision is made and will not change.'

It had not taken Peter long to figure out why West could not visit him and his mother, especially after his political career started to take off. The continuing rule of Queen Victoria's Summer Court guaranteed that in polite society, propriety was everything. Still, the man could at least acknowledge that a bond existed between them.

The anger gave Peter the strength to speak.

'Perhaps you fail to recall the conversation I was referring to. You described a situation where you had been wrong, yet unable to admit it. Well, sir, in this case you still have the opportunity to do so.'

'That is quite presumptuous of you, Mr Bloom.' West's soul-spark looked like a fortress now, pale grey blocks arranged in concentric rings, with faint orange light in the centre. 'Why do you think I am unable to admit that I am wrong?'

'Because you think the Summer Court has grown too powerful, and you need to show them that you are still in charge.'

'Hmm.' West sounded bemused. 'That is an interesting argument. Unfortunately, it is also incorrect. There is a bigger picture that you cannot see, which informs my thinking. I suggest you—'

Suddenly, the prime minister's soul-spark flickered, just as it had before. West made a small coughing sound. The thought-curtain surrounding the central spark of his mind opened.

A bigger picture, Peter thought.

And for a heartbeat, West's thoughts were unguarded.

Peter dived forward and stared directly into the prime minister's soul.

In Summerland, living souls were things of light: glowing polygons, flames, bubbles and very occasionally recognisable images. Soul-readers had compiled a basic dictionary of emotion over the decades, but every soul had its unique language of thought-forms.

Peter had never seen a soul like Herbert West's.

It resembled a miniature cinema or a diorama. In the centre of it was a silver city of towers and buildings, layered like a wedding cake, with countless tiny sparks in every window and street. Giant faces hovered in the sky above the city: West himself and two others, Lodge and Marconi. Peter realised he was looking at the Summer City.

As he watched, a dark tree grew from the abyss beneath the city. Its black branches pierced the silver buildings and twisted themselves around the towers. Wherever they touched, sparks flickered and died. In moments, the city was a shrivelled husk, like an abandoned beehive stuck in a tree, grey and crumbling. A jagged, purple, insect-like thing hatched from it, and distantly, Peter recognised it as the thought-form for guilt.

Then the vision disappeared, replaced by the usual kaleidoscope of consciousness. Whatever tremor in West's ailing brain had caused the images to manifest was over.

'Camlann,' West muttered. 'Camlann, Camlann.' He

took a deep breath. 'I am sorry, Mr Bloom. What were we discussing again?'

Peter hesitated. Then: 'I presented my argument for allowing the Summer Court to continue running the Dzhugashvili operation and you rejected it, as is your prerogative.'

His voice was shrill. The vision in West's soul burned with a cold fire in his mind and the fear shrank his self-image into boyhood again. He was glad West could not see into the aether.

'Indeed. Then I think we are done. I have one more meeting tonight. No rest for the wicked, eh?'

Had Peter witnessed the fevered imaginings of a senile author? No, the images had been too powerful, too all-consuming. Somehow, they had to represent the bigger picture West had mentioned. He might have lost the operation in Spain, but perhaps gained something even more valuable to the Presence.

'Thank you for your time, sir,' he said aloud.

'Mr Bloom? I do remember our conversation. You have to understand that the higher you climb, the more eager people are to push you off your pedestal. And I am presently standing on one leg. Under other circumstances, I might have viewed your argument in a different light. Is that understood?'

'Yes, sir.'

'Capital. Do keep up the good work.'

Peter watched the prime minister's soul close up into a golden ovoid like a Fabergé egg, sealing away all its secrets. Then he entered the Chimney, shrugged his self-image back into adulthood and started the descent into the Summer Court to tell C the bad news.

TEN

Soul-Reading, 11th November 1938– 12th November 1938

The Finance Section of the Winter Court was dreadfully cold, and Rachel White had a hangover.

The white noise of the typewriters rolled over her in painful waves. She had been unable to stomach the morning tea in the staff room and her mouth was dry. She hunched over her desk: it seemed to help with the nausea. Thankfully, there was barely any light from the converted prison canteen's gridded windows. The electric heaters were on full blast and dried up the damp air, but even so, she had to wear a thick scarf and fingerless gloves.

Very slowly, she took a purchase order from her in tray, rubber-stamped it and punched the serial number into her ectoterminal, one digit at a time. Later, she decided, she would start her path towards treason by seeing if there was a cash stream that could be diverted from a particular, little-used Cresswell & Pike account to fund Max's small but growing operation. But that would have to wait until her brain dealt with its chemical imbalance.

One more reason to be jealous of the dead like Bloom.

Joe had heard about what happened at the Harrises', of course.

Rachel was not sure who had called him: quite possibly it was Philby. When she woke up to the harsh clanging of her alarm that morning, still in that numb, semi-drunken state that preceded the main event of her hangovers, he was already up.

She found him downstairs feeding the finches, already fully dressed but unshaven. The birds were cold and sat still on their perches, fluffed up into feathery balls.

'We need to keep them warm,' she said hoarsely. 'Let's move them closer to the fire.'

After the ectoplasm incident, they had somehow reached a mutual, unspoken agreement to pretend it never happened. However, he had started taking care of the finches with a dedication that had the tang of penance.

'I am not sure the female is well,' Rachel said. 'I am going to take them to Max's tomorrow, see what he thinks.'

'That sounds like a good idea, love,' Joe said. 'I could do it, too, if you want to rest.'

'No, it's fine. It gives me something to think about besides work.'

'How are you feeling this morning?'

Rachel wrapped her dressing gown around herself tighter and huddled close to the gas fire.

'A little worse for wear,' she said. Her head was starting to have that feeling of fractured glass. Memories of the previous night emerged from the cracks, and she did not like the look of them. Had she really said all those awful things? Master plan or not, it had better be worth it.

'Your mother tried to call last night,' Joe said.

Her mother's calls had been more frequent lately. She was clearly bored, with Rachel's father travelling.

'Of course she did. Did she actually speak to you?'

'No. Gertrude picked up. Maybe you should give her a call tonight.'

Rachel had not returned her mother's calls for the past two weeks. She was not sure how she would even begin to explain what had been happening. Telling white lies to her mother had been difficult even before she passed over, but now that she could literally see into Rachel's soul, it was practically impossible. And when she was bored, she had a habit of spending some of her *vim* pension on thought-travel to hover around Rachel whenever she was in public spaces after sundown. Rachel alternated between finding it comforting and annoying.

'I will get around to it, dear,' she said aloud.

'How is everybody in the Group?'

'Oh, they were a bunch of pussycats as always. Guy Liddell asked after you. And, you know, people made a few suggestions that I might look into later.'

'That's wonderful.'

Joe's voice was flat. He pushed his hand into the birdcage to change the droppings-covered newspaper at the bottom. It sent the finches into a fluttering frenzy for a moment. The noise made the first ray of pain penetrate into Rachel's head.

Suddenly, Joe's manner infuriated her. It was always like a dogfight with him. He circled around a subject in figures of eight, and only when there was no escape would he fire his emotions at you in a single machine-gun burst. And even then, there were things he would simply not speak aloud.

'Joe, if you have something to say, please say it. I need to go to work soon.'

It was the wrong way to go about it, she knew. She had tried to get him to open him up before and pushing him never worked; he just became quiet or disappeared to his club.

'Look, Rachel, I just think ...'

'What?'

'Maybe we should take some time off. You've been under so much pressure, and we haven't been to the Atlantic Coast for a while. My doctor was saying that it could do me good.'

Gertrude came in with a full English breakfast on a tray. Rachel thanked her, but knew immediately there was no chance of getting it down.

'I don't know,' Rachel said after the housekeeper had gone. 'It feels too early to take leave, with the new job and everything.'

'I'm sure Miss Scaplehorn will understand.'

'Have you *met* the woman, Joe? She is not the understanding kind. I would love to go, but ... it just isn't a good time. I'm sorry.'

The bacon smelled delicious, so she hazarded a nibble. An acidic taste rose into her mouth immediately. She leaned back in her chair, closed her eyes and waited for the heaving in her stomach to subside.

'Don't take this the wrong way, Rachel,' Joe said slowly, 'but is there something I should know? Something keeping you here?'

For the past few months, she had suspected Joe of seeing other women. It might not even have been a flesh and blood woman. There were places in the East End where spirits and mediums conjured alluring feminine phantasms out of ectoplasm for the discerning gentleman who worried about disease. Or it could simply have been a secretary in Blenheim.

Rachel was not sure which option was the worst, and so she kept the jealousy locked up in a cage, where it stayed still unless disturbed.

She opened her eyes and gave him a pained smile.

'Just this terrible headache, dear. Would you be a darling and get me some aspirin so I can face Miss Scaplehorn?'

Joe nodded, touched Rachel's hand briefly as if an after-thought, and went upstairs to fetch her medicine.

Rachel managed to get to the third invoice when somebody placed a hot cup of tea on her desk. Startled, she looked up and saw Roger Hollis.

'How are you, Rachel?'

She picked up the teacup and smelled it. 'You made it too strong. And without any lemon. But thank you.'

'I suppose you would have preferred proper chai. But you're welcome.'

Rachel massaged her forehead and sipped the hot tea.

'I'm sorry about last time, Roger. I was tired, and didn't want anyone explaining things to me. Especially things I did not want to hear. What are you doing here, anyway? No flowers for anyone this time?'

For a moment, Roger was consumed by a hacking, painful coughing fit and had to wipe his mouth with a handkerchief. The other Finance clerks turned to look. The cold weather had not been good for his health. In all likelihood, he did not care any more and was just waiting for his transition to Summerland.

'In fact, I am here to see you,' Roger managed.

'Then you can clearly observe that I am taking your good advice.'

'I couldn't help hearing about last night. I spoke out of turn earlier. I want to make it up to you.'

Of course. Philby would have already turned her escapade into the talk of Blenheim, with that gift of the gab of his.

'All right,' she said. Miss Scaplehorn was looking at them pointedly over the thick rim of her glasses. 'Let's go somewhere else. It is only a few minutes until the lunch break anyway.'

They huddled on couches in a corner in the staff room – it was empty with everybody at the canteen for lunch. Rachel drank her tea and offered Roger some dry biscuits from a tin. She took three herself, and then a fourth: her stomach felt able to handle them.

Roger nibbled a brown disc delicately.

'Rachel, before you say anything, I heard Philby's version of what happened. He loves to embellish, so I am giving you the benefit of the doubt. I have been thinking, and I may be able to help you.'

'Well, I have a few hundred purchase orders that need stamping if you are free after this.'

'I am being serious, Rachel. I thought about what you said, and there is someone I know in the Summer Court who agreed to look into this imaginary mole. One of the Young

Turks, in fact. It's all rather … unofficial, but he thinks there might be something to it.'

'Why doesn't your Spook friend just request my report?'

'Yes, well, you know how it is, not everything gets put into the reports. Besides, like I said, it is all a little unofficial. So I was wondering if there is anything else you remember about this FELIX, anything else that might help.'

Rachel stared at Roger's familiar, boyish face, his friendly smile.

I could let it go, she thought. *Someone would take care of it. I could go to Liddell, accept the transfer back to the Irish Section, tidy up here and no one would ever know.*

Then the anger she had felt at the Harrises' came back. *Bloom is untouchable*, Max had said. For all she knew, Roger was working for the forces who chose to shield Bloom from discovery. This was her operation, Kulagin's gift to her, her chance to show the Service what she was made of and maybe get her job back.

'No, I'm afraid there is nothing I can think of,' she said. 'Much as it pains me to admit it, Harker was probably right about it being misinformation. Even a broken clock shows the correct time twice a day.'

Besides, it would be exactly like Roger to do her a favour to win her affections before his time in mortal flesh ran out, their long platonic friendship be damned. Sometimes she felt that the carefree way he flaunted his affairs was meant to make her jealous. Maybe she was just flattering herself.

I could use a little flattery, Rachel thought.

'Rachel, you do realise that this is not the worst position for you to be in. I really want to help you.' He frowned. 'At least with table manners, if nothing else. You have crumbs on your lips. Here.'

He handed her a clean handkerchief. For an instant, they both held on to it, their fingers almost touching. Then she pulled it to her and dabbed her lips with the silky cloth. Absurdly, she felt guilty at the touch. She put it down on the low table between them, next to her empty cup.

Even if what he offered was genuine, she could not accept it. It meant getting too close.

'I appreciate it, Roger, I really do. I understand that you want to climb up a spirit spy's trouser leg, and I wish you all the best. I just can't help you get any higher. I'm sorry.'

Roger frowned and stood up abruptly. 'I think you are making a mistake.' He sounded hurt.

'I have been making mistakes all my life, Roger.' She sighed. 'For what it's worth, I will miss you after you are gone.'

'All right, old girl,' Roger said. He suppressed a cough with his sleeve. 'I guess this is a goodbye, then.'

'Goodbye, Roger.'

Max Chevalier leaned closer to the birdcage and peered at the finches. The female was morose and sat in a corner, all fluffed up, while the male jumped up and down and pecked at seeds as heartily as ever.

'The females are a bit more fragile, I'm afraid. You have to watch out for tumours, the swollen belly may be a sign of that.'

'Can we get to the matter at hand?' Rachel asked. Although the bird *did* look unwell.

'Tut,' Max said. 'Priorities, Mrs White. Living birds trump dead spies.'

'Maybe this is all for nothing. Maybe Bloom was simply being polite.' Her mood had not substantially improved in the past day. Joe had slept in the guest bedroom, blaming chilly sensations again.

Max had scheduled their meeting at Sloane Square that Saturday before a social outing. He wore Henry's body and evening wear. His hair was waxed and he smelled of strong cologne. If not for the slackness of his face and dead eyes, he would have been one of the most handsome men Rachel had ever met, but on the whole, she preferred the Edison doll.

'Poor wee beastie,' Joan said. 'I wonder if it has a soul.'

She was one of Max's agents, a blonde, birdlike woman with a faint Scottish accent who was, based on the looks she gave Max, at least a little in love with the dead spymaster. The other agent present, Helen, a surprisingly senior lady with a cockney accent and a fearsome, feathered hat, sipped tea and fed sugar cubes to the foul-mouthed Amazon parrot on its perch. Max had sworn over everything he held holy that both of them, as well as Henry, could be absolutely trusted, but the two ladies still made Rachel a little uncomfortable.

She gave Joan a pointed look. 'I am more concerned with espionage than eschatological ornithology right now,' she said. 'How long should we wait?'

'Why the hurry, Mrs White?' Max asked, 'Softly, softly, catchee monkey.'

'Roger Hollis, my former secretary, came to see me yesterday. He claimed to be investigating the mole as well, on behalf of a patron in the Summer Court. He wanted me to help him.'

'Isn't that interesting?' Max said. 'What did you tell him?'

'I said I did not know anything. I believe he had … ulterior motives for offering his help and is not serious about the investigation.'

Helen let out a bright giggle. 'Oo-er,' she said. 'Somebody after the old slithery?'

Rachel blushed. 'Either that, or he is simply courting favour with Bloom's protectors.'

She had been surprised to learn that Helen had infiltrated a Luddite group run by a Soviet agent and was a safe house and logistics expert. Joan had been the key witness in the famous Russian Tea Room Case a few years ago. A keen automobile enthusiast, she was to be their driver. At the Winter Court, Max had preferred such part-time agents over professionals, praising their dedication and lack of careerism.

It all seemed jolly and eccentric, but Rachel remembered the story about the fox that Max had shot. She had no doubt that, if necessary, he would treat his agents with the same combination of tenderness and ruthlessness.

'Very well,' Max said. 'We shall watch out for Mr Hollis. As for Mr Bloom contacting you, no need to fret. I suspect he is going to follow the pattern of classic asset development – which is not dissimilar to seduction, incidentally. I could practically write you a script, if it wasn't for the soul-reading.'

Rachel blinked.

'Ah yes, Mrs White. Like all of us post-mortals, he can see into your head. *That* is what makes this interesting.'

'All right,' Rachel said testily. 'So how am I going to stop him from seeing my deepest and darkest secrets?'

'Well, soul-reading is not thought-reading. A spirit can see the aetheric shape of your soul, and that is a very transient thing, not verbal at all, more like a Cubist painting that moves. Even with just a little training, most emotions can be identified. That makes the Spooks very good at talent-spotting and asset development. However, there are counter-techniques related to Stanislavski's acting method: using your memories to create powerful emotions to fool the observer. Let us try a little experiment.'

He touched a switch on the spirit crown. Henry stiffened, and then his face returned to normal.

'Just wait a minute, my dear boy,' Max's voice echoed from the Edison doll. The medium sighed and leaned back. On the few occasions when Max was not inhabiting him, the young man said as little as possible.

'Now, think of something happy, please.'

Rachel stared at the doll blankly. *Happy*. Childhood memories flashed in her mind. Listening to her *ayah*'s stories. Tending the garden with her mother. Joe's proposal on the Atlantic Coast in France. The images felt cold and distant. Her eyes burned all of a sudden, and she had to squeeze them shut to keep from tearing up.

Rachel stood, embarrassed.

'I don't think I am naturally a happy person,' she said in a choked voice.

'I should say so.' Max's voice was soft. 'Whatever that was, I wouldn't use it.'

'There, there,' Helen said. 'It's all right, dearie-dove. Sit down. You're amongst friends here.'

Looking at her beaming, ruddy face, Rachel was suddenly glad that Max had not recruited traditional Court hard men.

'Obviously, we have our work cut out here,' Max said. 'I may have to cancel my dinner. Oh well. We might try anger instead. Or, better yet, guilt. Guilt is always reliable.'

ELEVEN

An Affair in the Registry, 14th November 1938

Peter Bloom entered the Reading Room of the Summer Court Registry to look for the file on the last battle.

Only a handful of the thirty ink-spattered desks were occupied. There were four archivists' counters and a small break area. It could have been a library in any civil service building of the living, unless one looked to *ana* or *kata*. Even rudimentary hypersight revealed the endless spiralling stacks with their labyrinth of secrets. Peter liked the Registry; it reminded him of the college library in Trinity, although it lacked the smell of paper and dust.

Ostensibly, he was here to compile material for the briefing on Spain for the Winter Court. C had been furious after Peter reported the outcome of his private session with West. The old man sealed himself into his office for two days, refusing to see anyone except the stone-faced Hill. The Special Committee was due to meet in another week, 21st November, and Peter suspected the Chief was girding himself for another confrontation with Sir Stewart. His absence left Peter to deal with the details of transferring the operation over to the Winter Court. A young officer called Hollis kept bombarding him with requests for information. Dutifully, Peter was in the process of preparing an information package – which would also be delivered to Otto and Nora via the Listener.

But the real reason he was in the Registry was the word West had spoken: Camlann.

Camlann was the battlefield where King Arthur and evil Mordred perished by each other's hand, ending the golden age of Camelot. Was West haunted by the possibility of a world war precipitated by conflict between the Soviet Union and Britain? Did the image represent the Presence invading the Summer City?

Yet that did not explain the guilt West felt. Camlann – or CAMLANN – had the ring of a code name for an operation or an asset. Arthurian code names had been a fad in the early days of the SIS.

If there was an SIS file documenting plans of a war with the Soviet Union, obtaining it was of paramount importance – especially if there was a risk that the fire burning in Spain would spread to the rest of the world, and Summerland itself.

It had to be worth the price he was going to pay for it.

Peter went up to one of the archivists, Astrid, a young woman who had gone through a premature Fading during her time at the Registry. When he joined the Court, she had been pretty, with auburn hair, a prim figure and legs with the perfect geometry of sharpened pencils. She still wore white blouses and short skirts, but her hair was now colourless and her face had become a translucent oval, illuminated from within by the faint prismatic glow of her *luz* stone.

'Mr Bloom,' Astrid whispered. Her voice was nearly gone

as well, a barely audible vibration in the aether. 'How have you been?'

'Too busy to see you, I'm afraid. Visiting the living.'

'No wonder you look pale.' In spite of her condition, Astrid was sharp as a tack, and even liked to joke about it.

'Merely looking forward to forgetting our first meeting so I can experience meeting you again.'

Astrid laughed, a gentle, tickling sensation in the aether, like leaves brushing Peter's face.

'And here I thought today might finally be the day.'

Fading affected everyone differently, and even a regular intake of *vim* did not necessarily protect you from it in the long run. Before Tickets, it happened very quickly, and it was no wonder that early mediums were accused of being charlatans when the spirits they channelled could only recall fragments of their past lives. Sometimes Peter wondered what it had been like for his father, and what was the last thing that had remained with Mr Bloom at the very end.

Peter sighed. 'I'm afraid not. I need a couple of files.'

'I heard you were moving up in the world.'

'I wish. If I make a mess of this one, C will have my head.'

'Only your head? He is getting soft in his dotage.'

Peter grinned and took a request slip from Astrid's desk. He scribbled keywords and an operation code on it and signed it with his *luz*. It was for an early report from BRIAR.

Astrid glanced at the slip briefly and stood still for a moment. The memories she had lost via Fading had largely been replaced by the vast and complex index of the Registry.

She conjured a Hinton Cube from the aether, a flowing, shifting crystal the size of a small die. It represented a unique four-dimensional address that one could thought-travel to, just like the Tickets and ectophone beacons.

Peter made a show of frowning at the Cube. 'You know, Astrid, I am not feeling terribly well. I had a bad connection with a medium, gave us both a headache the size of Gibraltar. Would you mind helping me with this?'

'Of course,' Astrid said. She leaned closer. 'It would be my pleasure.'

Peter winked at her. You could find a flaw in any system, no matter how carefully constructed. That was what the philosopher Ludwig Unschlicht had taught him.

It was seven years ago, during Peter's second year at Cambridge.

The lecture had been strange from the start. Dr Unschlicht walked into the seminar room at Trinity, pushed a chair to the centre of the small space and sat down. He sat quietly for a while, face tense in extreme concentration. The German philosopher was almost fifty but could have passed for thirty. He had an aquiline profile and a mass of brown curly hair atop a high forehead.

Finally, he began chopping the air with his right hand.

'I shall try and try again to show that what is called a mathematical discovery had much better be called a mathematical invention.'

That made Peter grip his exercise book and fountain pen with anger. Of *course* mathematics was discovered, not invented! Invention was a degrading word, better suited to engineers. Mathematics was about how things *were*, in every possible world. He looked around at the handful of other students and fellows in the room and was disappointed when he did not see other expressions of outrage.

Still, Dr Unschlicht's presentation was as compelling as it was strange. He had no notes; he simply talked. Every now and then he stopped and muttered briefly to himself, brow furrowed as he attempted to pull a thought from some unseen well with the sheer force of his will. When he spoke again, his next statement was perfectly coherent, logical – and to Peter's ears, blasphemous.

'Think of the case of the Liar's Paradox,' Unschlicht said. 'It is very queer in a way that this should have puzzled any-one, because the thing works like this: if a man says *I am lying*, we say that it follows that he is not lying, from which it follows that he is lying and so on. Well, so what? You can go on like that until you are blue in the face. Why not? It doesn't matter. It is just a useless language game. Why should anyone be excited?'

'Because it's a contradiction!' Peter shouted, unable to contain himself. 'If mathematics allows statements that can be both true and false, it all falls apart!'

Unschlicht looked at him, eyes blazing. His thin-lipped mouth curled into a smile.

'Why?' he said. 'Why does everything fall apart? Nothing has been done wrong. Why is this young man so afraid of contradictions?'

Peter blushed. 'Well, if you can't build mathematics on logic, then what is it built upon?' he asked. 'Russell and Moore showed that—'

'I am very familiar with their work. But you haven't answered my question. What harm is there in a contradiction?'

'What about a situation where you are building a bridge?' a new voice said, high and full of enthusiasm.

The owner of the voice was one of the first New Dead Peter had seen. He, or his medium, wore full spirit armour, a bulky contraption like a diving suit covered in wires and coils. A faint smell of burning dust emanated from it.

'If you want to build a bridge,' the armoured stranger continued, 'you want to make sure your calculations are correct. And how can you make sure it won't fall down if there is a contradiction in your calculus?'

'Doctor Morcom,' Unschlicht said, 'don't you give a class on this very topic? Perhaps you would like me to enrol.'

Peter recognised the name. Dr Christopher Morcom was a mathematical prodigy who had passed over at a young age but continued his work in Summerland and even obtained a posthumous fellowship at Trinity.

'I am indeed teaching a class on the foundations of mathematics,' Dr Morcom said. 'But I was intensely curious about your approach.'

'You can educate me in turn, then! Has a bridge ever fallen down because of the Liar's Paradox?'

'Of course not. But mathematics and physical reality *are* intimately linked. At the end of the last century, we saw the Scottish mathematician Tait's perfect correspondence between classification of knots and the periodic table of elements. In Summerland, we are discovering even deeper links between geometry and the nature of souls. How can we continue this journey if our entire edifice of logic rests on a shaky foundation?'

'Your argument is irrelevant. The process of mathematics is agnostic to its material or aetheric nature. It is a language game, nothing more than a matter of grammar, social conventions and practical demands. Doctor Morcom, you will have to agree with me that our bridges stand. If they fall, it is not due to a flaw in the foundations of calculus. Find me a perfect bridge made of mathematics in your Summerland that collapses under your weight. Then I may look at things differently.'

'Let us hope our aetheric bridges continue to carry us, then,' Morcom said.

He sat down, conceding a stalemate. Unschlicht followed suit, brow furrowed, and continued his lecture.

Afterwards, Peter followed him across the verdant expanse of Trinity's grand quad.

'Doctor Unschlicht.'

The philosopher turned around, head cocked to one side like a puzzled bird of prey.

'I didn't understand the point you were trying to make,' Peter said. 'Are you saying that mathematics is true, or that it isn't?'

'My point is that there is no point. I won't say anything which anyone can dispute. Or if anyone does dispute it, I will let that point drop and pass on to say something else. Learn to embrace contradictions, young man. Once you do, perhaps we can have a serious discussion, hmm?'

He walked away and left Peter standing there, his thoughts unmoored and lost, like a kite whose string had been cut.

Seven years later, Peter walked in the midst of mathematics made solid, in the heart of the Registry.

Astrid guided them to the first file with blinding speed,

holding his hand in a featherlike grip. Their thought-travel blurred the colours of the files into a fuzzy grey which then resolved into a cubical space surrounded by shelves on all sides and illuminated only by amber hyperlight. The angles and the corners twisted whenever Peter turned his head. They were inside one of the countless interconnected tesseracts that made up the stacks. It was hard to believe that as little as thirty years ago, the Service had got by with a small building on Charing Cross Road.

Astrid floated up to a high shelf close to the ceiling and pulled out a thick file. She handed it to Peter.

'There you go, Mr Bloom.' Her blank face glowed with rosy light. 'Is there anything else I can help you with?'

Peter let the file drop and drew Astrid to him. He kissed her mouthless face. Her skin felt like a soap bubble, slippery and yielding against his lips. He licked the nub of her *luz* and she moaned softly.

Peter had not taken many lovers in Summerland. Privately, he considered the Victorian morals that discouraged pleasures of aetheric flesh ridiculous. Except in Summerland, naked-ness would have meant literally baring his soul, and his secrets with it. And so, even now, his self-image stayed clothed and distinct. He pushed his own *luz* deep into Astrid's aetheric flesh, but only caressed her soul-stone without letting it in.

It would be so easy to allow them to become one. What was the Presence but the logical end point of a union like this? She pulled him closer and ground her *luz* against him. Her fingers melted into aetheric tendrils that flowed down his back. For a moment, it was excruciating to close him-self to her. There, in his arms, was a cure to his solitude, an opportunity to share himself fully with another being. As for Astrid, she yearned for his memories of the flesh, of the living world, of all the things she had lost. And he could not give them to her.

He could only take.

While Astrid clung to him, lost in passion, he focused on his *luz* inside her, reached through it for the Registry index that filled her mind like sawdust packed inside a toy. He whispered the word CAMLANN, and suddenly a Hinton Cube blazed in his mind, leaping up from Astrid's vast memory.

He continued to caress her for a few minutes, but with less enthusiasm. Astrid grew increasingly frustrated and finally pulled away.

'I'm sorry,' Peter said. 'I'm sorry, I don't know what came over me. This isn't right, we shouldn't—'

Astrid's egg-smooth face betrayed no emotion but her voice was cold.

'It is perfectly all right, Mr Bloom,' she said. 'You did say you had a headache from your medium. It must be nice for you boys, being able to visit the living. I thought I could help you grow up a little, but I see I was mistaken.'

Peter blushed. Astrid gathered her flowing form into her previous prim self-image.

'I'm sure you can find your own way back.'

The aetheric current from her sudden departure sent the pages of the file flying all over the tesseract.

Peter gathered the sheets of the Spanish file from the floor. Then he focused on the Hinton Cube from Astrid's mind and thought-travelled. The tesseracts and files blurred. There were cross references, several streams of thought that pulled him in different directions. Lacking the archivist's instinctive skill, he concentrated on the strongest one, holding on to the image of the Cube like a swimmer to a branch in a current.

Then he was in front of a shelf full of files. *There*: the pull of the Cube guided his hand to a folder with a green cover. He took out the sheaf of contents and put the empty cover back on the shelf.

For a moment, he thought about the texture of the paper between his fingers. Even now, the Empire's aetheric technology clung desperately to the conventions of the living.

Of course, nothing was what it seemed. Somewhere within the files was a *luz* fragment, the ultimate result of Fading, an ancient soul-remnant brought up from the mines in the *kata* depths and put to use as a scaffold to hold together a bit of aether that thought it was a piece of paper and ink. Did a glimmer of the original consciousness remain? Did the old soul within feel anything when the file was read?

Too bad souls that were still human did not have their thoughts and desires spelled out so clearly.

Peter concentrated. The stack of sheets curled up as if burned by an invisible flame. It became a glowing bubble of aether around the *luz* shard, an apple of light and air in his hand.

He swallowed it. The tiny *luz* shard nestled into an orbit around his own soul-stone. Suddenly, crystalline information filled his memory: photographs, reports, transcripts. It was too much to process all at once. He would have to examine it carefully later.

At least he would carry this one Faded soul with him to join the Presence.

*

When Peter returned to the Reading Room, he felt thin and hollow, frayed at the edges. Obtaining more *vim* had to wait, however. It would not do to leave just yet. He avoided looking at Astrid, found an empty desk and made a show of reading BRIAR's report.

It pulled his thoughts away from the tantalising weight of the CAMLANN file in his mind and back to the situation in Spain. Besides Inez, he had been running two other agents, a secretary in the POUM party and an Anarchist barber with an influential and loose-tongued clientele. Handing them over to someone else felt like a betrayal.

Peter knew his guilt was completely irrational. Shpiegelglass was undoubtedly going to try to liquidate Dzhugashvili using the information Peter had provided. That was the first step in bringing the Republic under the Presence's influence. And surely, that was the only way to end the needless fighting in Spain.

Or was it?

'Hullo, Blooms, old boy!'

Peter lifted his gaze and looked right into the eyes of Noel Symonds.

Noel grinned. He was lean and slight with an impish face framed by unruly curls. In death, he did not look much different from their night-climbing days together in Cambridge. Although, of course, he now worked in Section A of the Summer Court, specialising in counter-intelligence.

'I have been looking for you all over,' Noel said. 'Would you be so good as to come with me, please? We'll get you a cup of *vim* on the way.'

He clapped Peter on the shoulder.

'You look like you could use it.'

*

Noel's office was in the upper floors of the Summer Court headquarters, in the warren of corridors that indicated prestige by their proximity to C's office. It was small but tidy and decorated with colourful old adverts for Symonds Soups, Noel's father's company.

Peter was tense when he sat down. Noel leaned on the windowsill and looked out at the view to Albert Park.

Noel was the one they would send, Peter knew. He thought about escape. He had an emergency Hinton Cube address that he could thought-travel to, given to him by George in case he needed extraction. But he was dangerously low on *vim* for thought-travel, and if this was going to be where they took him, there would be expert spirit Watchers everywhere, able to track him anywhere with hypersight.

He pretended it was a logic problem. Had they known he was going to use Astrid? Was it possible that West himself had set a trap for him? It seemed absurd, but not completely impossible. The CAMLANN file burned in his mind.

'How are you, old boy?' Noel asked.

Peter sighed. 'Worn out. C is sulking, and now I have to hand my entire operation over to the grubby hands of the Winter Court, gift-wrapped with a bow on top. I don't even want to know how badly they are going to bungle it.'

'Well, Harriet is bringing you some *vim* to perk you up. How's the love life?'

'Drier than a desert, I'm afraid.'

'I know what you mean.' Noel sighed wistfully. 'It's a complete monkey show here, and Father is trying to pull me back into the soup business, would you believe it? I thought I left it all behind. People say some things you can't escape even in death, but I didn't think soup was one of them.'

'How about your writing?'

'Oh, I tried to get that book of photographs published but it didn't work out. The editor was worried that encouraging Cambridge students to do things like climb on rooftops at night was not kosher. I may just put it out with my own money in the end.'

'I'd love to see it. For old times' sake.'

Noel smiled. 'You'll be the first one I'll call when it's done.'

He turned his back to the window, leaned against the glass and folded his arms.

He is about to lie politely, or get to the real business now, Peter thought.

'Listen, there is something I would like to run past you. There is a young chap at Blenheim who occasionally tells me things, on the q.t., you know.' Noel tapped the side of his nose. 'So, a month back, the Winter Court catch themselves a big fish and forget to tell us about it. A defector does a walk-in. It's all kept very hush-hush, only Section heads and the deputy director involved, and a couple of Watchers. Except it doesn't work out. The man just tells them things they already know, strings them along for weeks.'

Peter laughed, masking his relief. 'That sounds like business as usual at the good old Water Closet.'

'Indeed. In any case, they are getting ready to throw the fish to the cousins for some chickenfeed, and suddenly the defector decides to off himself in his hotel. Just like that. Doesn't have a Ticket. Disappears like a fart. The cousins get angry. Heads roll. It's a terrible mess.'

George had killed himself? Peter reeled. He really had not known the man at all.

'Does C know?' he managed. 'We should take this to the PM, to argue he can't give our Spanish operation to these bunglers.'

'We should! But here's the rub. My man told me something else. Apparently the last thing the defector said was that somebody over here is playing for the wrong team. What do you think about that, old boy?'

TWELVE

The Night-Climbers of Cambridge, 14th November 1938

Peter and Noel Symonds became friends seven years ago, on the same day he had attended Unschlicht's lecture.

He spent the evening wandering around town in shock, trying to gather his thoughts. It was late when he returned and he had to pay the porters some gate money to get in.

As he stomped across the grounds towards the corner staircase where his small room was located, he heard a rasp from above. He looked up, expecting to see one of the black squirrels that lived in the college grounds.

A young man in a Trinity Hall scarf and a suit hung suspended between two thick pillars that bulged from the brick wall. It appeared he had been shimmying up the groove between them, with his back against one pillar and his feet against the other. But now he was stuck halfway up.

'Ho, there,' Peter whispered. 'What are you doing?'

'Nothing,' came a pained response.

'You had better not be trying to get into my room. I *will* call the porters.'

'I'm not, honest! I'm just climbing.'

'You don't appear to be going upwards at the moment.'

'That's a good point.'

'It's Noel, right? Noel Symonds?' Noel had borrowed Peter's notes once after missing a class, for 'an important engagement', he'd said. Peter now suspected it had involved scaling vertical surfaces.

Noel grimaced. 'Hullo, Blooms. Say, do you see a coil of rope there, on the ground? I don't suppose you could be a nice chap, take it up to that window, tie one end somewhere and toss the other end to me? I don't think I can hold on much longer.'

His legs were shaking now, and he was quite high up.

'All right,' Peter said. 'But then we are both going to the roof.'

'Like this?' Peter asked and leaned against the rope.

He was trying to get around a statue of a saint protruding from the wall. He was high up, nearly thirty feet from the ground. He was sweating and his arms ached, but it did not seem to matter. It was all so irrational that it was as if he was outside his body, weightless.

'Yes. No. Move your feet to that ledge. There is a drainpipe next to you, grab it with your other hand. Now let go of the rope and take my hand. Don't worry, I'll catch you. One, two, three—'

Peter released the rope and reached for Noel. For a terrifying moment, he clung to the wall by his toes and the drainpipe. Then their palms smacked together and Noel gripped his hand firmly. Balancing on the ledge, Peter let go of the drainpipe and caught the roof's edge with his other hand. He pulled himself up while Noel strained under his weight, red-faced. Finally, Peter got one of his feet onto the roof, squirmed over the edge and collapsed next to Noel. A tile slid off and fell to the courtyard below with a terrific clatter. They both froze and held their breath for a moment. When no porters appeared, Noel grinned at Peter.

'That was not bad for a first-timer,' he said appreciatively. 'We usually do it like this, in twos, but Bunny, that bounder, thought he saw the porter coming and bolted.'

They leaned their backs against a large chimney. It was silent and the air was cool, and the lights of Cambridge shone all around.

'So how do you get started?' Peter asked.

'You need to have proper gear. A smooth, good quality jacket is a must – it won't get caught on things. And rubber-soled shoes, if you want to be serious.'

'My God, you do this it a lot, don't you?'

'Nearly every night. I'm even writing a book about it.' Noel grinned. 'It may be the high point of my life.'

Noel was the unofficial chief of a dozen climbers who, between them, had scaled every building of note in Cambridge. Peter listened to his stories with wry amusement.

'Why do you do it? Isn't all this stupidly dangerous?'

'Of course it is! But, you know, it's not like we have that much to look forward to. I'm going to end up running a soup business, can you imagine that? I've been trying to write poetry, but let's be honest, I'm no good. There's always politics, but that sounds like an awful bore. I *am*, however, pretty good at climbing, in spite of the state you caught me in. It is nice to be good at something.'

Noel looked at the city lights thoughtfully. 'You know, they say that the state you are in when you die affects what happens to you in Summerland. Sometimes I imagine it would be nice to fall, hit the ground and just keep falling, straight through the Earth. I could spend eternity trying to climb back up. That would not be so bad.'

He grinned. 'And climbing makes it easy to impress girls, of course.'

'Really?'

'Not really. In fact, I have yet to encounter any lady climbers, and most members of the fairer sex tend to regard our obsession with tall, pointed objects as being rather unhealthy and something Doctor Freud would have some thoughts about.'

Peter laughed.

'What about you?' Noel asked. 'Why did you climb up here? I'm sorry to be forward, but a person who takes such meticulous notes as you does not strike me as someone who suddenly has an urge to sit on a rooftop.'

'You wouldn't understand.'

'Try me.'

'It's silly. I was at this lecture earlier today and something Doctor Unschlicht said upset me.'

'Really? I usually have trouble even staying awake at lectures, let alone getting upset.'

'It's just that ...' Peter waved his hands in the air in frustration, looking for words. 'He was saying that mathematics does not mean anything, that it's just a language game, that there is no truth behind it. I thought he was wrong, but it was so hard to argue with him. I wanted to be a mathematician, but now I don't know what to believe.'

Noel looked at him curiously. 'A mathematician? You

know, a lot of the climbers are doing the tripos. I think you lot use your brain so hard that night air does you good. Why don't you try it?'

'Climbing?'

'Yes, why not? You definitely have what it takes. We've written a manual of sorts – I'll bring it to you tomorrow and you can have a look.'

Noel's teeth flashed in the dark.

'Of course, there is one thing that every beginner has to do for themselves. An initiation ritual, if you like.'

'What is that?'

Noel got up, gathered the rope and tied it around his waist. Then he walked to the roof edge, leaned over, grabbed a drainpipe and started climbing down as nimbly as a monkey. He paused and peeked over the edge, eyes full of mischief.

'Getting down,' he said. 'Good luck!'

And then he was gone.

Sitting in Noel's office seven years later, Peter remembered that feeling, being left on the roof all by himself. It had been a test, of course. He had got down, in the end, after crawling around the pitch-back roof on all fours for a while.

Noel liked tests. But if this was one, passing it required more than shimmying down ornamental stonework and a broken fingernail.

'One of us playing both sides?' Peter said finally. 'That sounds unlikely to me. Are you sure that was not just some Russian ploy?'

'That's what the Winter Court bigwigs are saying, too. I just wanted to know what you think.'

'Why me?'

'You were always the clever one, old boy. And Spain is where we've been having the most trouble of late. Anybody in your Section we should be worried about?'

Peter looked at Noel. He had that same confident, carefree look as when he was making his way up the Old Library chimney all those years ago. That meant he did not entirely know what he was doing but thought he was on the right track.

'This source was sure that the mole is in the Summer Court?'

'I think so – why do you ask?'

'Well, to be honest, I have been wondering about BRIAR. There is a strong NKVD presence in Madrid, and he *is* in a Communist volunteer unit. The Winter Court could be wanting to put the blame on us when the fox is in their own henhouse.'

'Good point. I am going to press my source on that. Anybody else?'

'Not that I can think of.'

'All right, then. I just thought you should know, in case a witch hunt is imminent. We have been in this together for so long that I wanted to come to you first.'

Noel's face was unreadable. It would be very like him to give a warning even if he suspected Peter. Or was he offering Peter a chance to come clean?

'Does C know?' he asked.

'Not yet. I want to keep it that way until I have something more solid. It may turn out to be nothing.'

When their Director of Studies, Mr Jepson, had recruited Noel for the Service in their third year at Cambridge, Noel had finally found something more thrilling than night-climbing. Peter had followed him soon after, via a slightly different route.

Not for the first time, he wished things had been otherwise. Noel's friendship was the one thing he had not wanted to sacrifice on the altar of the Presence. George had advised him to continue the camaraderie, keep as close to Noel as possible, as if nothing had changed. He had been unable to do it. Noel had felt some unspoken thing between them, a stone in the current of their friendship, and it had pushed them apart.

The irony was that it had been the night-climbing and their friend Cedric that set Peter on the path that finally led him to the Presence.

The day after their first meeting, true to his word, Noel came to see Peter and brought him the Climbers' Guidebook, a stack of typewritten pages, handwritten notes and photographs. Try as Peter might, he could not be angry with Noel for abandoning him on the roof: the shared nocturnal activity made him feel part of something special.

Peter met Noel's friends, James, Bunny and Cedric, who also spent their nights hanging off Cambridge's architecture. They exuded a potent mixture of enthusiasm and sheer insanity. The climber community was small and secretive. Noel claimed that there were often climbers in the same college who never knew each other.

Under Noel's tutelage, Peter practised on the roof of the Old Library. Noel called it the nursery for climbers: a jumbled confusion of slopes, leaded walks and iron ladders.

A month later, Noel deemed him ready to attempt the Library's Tottering Tower. It was a twenty-five-foot-high structure, a thin stone needle with a collar of gargoyles and a sharp cone on top.

Peter gasped when he saw it, but it was more of a mental challenge. You had to leap across a chasm to start, but once you did so, the tower itself had miniature carvings that made the rest of the climb easy, like going up a stepladder.

Then they were both at the top of the tower, standing on carvings and holding on to the spike at the top.

'Look at this view,' Noel said. 'It was worth the effort, wasn't it?'

The massive edifice of King's College Chapel loomed ahead, so gigantic that even at their height of sixty or seventy feet, Peter felt like he was still looking at it from the ground. To the north, St John's Chapel rose above a sea of rooftops. Directly below was Trinity Hall, with the speck of a porter walking across the quad. Peter felt like a bird, soaring.

Maybe Unschlicht had done him a favour. If you were rooted in something solid, you could never truly fly.

After that, he embraced climbing wholeheartedly. It took his mind away from doubting mathematics. It was good to feel red brick against his body, and to solve one problem at a time – hand here, foot here – and see how far up he could get. His studies suffered. The days became blurry, sand-eyed intervals between climbs, and he spent more time adding entries to the Guidebook than he did with his homework.

And that was the way it was until September, when Cedric died.

*

After Noel, Cedric was the climber Peter came to know best. He was a tall Trinity boy who dressed in ridiculously high-waisted trousers and braces and smoked a pipe. In tutorials, he was completely silent, folded his lanky frame into his bench with great difficulty, and squeezed his pencil nub so hard it looked as if his long, flexible fingers might snap like twigs at any moment. During climbs, he became alive and talkative, telling Peter about growing up with his six rugby-playing brothers and his plans to open a store selling American comics.

One night, Cedric tried to solo-climb one of King's College Chapel's spires. It started to rain, he lost his footing and fell more than a hundred feet. A proctor found his body lying in the courtyard the next morning.

Two days after his funeral, Noel organised a night expedition to scale the spires of the Chapel in Cedric's honour. The party got their hands on an ectophone and ran the wire up all the way to the top. The climb was difficult – the first frost had settled – but there were ten of them, with lots of ropes. They attacked the Chapel as if it was a mammoth, to be tied down and sacrificed in their comrade's memory.

At the top, Noel called the ectophone exchange and waited. The sombre mood evaporated when Cedric answered from Summerland. Noel sat atop a gargoyle like some sort of demonic cowboy, lifted the phone and hooted.

'Here we are, old boy! Here we are!'

Down on the rooftops, the other climbers patted each other on the back and shouted greetings.

Noel waved at Peter, inviting him up to speak to Cedric. He climbed the spire accompanied by the climbers' cheers, joined Noel at the top and accepted the heavy handset.

'How are you?' he asked Cedric.

There was static on the line. Then the dead boy's voice spoke, more hollow than in real life, but recognisably Cedric.

'It's great here, actually. The lectures are still boring even via ectophone. Not much climbing going on. But thought-travel is amazing. And you can shape things with your mind. Need to pay attention, though. If I'm not careful, my head starts to look like a crushed plum. I kind of wish I had got here sooner, to be honest, just not by falling on my noggin.'

As Peter listened, it suddenly felt like the spire was inverted, and the night sky was some unfathomable abyss below him.

'I'm happy for you,' he whispered and passed the handset back to Noel.

Ignoring his friend's surprised look, he descended alone, all the way to the alley behind the Chapel, and ran to Trinity without stopping.

Back in his room, he lay down on his bed and closed his eyes. It was so unfair. His father had tried to make a dif-ference all his life and disappeared without a trace. Cedric had just drifted through life without purpose, and to him, Summerland was like a holiday resort.

Was this what his mother had tried to tell him? There was no point in climbing when nothing changed if you fell. There was no point in mathematics if it was just a game, with no stone-hard truth beneath.

Noel and Cedric and the others would never understand that.

For the first time since he started night-climbing, Peter felt completely alone.

*

During the years that followed, Peter had come to terms with solitude, but it still stung a little to sit with an old friend over cups of *vim*, conscious that a slip of the tongue would open up an abyss beneath him.

'I'm glad you came to me with this,' he told Noel. 'Do keep me posted.'

'Of course.'

'Incidentally, did your source find out anything more about this defector character?'

'Not much. The Watcher he spoke to said the Russian was a rowdy blighter. Punched a poet, apparently.'

Peter forced a smile. 'Punched a poet? That's a good start. I don't remember anyone ever punching you.'

'Well, there was that scoundrel Caldecott. But that was over a girl.'

They both laughed at the memory.

'We should really get together after work sometime,' Noel said. 'Maybe even bring Cedric along. Say what you want about the Winter Court, but at least they don't have to pay an arm and a leg for a medium to get a drink.'

'How is the old devil?'

'Oh, you know. All business these days. Always asks about you.'

'We had some good times, didn't we? Once in a while, I still think about that night we climbed the Tottering Tower. Are you going to put that in your book?'

'I don't think so,' Noel said. 'Some things people have to discover for themselves.'

*

The rest of the twilight day in Peter's own Section lasted for ever. He had to finish his briefing for the Winter Court but it was difficult to concentrate. The CAMLANN file burned in his mind like a tantalising hot coal, but he did not dare to examine it in his office. More than once, the words flowing from his aetherpen became complete nonsense and he had to put it down.

Finally, he was done and sealed the ectomails to Hollis with his *luz*.

On his way back to Undermay, standing in the fourtube car, he kept hearing Noel's words over and over again.

I thought you should know, in case a witch hunt is imminent.

Every evening commuter who threw him a passing glance looked like a Watcher. Once, his hands on the bar near the ceiling became those of a young boy again, small and pale, with chewed fingernails. He quickly stuffed them in his pockets until he had his self-image under control. It was impolite to remark on drifting appearances, but it would not do if someone who knew him noticed he was in distress.

His *luz* pulsed with fear to the rhythm of the four-rail's clatter. The Summer Court had soul-surgeries that could dig secrets from his mind, no matter how well he hid them. And after he was bled dry, there was the judgment of *kata*, the abyss from which no one had ever returned.

For the first time in seven years, doubt crept into his mind. Not only had George fled the Termin Procedure, he had killed himself. Why would anyone choose a Ticketless journey into the *kata* depths over joining the Presence?

Peter really had not known George at all.

You can prove anything from a contradiction.

Was it possible that it had not been a suicide after all,

175

that Shpiegelglass or someone else had liquidated George and the Winter Court was covering it up? But why would Shpiegelglass keep that from him?

Peter sat down and watched the fourtube's pale, dark-suited men and women returning from the upper *ana* levels, or from long, tiring journeys to do aetheric work in the living world, and felt jealous. Their lives might be meaningless, but at least they weren't troubled by unanswerable questions.

Back in his flat, he finally took out the CAMLANN file. It was not so much like unwrapping a present as he had anticipated, but rather pulling out a tooth: it had tangled up with the doubts and fears in his mind during the course of the day. He focused on the bubble of aether with its tiny *luz* kernel and fanned out the documents it contained like a magician's oversized playing cards.

There was a budget with deliberately obscure line items, a list of personnel – twenty researchers and support staff, both living and spirits – and a contract with Marconi for aetheric instruments. No names of the staff were included, a standard practice in defence-related contracts. Still, it looked like a significant effort: the total cost was more than a million pounds. An impenetrable one-page executive summary talked about research into 'deep *kata* phenomena', whatever those were.

The project was commissioned by West himself in January 1928 – then a freshly minted prime minister – and terminated in August 1928. It had been supervised by a steering committee including West, the Royal Eschatologist Sir Oliver Lodge and Guglielmo Marconi. The minutes from the committee's final meeting were sparse but indicated that the project had been shut down due to 'inconclusive' results – Lodge and Marconi had overruled West. Peter perked up at that. There were rumours that the original three who were present during Colonel Bedford's first journey to the afterlife in the late 1890s had suffered a falling-out. It was certainly true that West, Lodge and Marconi had not been seen together for a while.

The rest of the file – the actual research – was a blur. Peter swore. Either the aetheric record had degraded over time, or the Zöllner camera – which recorded images in aetheric patterns that could be transported to Summerland – had not worked properly.

Or someone had made sure it had not worked properly.

He paced around in frustration. Then it occurred to him to look at the cover sheet of the file. Yes, the file *was* an aetherised version of an older paper document, which was stored in the *original* Registry. Which was now in St Albans, a small town outside London, where it had been relocated from the original Charing Cross site in 1932.

It would not do to send an official request for the file, especially if Noel and his Section were watching him.

Then it struck him. The answer was obvious. He needed to find out what the Winter Court knew about him, and what had happened to George. He needed access to the Old Registry.

In other words, he needed a source inside the Winter Court.

He remembered the night Noel had left him on the roof-top alone. It was so dark he had crawled around on all fours, looking for routes down. Then the clouds hiding the moon passed and it became an algebra problem, putting a series of simple steps in the right order. Go down a drainpipe close to a window with ornamental stonework. Jump onto a ledge, hang from it, drop. And then his feet were on the ground.

Peter poured himself a cup of *vim*, sat down, took up his aetherpen and started drafting an ectomail to Rachel White.

THIRTEEN

Asset Development,
16th November 1938

At the top of the Marconi Tower, Rachel White looked at London through the November rain and steeled herself for her new career as a Soviet source.

Bloom had suggested having the call there early in the evening, after she finished work. 'Talking on an ectophone is rather dull,' he wrote in his ectomail. 'I would rather go for a walk with you, somewhere we can look at the world from different perspectives.'

Rachel buttoned her raincoat tightly against the wind-tossed droplets and wished she had not agreed so readily. Spirit spies did not get colds. She sniffed and waited for the ectophone in her handbag to ring. Bloom was late.

The Tower stood near the Embankment. One of Gustave Eiffel's posthumous projects, it was a triple-pronged radio mast, a monstrosity of wrought iron and steel that smelled of rust. It had started to rain the very moment she began to climb the steps in the central spire. All the tourists and visitors came clambering down in the opposite direction, holding umbrellas and leaflets over their heads. Rachel gritted her teeth, forced her way up to the central gondola and showed her SIS identity card to the watchman, who touched his cap and returned to his glass-walled booth and a cup of tea.

It was a perfectly logical meeting place, of course. The Tower was a hub of spirit messenger and ectomail activity, a giant instrument attuned to the aetheric signals that tied the worlds of the living and the dead together, and meeting there was the Summerland equivalent of a discreet encounter in a crowded, public space. Bloom was being careful.

Below, the Thames was a pitch-black, flowing fracture that bisected London into two lobes of a brain made of street lights, people and electricity. Momentary vertigo grabbed her and she clutched the railing with one gloved hand, struggling to hold her umbrella with the other.

At that very moment, her phone gave a tinkle. She let go of the umbrella. The wind seized it and it blew away, rising upwards in a chaotic, tumbling motion. Her hat and face were instantly wet. She fumbled with the earbuds and the tuning dial until she heard Bloom's voice through the hiss of static and the rain.

'Tell me, Rachel,' he said, 'what do you see?'

She sniffed. 'Rain. London. And an abyss that will allow me to join you over there if I take just one more step.'

Bloom laughed, a soft, whisper-like sound. 'I apologise. I should have checked the weather forecast. One tends to forget.'

'I understand.'

'If you prefer, we can go somewhere else.'

The wind had eased a bit. 'I am fine for now,' Rachel said.

'I climbed all the way up here so we might as well enjoy the view. What is it that *you* see, Peter?'

'Over here, the Tower is like a giant firecracker and we are right in the heart of it. It's noisy. There are spirits everywhere, flitting back and forth, carrying letters and messages.'

Max was nearby in Summerland, too, watching. She tried to sweep the thought from her mind, in case Bloom noticed anything. Right now, it was easy enough to focus on the chill and the discomfort, and the view below.

'And you can see the souls of London from here, moving like impulses through nerves. It really is like one vast creature, alive and sentient.'

'Does death turn everybody into poets, or just you?'

Bloom laughed. 'My apologies. Poetry does not keep you warm, does it?'

'Not that kind, anyway. Tell me, then – what can I do for the Summer Court?'

'I would rather discuss what the Summer Court can do for you. You have had quite a career, Rachel. The Registry, the Irish Section, Counter-subversion. And you even married into the secret world. That happens often, of course, although usually it's the secretaries, no offence. Your husband used to be a liaison officer for the RAF?'

'Formerly,' Rachel said. 'He has some health issues.'

'Ah. I was wondering why he was not at the party. I am sorry to hear that.' There was genuine concern in his voice. The idea that her private darkness was visible to him made Rachel angry. That was good. She seized the emotion and brought it out in her voice, just like she had practised with Max.

'I did not think we were here to discuss my husband.'

'Of course not. It is just that I am aware of your pension and Ticket issues.'

Rachel said nothing. The rain had nearly stopped. The tiny raindrops that remained felt almost pleasant on her face.

'I'm sorry,' Bloom said. 'I did not mean to overstep.'

'You did not. Things are ... complicated at the moment.' She paused. 'Can you tell me more about what you see? What is it like over there?'

'Well, it is more or less as they describe in the books. I believe your mother is in a Summer Home?'

'Peter. I don't want to hear about four-dimensional captains and three-dimensional ships, or any other broken metaphor. Tell me stuff I can't read about in books. What is the worst thing over there?'

Bloom considered. 'That would have to be the Fading. It's terrifying. One does not notice it at first. *Vim* – aetheric energy – stops it, for a time. Thought-travel and aether-shaping make it worse. The aetherologists claim that the aetherbeasts used to be human spirits, too, only they forgot their true natures aeons ago.'

'That sounds terrible. I have heard the word but did not realise what it meant.'

'The National Death Service does not advertise it. But with enough *vim*, it is barely noticeable, a tiny memory here and there over the years, and it does not happen to everybody. There are beautiful things, too. The Summer City sings to itself sometimes. It sounds like musical rain. There is a man, a Faded person, who tells fortunes near the Fortress. He listens to the *luz* bricks. I thought he was mad at first, but if you listen closely, you can hear the soul-stones mutter in the walls.'

'So it sounds like being dead is no simpler than being alive. Good and bad.' In spite of herself, Rachel was fascinated. Spirits rarely discussed Summerland – they were always hungry to hear more about the living. She chided herself for getting too distracted: she was no longer a little girl who believed in magic kingdoms.

The rain had stopped. The clouds were a mixture of red and grey, reflecting the city lights. Near the horizon, a solitary star winked over the skyline.

'The longer I spend in the Summer City, the more I notice the bad,' Bloom said. 'Some parts are not pleasant. There are whole Circles of Faded that are like madhouses, and no one gives them *vim*. Then there are the soul-mines, deep in *kata*. The whole city is built on the labour of the miners, but they get little recognition for it.'

'You sound like a Communist,' Rachel said. It was a trap: he was probing for Leftist sympathies and she had no real way to deceive him. Max had told her to expect it.

'It used to be somewhat fashionable, once.'

'Well, the Dimensionists always had Socialist ideas,' Rachel said. That was true enough: Herbert Blanco West had spun the political party out of the Fabian Society, back in the day, and some of that heritage still remained, no matter how much they emphasised liberalism, reason and science in their rhetoric. 'I joined the Service during wartime. We did not think too much about politics back then.' She paused. 'This is a very strange sort of interview, Peter.'

'You are a strange sort of person.'

'Should I take that as a compliment?'

'Absolutely. It is a rare individual who follows an unconventional path as far as you have. And I do share some of your concerns. See how hard it is for us to understand each other's worlds? No wonder we have inter-Court rivalry. We have no idea what goes on over there, and you cannot comprehend what it is like to be dead. Yet we should be the right and left hands of the Empire, dexter and sinister.'

'So you would like me to keep tabs on the Winter Court for you, is that it?' She thought of Roger Hollis, and there was nothing fake about her indignation.

'You do not sound very enthusiastic.'

'I am angry at some of my colleagues, yes. It does not mean that I will betray them.'

'Really, Rachel, I said absolutely nothing about betrayal. But tell me – why are you angry at the Winter Court?'

'Because I am not appreciated. I am given menial tasks a schoolgirl could do in her sleep. Yet I have nowhere to go. If I leave, I lose my pension and my Ticket, and then my destination is to become one of your Faded. My husband is unwell, and—' She seized the iron railing with both hands. 'I am trapped,' she said in a choked voice. 'Do you have any idea how that feels?'

'As a matter of fact, I do.' He paused. Then: 'I was a student. There was a group of us who liked to scale college rooftops at night. We did not really have anything better to do. We all knew it was dangerous, but no one cared: Summerland awaited us all anyway.

'Then a boy I knew, Cedric, fell to his death while trying to climb to the King's College Chapel's spires. No one thought it was a big deal. We carried an ectophone – you know, one of those big, old Marconi models – to the Chapel roof and held a party there in his memory, while he was laughing with us on the Other Side.

'That was when I realised everything would go on exactly the same, for ever. Our fathers – our parents – mostly on the Other Side already, ran their businesses and would keep running them. It did not matter what we did, not in the slightest. I was destined to be … I don't know what, a civil servant, for ever. A nothing.'

Rachel was certain this was not the whole truth. Was Bloom turned at Cambridge? That meant the Soviets were on the lookout for talent years before the candidates even joined the Service. It required a four-dimensional mind to take a long view like that.

'You seem sceptical, Rachel.'

Rachel swore. It was too easy to forget that to Bloom, her head was a glass vessel, with coloured emotions visible inside.

'I am merely cold.' Her breath had begun to steam. 'I am afraid I will have to go soon. How did you escape your dreadful fate?'

'I found something to believe in.'

Rachel sighed. 'The Service. I see. Something bigger than yourself, something truly immortal. I used to think like that, but I am tired, Peter. My faith is weak. Maybe it always was. The Service is not what I hoped it would be, especially if you are a woman.'

'What would you do to make it better?'

Rachel gritted her teeth. 'I would see men like Harker … well, humiliated. Revealed for the fools they are.'

'Revenge?'

'Fair play.'

'Rachel, here is what I propose. Keep a diary and share it with me. Include what you want in it, leave out whatever you wish. Write about your colleagues. Observe them. We will sort out some unofficial means of compensation and take it from there. How does that sound?'

'It sounds like a good first step.'

'Every journey begins with one, Rachel. Goodbye. We will speak again soon.'

'That was completely useless,' Rachel told Max Chevalier. She walked briskly along the Embankment, still shivering, keeping an eye on the road for cabs. 'The only thing I got out of this was a cold.'

Max's voice on the ectophone was calm. 'It's all going according to the plan. He found commonalities, built some trust, asked for a small thing that is not difficult for you to provide – but which is sufficiently dubious for you to keep it a secret. You need to think like a naturalist: you establish certain behaviours, make them natural, and then—'

'Then the frog cooks, is that it?'

'Exactly. The next time, or the one after that, he is going to ask for something more substantial, and we are going to give it to him.'

'We can't give him anything. That would be treason! And we can't keep this up for much longer. He is in the Iberian Section, for God's sake. The newspapers are speculating that West could send troops there if things get worse. We can't put our boys in harm's way.'

'Mrs White, every castle that defends this kingdom of ours is built out of a thousand little treasons, you should know that by now.'

Rachel stopped and looked back at the Marconi Tower, looming over the river. Like a firecracker, Bloom had said.

She imagined it burning and falling like a flaming tree, crushing buildings beneath it.

'We will get him, don't worry. You have done a fine job, a fine job indeed. He was more aggressive than I expected. I wonder if he is under pressure. Until now, he has been so very flighty, our little Bloom bird.'

'Fine,' she said. 'But if it ever looks like we are going to risk the lives of good Englishmen, we will have to rethink this.'

'Of course.'

'In any case, it is easy for you to talk, Mr Chevalier. What have you been doing in this enterprise so far?'

'Oh, just what I do best,' Max said. 'Watching. Watching and listening.' He made a little trilling sound, like a bird. 'Speaking of which, there is a spirit not far away, watching us. Quite a solid self-image – and a family resemblance, I'll wager.'

Rachel sighed. The spirit Watchers of the Summer Court had nothing on Henrietta Forbes-Smith. 'That would be my mother. I will deal with it.'

Rachel pressed the preset button that activated the beacon for her mother. Then she used the alphabet rotors to spell out a message.

MOTHER. NOT A GOOD TIME. WORKING. DO NOT SPEND *VIM*. WILL CALL SOON.

In a few moments, the phone rattled and the rotors spun back a response.

WEAR RUBBER BOOTS, BBC SAYS RAIN.

FOURTEEN

The Final Exam,
29th November 1938

Most of the high-level intelligence briefings Peter Bloom had attended during his career would have sounded dreadfully dull to an outsider. No raised voices, a careful consideration of facts, all the passion and excitement of a Tuesday morning meeting in an insurance company.

The second session of the Special Committee for the Iberian Problem was not like those meetings.

'You are telling me we just handed you our best Spanish assets, and you, you—'

C's fury was beyond belief. Peter had never seen him lose control of his self-image, but right now the Chief of the Summer Court was a pale, mangled corpse whose right leg ended in a chewed stump crusted with black blood.

Sir Stewart's soul-spark was tiny and fearfully blue. 'We used the intelligence we were given,' he said, mock bravado in his voice. 'It is not our fault if it was not particularly intelligent.'

'Gentlemen,' the prime minister said wearily, 'stop arguing

and explain to me how this happened.' There was a shrill note to his voice on the ectophone. This time, Peter Bloom could actually see his round, blurry figure, drawn in the aether by the vortex lines of the nyctoscope in his office, like looking through a grilled window into a black-and-white version of the world of the living. It was hard to make out his face, but as he paced around, Peter recognised his familiar waddle.

'We are still trying to compile a full picture,' Sir Stewart said. 'It is true that we ... no longer have many intelligence assets in the region. It appears that a power struggle has erupted in the Republican Party between POUM – where our asset CARRASCOS operated and which supported Dzhugashvili and the Communists. The meeting between Mr Dzhugashvili and our delegation, led by Mr Nicholson here, was disrupted by a shoot-out between the two factions. There is now open fighting between Republicans on the streets, and the Communists are purging anyone with suspected ties to Dzhugashvili—'

'I say *it appears* there is a leak in the Winter Court,' C interrupted. 'This was no power struggle. The NKVD engineered it and used our meeting with Dzhugashvili as an excuse to eliminate the opposition to the Communists.'

'Where is your evidence for that?' Sir Stewart said. 'The Republic has been a gunpowder keg for years! We just stumbled into it when the fuse was burning.'

This was not how it was supposed to go. Peter had thought Shpiegelglass would use Inez and the rest of the information he had provided to liquidate Dzhugashvili, with no collateral damage necessary. Instead, the NKVD enforcer had somehow poured petrol into the fire and started a civil war within a civil war.

'Harold, what do you think?' West asked.

Harold Nicolson was a career politician and a long-time friend of the prime minister who had been sent to Spain to treat with Dzhugashvili. His self-image was that of a fresh corpse, wearing a white linen suit riddled with crimson bullet holes. The aetheric image of a cigarette dangled from his fingers.

'Something was off, HB,' he said, using the prime minister's famous nickname. 'We waited at the Telefónica for hours, but Dzhugashvili did not even show. A young Spanish lady was there, a POUM member. I talked to her through an interpreter, she kept assuring us the great man would be there any minute. Then the Communists stormed the building and the shooting started. Nobody from our party or POUM made it out alive.'

In a Small War game, Peter knew, you did not mourn the loss of an individual piece, but he could not help seeing Inez's soul-spark, the green sphere of trust and certainty, when he promised her there would be peace in Spain.

The Presence must have known this would happen. It would have calculated the best outcome already. Surely that was the case. The Communist Party would stabilise Spain and defeat the Francoists. It would all turn out fine.

Only ... human error was always possible. Shpiegelglass could have misinterpreted the Presence's instructions. Peter shuddered at the thought.

'What about Dzhugashvili?' West asked.

'We are looking for him,' Nicolson replied, 'but like I said, we need more assets in the area before—'

'Please,' C said. 'We are scouring the aetheric landscape for signals intelligence. We are going to find him.'

Peter frowned. Dzhugashvili had a legendary ability to avoid capture, but Spain should have been a large enough prize to lure him out of hiding. Had he been warned? Who could possibly have known about the meeting?

'So, we are down to reading newspapers,' West said. 'Let me give you a few headlines.' The tiny figure in the nyctoscope image put on round glasses and studied a pile of news-sheets. 'COMMUNISTS TAKE OVER MADRID. MADRID PAINTED RED. SOVIET SPAIN. And so on and so on. That is, I believe, roughly what you gentlemen are saying.'

The prime minister's soul-spark was wrapped in an opaque shell, but hair-thin cracks ran through it, and an ominous red light emanated from them.

'I am going to have to take this to Parliament. This is no longer just an intelligence matter. Socialists recruiting volunteers from Britain to fight Franco is one thing. Communists shooting British diplomats is another. I wish we could be better than this. Truly, I do. My dream has always been to look beyond the small problems of humanity. But right now I see no alternative. We will have to go to war in Spain.'

West stared right at the nyctoscope, and even through the blurry vortex lines, Peter could see the pain in his silver eyes. He was sure he imagined it, but they appeared to be looking straight at Peter, expectant, as if the prime minister was a tripos examiner and he was a student again.

Peter spent the year after Cedric's death studying for finals at Cambridge. There was a kind of solace in the work, even though he constantly felt like he was walking on something eggshell-thin.

Perhaps that was why he forced himself to work faster and harder, studying twenty hours a day, going through the infamously challenging Tripos Part III questions, in the vain hope that something would emerge out of geometry or algebra or functional analysis to refute Unschlicht's argument.

He kept himself awake at night by wrapping a wet towel around his head and drinking coffee until there was a constant burning feeling in his belly. When he nodded off, his fitful dreams were full of elephant pyramids and flies balancing on vibrating strings and the Chinese Remainder Theorem and its applications.

Three days before the exams, on a cool May morning, he woke up at four a.m. having hardly slept at all. He dressed and wandered through empty streets that were just starting to fill with soft light.

He found himself at St John's Tower. It was kept locked whenever the exam period approached, but the iron railing was no obstacle to a former night climber of his calibre. A chimney and an open window later, he was in. At the top, there was a small ledge between the stone railing and the sloping roof of the college chapel. Peter balanced on it and walked to the edge, where the abyss waited.

As always, the world looked different from above. The faint outlines of the city had a perfect order to them, a geometry that was not apparent at night. He could almost believe that the world made sense.

But that was a lie. Reason itself was cracked like Humpty Dumpty fallen off his wall, and there was no way to put it back together again. His mother had it backwards. There was nothing in this world, either, and what awaited the Ticketless in Summerland – the forgetful sleep of Fading – was a gift.

After Cedric died, he had burned his Ticket. Now, he doubted he could recall it even if he wanted to. Just one step separated him from the place where his father had gone before him, the raw, unshaped aether without meaning.

Peter closed his eyes and took one deep breath.

Suddenly, he heard a shout from below.

'Mr Bloom!'

It was Unschlicht, in his shirtsleeves, standing directly below him.

Suddenly, it did not feel right to jump when someone was looking; it was a private thing, between himself and the world. He thought about hiding, but it was too late.

'Mr Bloom, if you are quite finished up there, I would like you to come with me, please.'

Unschlicht leaned back in his chair, fingers steepled, and looked into the distance with his clear bird-of-prey eyes. They sat in his rooms in one of Trinity's towers. There was a table, two folding chairs and virtually nothing else, no curtains, and no books. On the desk rested a foolscap-sized journal, bound like a ledger, and a fountain pen.

Unschlicht was quiet and still for so long that Peter began to suspect he had been forgotten. He looked dishevelled. A leaf clung to his shirt, and the knees of his trousers had grass stains. Then the philosopher looked up and cocked his head to one side, like Peter had seen falcons do.

'You are a very lucky boy, Mr Bloom, that my friend and I spotted you from the green. What are we going to do with you?'

'I won't try it again, sir,' Peter said. 'It was just a silly thing.

A whim. A dare. I will sit my finals on Monday, like I am supposed to, I promise—'

Unschlicht made a chopping movement with one hand.

'That is not my meaning. You appear to have taken my philosophical commentaries very seriously. That is good. That is very good. But I fear it has made you too much possessed by death.'

Peter said nothing.

'That is foolish. We can never experience death. Death is not an event in life. If we take eternity to mean not infinite temporal duration but timelessness, then eternal life belongs to those who live in the present.

'But Summerland—'

'Summerland makes no difference. It is merely another construct, with no true eternity. It is the board for yet another linguistic game. But tell me, Mr Bloom, who makes the rules? Who stands besides the board, watching and judging?'

'I don't know.' Peter felt uncomfortable under his un-blinking stare. Unschlicht smelled faintly of grass and sex, and suddenly Peter realised what he had been doing in the grounds that had stained his trousers.

'Well, let me show you,' Unschlicht said. 'I am only the stepladder, boy. You must climb on your own, and then throw the stepladder away.'

He got up and pulled out a heavy-looking leather suitcase from under his bed. He lifted it with some effort and placed it on the table in front of Peter.

Then he opened it.

Inside it was God.

FIFTEEN

At the Blue Dog Pub, 30th November 1938

The Blue Dog Pub was on Cottage Place, off Brompton Road, away from the bright cafes and shops of Knightsbridge and the grandeur of the Victoria and Albert Museum. A high wind blew down the alley and made the bare trees in the private garden on the other side of the road wave their branches and whisper. In the November dark, the pub's windows were bright and welcoming.

When Rachel entered, the stifling heat of a gas fire and the smell of beer washed over her. The place was small and quiet, just a handful of tables and a large wireless set playing a German song, dog-themed paintings and posters on blue walls, a scuffed bar with brass taps. The landlord, an old man with a thick white moustache, looked up at her and then went back to polishing a pint glass.

She ordered half a pint of cider for herself and a pint of lager, peeled off her winter coat and sat down near the fireplace to wait. She had started to feel like she was fighting a cold and the warmth felt good. Fifteen minutes later, the bell above the door tinkled and Bloom walked in.

'Peter. It is good to see you again. I bought you a drink.'

This was the first time Rachel had seen Bloom in the flesh since the Harrises' soirée. As far as she could tell, he was wearing the same body as the last time, although he looked bearlike in his thick duffel coat and hat.

The barman frowned at Bloom and went on polishing his glassware. The New Dead were not welcome everywhere, especially not amongst German immigrants. The crushing defeat of Germany in the Great War and the role ectotechnology had played in it had left deep scars.

'This weather makes me appreciate your fortitude during our first meeting,' Peter said. 'Thank you for coming at short notice.'

In the last two weeks, Rachel had taken several more steps towards treason. At Bloom's request, she had jotted down notes on her co-workers. She found it cathartic, especially describing Miss Scaplehorn as a beak-nosed harpy. She chronicled rivalries between Section heads and affairs between junior agents and secretaries. She made most of them up, with enough half-truths to appear plausible.

She delivered her reports to Bloom via ectomail drops, which seemingly by accident established a reasonably secure covert communications protocol. They spoke briefly on the ectophone and went for a walk in Serpentine Park one Saturday, Rachel with the ectophone buds in her ears, Peter in spirit. There was little need to mask her emotions that time – she genuinely enjoyed his company. Like Joe, Bloom lacked the snobbishness that characterised many Court agents. He kept the conversation light, asking Rachel about

India and relating a few amusing anecdotes about C.

This meeting, however, felt much more serious.

'I did not expect to see you in the flesh again,' Rachel said.

'I was needed in Blenheim. Spain went pear-shaped so quickly it's all hands on deck. The Army might end up having to fight British volunteers, would you believe it? It's a mess. How we ended up in it is a textbook example of the problem we are trying to solve here, really – the lack of Winter and Summer collaboration. Your reports have been very helpful in gauging the temperature up here.'

He took off his mask but kept his hat on, and quickly donned a pair of tinted glasses that hid the medium's blank eyes. His charter-body's face was pale and rounded. He looked a little like a chubby boy wearing his father's hat.

Not for the first time, Rachel wondered about Bloom. In her experience, a double agent was motivated by ideology, sex, money or ambition. Peter did not quite fit any of them. Maybe he was simply a better actor than most.

'I'm glad to hear it. The Finance Section continues to be as exciting as always,' she said. 'Over time, I could even get used to it.'

'I doubt that, Rachel. I really doubt it.' Bloom sipped his beer and grimaced. 'I'm afraid I don't really like beer. Although this body appears to.'

She raised her cider glass. 'One more sip, for good luck?'

They clinked glasses.

'It is nice to meet like this,' Rachel said. 'The other times … well, I always felt sort of naked.'

'Really?'

'That came out wrong. But I knew you could see my thoughts.'

'Not your thoughts. Just a glimpse of your emotions. Your aetheric shadow. It is unfair, I know.'

'So, what did you see, Mr Bloom?'

Bloom sipped his pint and then stared at it. 'You are very unhappy. Not just angry. Something happened to you. Did you lose someone? Not that it is any of my business.'

'Yes. Yes, I did.'

'It is hard, isn't it?' Bloom said. 'Younger people do not even understand what death is any more. We have all become like children that way. That is probably why people are happy to send soldiers into harm's way in Spain. It's not real to them.'

'You lost someone, too,' Rachel said.

'My father. He never got a Ticket. He was too stubborn. I am not sure what happened to him. I expect he Faded quickly.'

'I'm so sorry.'

Peter emptied half his pint with one gulp. 'You know, this stuff is starting to grow on me. That happens a lot: the medium likes something and you start to like it, too. I now have a surprising fondness for orange marmalade, for example.' He looked at Rachel, his medium's blank eyes just visible behind the glasses. 'I'm sorry. I am rambling.'

Rachel smiled in spite of herself. A person who liked orange marmalade could not be all bad.

'No, no, it's absolutely fine,' she said. 'I would love to know more about you.'

Peter stiffened and cradled his pint in his hands.

A mistake, Rachel thought. *I went too far.*

She finished her own drink and ordered two more. Max had warned her about this. *He will share something. It will be*

198

calculated, not a lie but not the whole truth, either, designed to evoke sympathy.

Two could play that game.

'I lost a child,' Rachel said.

Bloom blinked. She lowered her voice.

'Looking back, I think we decided to have a baby for the wrong reasons. My husband – he has some issues. He needed something to ground him. It felt like the right thing to do at the time.'

Joe would have been a good father, Rachel knew, especially for a boy, with stories from his rugby days and flying. Sharing them with his son might even have helped him to heal.

'The pregnancy was fine, at first. Maybe it is a bit like being possessed by a spirit: a strange new being inside you, with its own desires. I can't say that I was any fonder of orange marmalade than I am now, but at one point, I did find myself nibbling at pieces of lavatory paper.' She laughed softly.

She had imagined a boy, someone with Joe's eyes and her own complexion, a mirror to them both. The child had grown in her mind before it was even conceived and quickly became the centre around which things revolved. Although she remembered the moment of conception itself very well. Their lovemaking was infrequent at best even then, but that evening they had been to the Harrises', were both a little drunk and Gertrude had the night off. Somehow Joe fumbling with the keys had transformed into Rachel kissing his neck and that led to a shedding of clothes and a furious coupling in the drawing room where the groans of the old couch mixed with theirs.

Rachel smiled a little, lost in the memory, and then

continued, 'I was going to call him Edmund Angelo, after my uncle. In all honesty, it took a while for me to stop feeling that the child would be a distraction from my work. Then I realised that having someone to protect would make me more dedicated than ever to keeping England safe. In any case, we planned to have nannies, and Edmund would look forward to me coming home. We had a little nursery set up. Joe was happier than I had seen him, well, ever. I bought Edmund books and clothes. I imagined reading to him, all tucked under the covers, eyes closed, asking questions, drifting to sleep. When he was old enough, I was going to read him *The Water-Babies*, and *The Velveteen Rabbit*.'

There were a few happy weeks after she realised she was pregnant, and then she bled on the bathroom floor. Nine weeks from conception meant no soul, according to the theory, no electrical net of the brain to catch a soul-star falling from the Unseen.

'It happened so quickly. I touched the thing that came out. It was so tiny, like a seed. And then—' She covered her mouth with her hand.

Dizzy from the blood loss, she had imagined planting it in a pot and growing Edmund like a flower.

Bloom took her hand. 'Ssh. You can stop there.'

She looked at him, tried to ignore the blank eyes and the doll-like face. Suddenly, the beer smell made her feel sick.

'It is quite all right,' she said. 'I did not lose anyone real.'

'I think you did. Of course you did.'

When she recovered, she studied the literature and tried to understand how her body had betrayed her, interrogated it as if it was an imprisoned suspect, but to no avail. All that was left was a sense of failure and a memory of someone who had never existed.

'Do you see now? Work was all I had left.' She squeezed Bloom's cold hand. 'And then those bastards took it away. Give me something to do, please. Something that matters.'

'Rachel. I understand. Believe me, I understand.' He gripped her hand back and held it tight. It looked like he wanted to say something but could not quite bring himself to do so. This time, Rachel did not dare to push, and the moment passed.

Peter let go of Rachel's hand and took a roll of papers from his coat pocket.

'There is something I didn't want to ask you, before. It is very important. I am running an operation in Spain and the Winter Court is not cooperating. I need a file I can't get hold of through official channels.'

He handed the papers to Rachel. There was a Registry cover sheet and a budget, a long list of line items related to a project called CAMLANN.

'There was a programme, ten years ago. I think someone who worked on it has been compromised by the Russians, but the full records were never aetherised. If I go through the official channels, the target will be spooked. But I need to know what they had access to.'

'Well, I should still know a few people who maintain the original Registry,' Rachel said. 'I will look into it for you.' She did not hide the eagerness in her voice.

'It is very urgent,' Bloom said apologetically. 'And confidential, of course. Anything you can give me will be a huge help.'

'I will need a couple of days.'

'Of course. Just let me know through the usual channels and we can make arrangements to meet again.'

'I would like that.'

Bloom removed his glasses and put his mask back on. 'All right. I had better return this gentleman I am wearing to his home, and make my way back to the madhouse.'

Rachel smiled. 'Travel safe, Peter.'

She watched him leave, waited for a while and then drank the rest of the cider to celebrate her victory.

It tasted flat, drinking alone in an empty pub.

Who would I even celebrate with? she wondered. *An absent husband whose nightmares come alive? A dead spy who keeps snakes in his bathtub? A former secretary who wants another notch in his belt before he becomes a ghost?*

She knew it was part of the game, but she had told Bloom things not even Joe knew, and he had listened, and understood. It made her feel better than she had in months.

It was hard to hate Bloom. He had his own wounds, it was clear. Was it worth destroying him just to show the old men at SIS what a mistake they had made? Was the story her *ayah* told her about a magic kingdom, the story she told herself, really worth it? Were Bloom's beliefs any different from her own? What had Kulagin said? *We are all comrades together, men and women, in the same shit.*

At death's door, with Kulagin's hands around her throat, she had not really fought for England, but for her own freedom.

She looked at the papers on the beer-stained table and her stomach twisted with guilt. What was wrong with her? For a moment, it had felt right to give Bloom what he wanted, to turn her charade with him into something real. For all she knew, giving him CAMLANN would mean countless deaths.

Her hands shook. She needed to ground herself before it was too late. Suddenly, she missed Joe very badly. There was a time when talking to him had made the world make sense.

It was not fair to her husband to tell a Soviet spy things she would not tell him. It was not fair of him to try to keep his nightmares inside until they spilled out when they were in bed together, dreadful and poisonous.

Rachel gathered the papers into her handbag and paid the barman. The wireless set coughed and wailed briefly, then resumed its song.

Catching Bloom could wait for one evening. She was going to have dinner with her husband, and they were going to have a conversation.

SIXTEEN

Das Dasein,
30th November 1938

After meeting Rachel White, Peter Bloom dined at the Lyons Corner House, near Tottenham Court Road, a comfortably middle-class but well-decorated place with modern bowl-like lamps and mirrors cut in Modernist waves.

Two tables away from Peter, Otto and Nora talked animatedly. She laughed loud and often, whereas he smoked a cigarette thoughtfully, staring at his cup of coffee, nodding occasionally.

They had set up a new protocol for in-person meetings which involved surveillance avoidance before making contact. Peter had requested a meeting because the Special Committee had sent him to Blenheim to try to prepare a comprehensive report on what had gone wrong with the Dzhugashvili operation. His day had been full of debriefings with shocked operatives, followed by a drink with Rachel White. He was looking forward to speaking to someone he did not have to lie to.

He was supposed to be alert and ready to move, but his thoughts kept wandering back to Rachel White.

She had opened up in the same way as others before her, when a bridge of trust suddenly crossed the chasm between the asset and the handler. Her motivations were classic: a feeling of being underappreciated heightened by personal tragedy. She was competent and driven, and the task of retrieving the CAMLANN file was well within her capabilities.

It should have been easy to maintain detachment, but there was a moment when he wanted to tell her the whole truth. It had felt unfair not to share something after she revealed the seed of her pain. It was like closing himself off to Astrid, only worse. He only wished there was something he could have given her in return, some reflection of the clarity he had found in Unschlicht's room in Cambridge years ago.

Unschlicht's suitcase had contained a machine, which Peter later learned was a predecessor of the Fialka: a typewriter keyboard with both Cyrillic and English alphabets, wired rotors and a long roll of typewriter paper.

Unschlicht flipped a switch and the machine hummed to life. Peter brushed the keys and then snatched his hand back. The metal was so cold it almost hurt to touch it.

'Go on,' Unschlicht said. 'Ask him anything.'

'What is it supposed to do?'

The philosopher made a face. 'Not it. Him. No doubt, with their usual imprecision, Doctor Morcom and his friend Turing would call him an oracle. A more accurate term is *das Dasein* – how do you say? – Ah yes, the Presence.'

Back then, Peter had no idea about the existence of the

Soviet overmind; Lenin's death and transformation had not been made public. For all the world knew, the great revolutionary was still alive, leading the Red Empire with inhuman efficiency.

'What should I ask?'

Unschlicht threw his hands up in frustration. 'Mr Bloom, it is utterly impossible for me to comprehend your interiority or, indeed, understand it even if I could access it. I can only state what I would ask, in identical circumstances: things which I would consider intractable to conventional reasoning. For example, is there a rhino in this room, right now? That is not something I can definitely, with human reasoning, refute.'

Peter stared at him. It would be very like Unschlicht to organise some kind of bizarre philosophical experiment, a teletype machine and a graduate student who provided answers.

Very well. He was going to put the experimenters to the test.

THE GREEK SAYS ALL GREEKS ARE LIARS, he typed. TRUE OR FALSE?

The keys were stiff and their chill stung his fingers. The machine made a moaning, otherworldly sound. Then it chattered and an answer appeared on the roll of paper.

BOTH, it said.

Definitely a graduate student, thought Peter. Well, at least Unschlicht had managed to provide a diversion from his despair. Peter owed it to him to play along.

PROVE IT, he typed.

With lightning speed, the paper started filling with symbols of predicate calculus. Peter watched, perplexed, as in an impossibly concise yet perfectly lucid fashion, the Presence proved the most beautiful theorem he had ever seen.

It stated that self-referential paradoxes like the Liar were inevitable in mathematics. If you started with self-consistent assumptions, you were bound to find them eventually, no matter how rigorous your thinking. But there was a way out. Every paradox hid a leap of faith within. You had to *assume* that the Liar was either true or false and take it as a new axiom – thus creating a new system of thinking which, in turn, had its own Liars. And so on and so on, a tree of branching paradoxes, for ever.

The Liar did not imply that mathematics was broken. It implied that mathematics was infinite.

And that was something true, not just in the world of the living or Summerland, but in all possible worlds.

Peter stared at the final line, transfixed. QUOD ERAT DEMONSTRANDUM, it said.

'That's impossible,' he said.

'Mr Bloom, I am not even going to dignify that statement with a remark.'

In *The Science of Death*, Mr West had speculated about the creation of artificial electric networks complex enough to bind *luz* stones as they fell from the Unseen, machines with souls. Was this one of them? If so, it was infinitely more advanced than the theoretical designs discussed in Dr Morcom's lectures.

Later, he would learn how far away from the truth his notion was.

'Tell me what this is,' Peter said. 'I will do anything. Please.'

Unschlicht looked at him, head in his curious bird-of-prey tilt.

'Why, Mr Bloom, he is the Presence. The only way to know him is to become him. Now, am I to understand that this is the extent of your curiosity? How very disappointing.'

Peter stared at the keyboard. It felt like the machine filled the entire world. Its humming song vibrated in his teeth and bones.

His second question felt small and meaningless, childish even. It was not the kind of question you would expect a soulful machine to be able to answer, no matter how intelligent. But Peter was exhausted to the point of delirium, adrift in a waking dream, and in dream logic it all made sense.

He put his hands on the keyboard and typed, WHERE IS MY FATHER?

When Peter asked for the bill, Otto and Nora got up and walked away, arm in arm.

Peter followed them carefully, keeping just within line of sight. They walked at a leisurely pace along the loud, busy street, crowded in spite of the chill and icy light rain. He ignored the sounds of electric buses and the colourful adverts for Dr Patterson's Pills, focusing instead on faces, coats and umbrellas that might have been following Otto and Nora.

After a while, they switched places, with Peter in the lead. He used Proops Brothers, a store that sold aether-mechanical and radio parts, as a choke point. Finally, Otto indicated satisfaction by sitting down on an empty bench under dead trees in Whitfield Gardens, a small public space surrounded by Victorian houses that provided some shelter from the cold wind. Nora took her place next to him and laid a hand lightly on his shoulder.

Peter joined them on the edge of the bench and rubbed his hands together. Rediscovering the sensations of the living had its pleasures, but in all honesty, he had not missed the London winter all that much.

'I need to come in,' he said.

'Already?' Nora said. She wore a thick fur coat that made her look even bigger and rounder than last time.

'I'm sure FELIX has his reasons,' Otto said.

Peter said nothing for a moment. Suddenly, the idea of joining the Presence did not feel as joyful as it once had. Maybe the oversoul itself was pure, but clearly operatives like Dzhugashvili could misinterpret its instructions. Was that why George had defected, in the end?

He wondered what would happen if he went back to Rachel White and confessed everything. He instantly recoiled from the thought. Being a triple agent was as close to Hell as Peter could imagine, and the system of Tickets and Summerland was something he had rejected long ago. Unschlicht would have admonished him for muddy thinking.

'There is an investigation in the Summer Court now,' Peter said finally. 'I have not dared to send regular reports since I found out. George told them that a mole exists, although apparently no more than that. And now the Dzhugashvili thing has everyone on their toes. Once C is less distracted by the war, he is going to turn over every *luz* stone in the Court. It will be dangerous to remain much longer.'

'Shpiegelglass will be disappointed,' Nora said.

'Have you heard from him? I cannot figure out who warned Dzhugashvili.'

'Our comrade is pursuing that question right now very ... zealously,' Otto said. 'He thinks there were Stalinists amongst the Communist Party in Madrid, although the Termin Procedure has failed to uncover them so far.'

Nora looked at Peter sharply. 'We all saw the Presence instruct you to keep your cover, Comrade. Are you telling me that you are questioning those instructions because things are getting uncomfortable? Or is the increased risk merely an excuse for your recent lack of results, like your failure to assume leadership of the Dzhugashvili operation?'

'No, of course not! I was ... distracted. Something else turned up.'

'I am sure Comrade Shpiegelglass would be *delighted* to hear about this distraction,' Nora said. She removed her mittens and flexed her strong fingers. Her palms were covered with callouses and there were black cracks in her fingernails.

This was not how it was supposed to go, Peter thought. This was not what George would have said if he was in danger. Then again, George was dead and Faded, and had betrayed both Peter and the Presence. Perhaps Nora's brutal honesty was better.

'There is a file,' Peter said. 'I saw it in the prime minister's mind. It is somehow connected to all his thinking about Spain and the war.'

'What is the subject of this file?' Otto asked.

'A scientific project in the twenties, investigating some little-known aspect of Summerland. I have a Winter Court asset trying to obtain a copy of it.'

Nora rolled her eyes. 'It sounds as valuable to the cause as the prime minister's used lavatory paper.'

'Please excuse my wife,' Otto said. 'However, you must consider the fact that extraction operations can fail and put us all at risk. Before taking that risk, I would strongly recommend obtaining ... more actionable intelligence. I am sure Comrade Shpiegelglass would appreciate it.'

'You don't understand,' Peter said. His hands were nearly numb and he stuffed them in his pockets. 'West is obsessed with it. It dominates his soul-spark, if you only could have seen it—'

'Obsession is not necessarily the same as importance,' Otto said. 'I believe the gentleman in question is also obsessed with little boys' war games.'

Peter blinked. Was it possible that he had misinterpreted what he had seen? Was CAMLANN some dead-end pet project, a senile old man's hobby horse? His own thinking on West could well be clouded, because of the Presence's answer to his second question, long ago.

He leaned back, thinking hard. The rain had stopped and he could see a clear patch of the evening sky, with a smattering of stars bright enough to outshine London's lights that spilled upwards. Peter had not seen stars for a long time, and suddenly they reminded him of a passage from *The Science of Death*.

There is no reason why life could not have evolved on other planets besides Earth. The soul-seeds fall upon the whole three-plane of our aether, as far as we know. Intelligence could have evolved anywhere, in our own solar system, and beyond.

So where are they? Where are the Martian ghosts? Some of the planets in our own system are much older than our world. There are stars much older than our sun. Summerland should teem with the spirits of otherworldly intellects. Yet it is occupied only by a narrow slice of humanity ...

The possibility that occurred to him then was colder than

the wind, sharp and terrible like Nora's chisel. In an instant, it pierced all his doubt.

'I think I know what project CAMLANN was about,' he said quietly. 'If I am right, it is infinitely more important than Spain or my cover.'

'Do enlighten us, FELIX,' Nora said.

Peter told them. At first, they were sceptical, but when he laid out the argument, even Nora's eyes widened – with fear or elation, he could not tell.

'I concur,' Otto said finally. 'If you can obtain proof for this hypothesis, Comrade Shpiegelglass would undoubtedly recommend applying the Termin Procedure to ensure the Presence has full access to it. When do you think you will be ready?'

'Less than a week. Three days, perhaps.'

'Very well. We will set up an extraction protocol. Nora will prepare a new set of emergency Hinton codes. They will take you to a temporary charter-body so we can transport you to a safe location for the Procedure.'

Peter frowned. He had imagined that once his task was done, the Presence would simply whisk him away, as if by magic. Then he realised he was being childish. It was not possible to thought-travel to the Presence – it was impossible to visualise His vastness. The Presence had to come to you, and the feedback loop at the heart of the Termin Procedure required a human body to anchor it.

Nora took Peter's hand. Her rough hands were warm.

'I was wrong about you, Comrade FELIX. I don't think you are a coward. I think you are completely mad. But it is a glorious kind of madness. Bring us CAMLANN. We'll be waiting.'

Otto and Nora left, arm in arm, and were carried away by the river of people on the street. Peter was cold but sat alone for a while, hands in his pockets, watching the stars and listening to the ticking of Pendlebury's spirit crown.

SEVENTEEN

Quo Vadis,
30th November 1938

After leaving the Blue Dog, Rachel found a telephone box, reached Joe at his club, booked them a table for a late dinner at Quo Vadis on Dean Street, and went home to change before heading to the restaurant.

She decided on just a trace of make-up and a blue dress she knew Joe liked. The restaurant itself was part of the plan: a public place would make it harder for him to run away when they got to the difficult topics. Besides, the pastel-coloured mosaic windows were glorious, a grid of green, salmon and orange.

She sat at the table alone and waited, a little cold, rubbing her bare arms.

'Madam? Would you like an *aperitivo* while you wait?' The maître d' – a small, neat Italian man – had appeared from somewhere.

'Hm? No, no thank you. Not right now. Maybe later.'

Truthfully, she was desperate for a drink, but her empty stomach was so tense she felt like she had swallowed an ice cube. Instead she waited, played with the edge of the flawless white tablecloth and thought about what she was going to say.

The problem was that Joe never talked about the war.

It was always there, from the first time they met: a secret whose presence she could sense with an interrogator's instinct. Against her nature, she left it alone. They shared understanding of the things that did not need to be said. It was enough to exchange a smile or a glance that said *look how ridiculous this world is.*

She even knew when he was going to propose, possibly before he did himself. It was a low-key thing. They were walking along a windswept Atlantic beach in France and huddled behind a rocky outcropping when he produced a ring from his pocket, cradled it in his palm like a child who had found a pretty rock in the sand.

'I have been thinking we should make this more permanent,' he said. 'What do you think?'

She said yes, and he hollered, threw her down onto the sand with a rugby tackle that made her whoop as well. The sand got everywhere.

The wedding was small. Rachel wanted to hire a medium for her mother to attend but Joe refused, and that was their first fight.

'Maybe an Edison doll if you insist,' he said flatly. 'But no mediums.' Eventually, she gave in. Her mother claimed she did not mind, but thereafter she pointedly ignored Joe whenever he tried to say hullo during Rachel's weekly ectophone calls.

They gradually got to know each other over the next three years. A trickle of small things they shared, usually after they made love or during long walks around the Serpentine. Rachel told him about the early years in India, and always feeling cold when she came to England. How she tried to fit in at the Court. Joe talked about playing rugby for England. How he got into flying, during an off-season when he was looking for a rush and found that he loved looking at the world from above.

But he never, ever said anything about the war. And when she lost the baby, there were suddenly two things they could not talk about, two large stones that filled the empty space in every conversation.

Maybe in the past few weeks, she had made things worse by adding a third.

Joe arrived a few minutes late. He was in full dress uniform, khaki and medals, clean-shaven, hair freshly cut. He looked better than he had for months, and if not for the grey in his hair, he could have stepped out of the day they first met.

He gave Rachel a curt nod and sat down.

'Was there a reunion at the club?' she asked. 'It's that – well, you look jolly dashing.'

Joe's face was set. 'No. I will tell you later. Let's get a drink.'

Cava materialised, and they drank it in silence. It tickled Rachel's belly. Then she reached across the table and took Joe's hand. He leaned back in his chair, but Rachel did not let go. She had to do it now, before she lost her resolve, before they fell back into their old pattern again like two gramophone needles in their own grooves.

'Joe, I know things have not been right. We both know why, I think. And at home, with my work, with you not

feeling well, we get stuck in a pattern, two gramophone needles going around in our own grooves. I thought we could ...
we could come out, somewhere different, somewhere nice,
and, well, talk about it.'

'Rachel, I ... Oh, hell. Is talking really going to solve
anything? What happened was my fault. Both with the baby,
and ... that night, when you brought the finches. Just let me
live with it, will you?'

'Joe, you can't just take the blame like that. The baby,
it was ... it was all normal, until it wasn't. Maybe if I had
been more careful, it wouldn't have—' Her voice caught. She
closed her eyes. 'Silly me. I brought us here so I would not
cry.'

Joe patted her hand. 'It's all right, now. It's all right.'

She kept her eyes shut for a while and heard Joe giving the
waiter their orders. Later, she had no idea what they were.
When he spoke again, his voice was gentle.

'I don't know what happened, not with you, and not with
me, the other night. I'm not a doctor. But I am pretty sure it
had more to do with me than you, both times.'

'That is not true. Maybe ... if you said something about it.
What happened. What they did to you. It would help me.
Help us.'

Joe said nothing for a while.

'We've been through this before. It would be unfair to the
lads, Rachel,' he said finally.

'I'm not one of them. But I comprehend duty, you know I
do. Maybe I could understand.'

'I really hope you do, Rachel.' He sighed. 'I really hope
you do. There is something I was going to tell you tonight
anyway. I re-enlisted. It sounds like there is going to be a

pretty good scrap in Spain. A lot of the lads at the club were raring to go, and so I thought, why not? And to be honest, I think it is best for both of us if I stay away from you for a while.'

Rachel covered her mouth with a hand. She felt the vertigo from the Tower again, a black abyss opening before her, except this time she was already falling.

'Joe. Please don't,' she whispered. 'It's not safe. There is—'

There is a traitor helping the Soviets. She bit her lip. She wanted to come clean about Bloom, about Max, about their operation. But there was no telling what he would do, what he would think. In many ways, they did live in different countries, with different languages, with glass walls between them.

In the end, the lifelong habit of not sharing secrets won.

'There is what?' he asked after she remained silent for several breaths.

'I just know it won't go well. From something I heard at work.'

'There are always rumours, Rachel. In any case, I can hardly withdraw now. Would make me look like a bounder. Bad for the old morale.'

'It's something else, it's—'

'Hush,' Joe said. 'Coming here was a good idea. But I think it is better if we don't try to say too much. I am not stupid, Rachel. I know there is something going on with you. I am not about to judge. I ... when things were really bad, I visited some places, in the East End, where you can ... well. Aetheric love, they call it. I thought it would make the nightmares go away. It didn't help, though. I am more sorry than I can say, Rachel.'

The jealousy fluttered in its cage in her breast, and she looked away. So it had been that, as she'd suspected: ectoplasm fantasies, nothing real. It still made her skin crawl.

'I'm sure it didn't,' she said quietly. 'I don't want to know about that.'

'And I don't need to know about your ... work. Or whatever it is.'

Maybe he would understand, Rachel thought. She pushed against the glass wall as hard as she could.

'It is not what you think it is, Joe. It really isn't. Let me explain what has been happening—'

Joe held up a hand. 'It makes no difference to me, really. I am going anyway.'

'Why?'

'Because I want to.'

'Joe, I need to understand why. Aetheric love I think I can just about live with, given time. But going away to a war, away from me – that is different. I deserve an explanation. And I might understand more than you think. I was a nurse for a while, remember? I saw injured people. But I've never understood what could have hurt you so badly you must keep it from me.'

Joe said nothing. He turned his cap in his hands and put it down. He ordered more wine and emptied his glass. Their first course arrived. Joe stared at the scallops on his plate and cautiously ate one, then put his fork down.

'All right, Rachel. All right, then.'

It took Joe a while to get to it. He talked slowly at first, about joining up, being shipped to France. Rachel held her breath as emotions from old memories played across his face like images from a magic lantern. She said nothing, only made small noises to egg him on, practically held her breath so as not to stem the flood of words.

'It felt ridiculous at first,' Joe said, 'wearing those contraptions. I did better than some of the lads: I was fit enough to carry it and walk. They did not work very well. One boy from Kent got electrocuted. I saw some films of the early experiments. One showed some poor bastard with ectoplasm pouring out of him but no control, flailing around, smashing the lab until they shot him in the head.

'We all got Tickets, of course – all soldiers did – but it was early days, we were still afraid. The officers would try to get the boys to charge across minefields, but it just led to more fear. The ectophones were poor, things did not work so smoothly in Summerland back then, and in any case we had all kinds of ideas about the place because we did not know any better. So there the soldiers all sat, in the trenches, in a stalemate.

'And that was where we came in, the ectotroops, tanks and flyers. I was always sensitive, even as a child, but only a little bit. Sometimes I would have this funny sensation, like a tickle in the back of my head, and see people who were not there, and crazy lights. But that was it.

'The first time they switched the armour on—' He shook his head. 'You feel this fist squeezing your head and everything goes cold, a bit like those ice-cream headaches you get as a child, but all over your brain. Then ... it comes. A door opens. You are ... throwing up, but the stuff that spews out becomes a part of you, makes you bigger, taller. You feel like you can do anything. Some of the lads grew giant legs and the tendrils – well, you have seen them. Some were more like giant beasts made of ectoplasm, or spiders scuttering through the trenches.

'As for me, I liked to make wings so I could fly. That was the only good part. If I had known what happened to our victims, the sources, I don't think I would have done it. But they only told us that the Huns we killed would die and go to Summerland, as per usual. It wasn't until our first proper scrap that we found out for ourselves how it really worked. And once we had a taste of it, it was too late to stop.'

Joe refilled his glass, drained it and took a deep breath. Rachel stared at him. She had seen the newsreels, of course, and had a vague notion of how ectoplasmic weapons worked, but had simply assumed they were powered by the energy released when a soul left a dying body. Horrific, but no more so than poison gas or artillery. Only it sounded like that was not the whole story.

Finally, Joe continued.

'Those poor Hun kids. They died twice, first on the battle-field and then we fed on their souls until only the soul-stones were left.' He lowered his voice. 'Sometimes they even got us going with some of our own boys. Deserters, usually. That was the worst part.'

Rachel had heard rumours that 'primers' had been required for ectotanks before battle, soldiers sacrificed to power the weapons, but it was a different thing to hear it from Joe. And if they completely annihilated enemy souls – that went completely against the Dimensionists' claims of humane warfare. She felt incandescent anger, suddenly. It would cause a scandal if it ever got out. Maybe it needed to get out.

'That is one reason you never talked about it, isn't it?' she whispered. 'You were told to keep quiet.'

Joe looked ashamed. 'We all agreed that you could never understand it if you weren't there. It was the only way out of that hell of mud and guts and worse – what else were we supposed to do?'

'I am not judging you, Joe. Thank you for telling me. Please go on.'

'The other reason I never talk about the war is I don't remember that much. You get lost in the flood when the souls come. There is this rush, like the best rugby match I ever played times ten, running forward, getting in a scrum, wrestling away the ball. And the noise, the gunshots, this howl that fills you. Here, back home, it is always too quiet. And I feel so weak. This is probably what it's like to be a ghost. Everything just passes through you.'

'You never seemed like a ghost to me,' Rachel said. 'Stay here. You don't have to go back to all that.'

'Rachel, I do. Not for our boys, not for duty. But because I miss it. Because it's too hard without it.'

Rachel stared at him. His eyes were red. He took a hand-kerchief from his pocket and blew his nose.

'There you have it,' he said.

She tried to feel sorry for him, tried to understand this had been done to him, he could not help it. But he was still choosing war over her.

The main course, braised veal, sat untouched between them, getting cold. The smell made Rachel nauseous.

She had thought herself so clever, so very modern, persuading him to open up, to talk about his emotions. Just because a traitor had tricked her into feeling better about herself. She had been a fool.

She stood up and flung her napkin to the floor.

'No, I *won't* have it,' she shouted. 'I will not have it. It's not fair.'

A soft muttering spread across the tables as the other diners turned to look at her.

'Rachel, please, sit down,' Joe said in hushed tones.

She could barely look at him. But she could not bear to storm out, with everyone looking. Avoiding that had been the whole point.

She took a deep breath and sat back down.

'This is what I was afraid of, Rachel,' Joe said. 'It's why I didn't want to tell you.'

'When are you leaving?'

'Wednesday next week. I can stay at the club until then.'

I don't want you to, Rachel wanted to say, but the words did not come out. She picked at the edge of the tablecloth again.

'It's no trouble, really,' Joe said. He was putting up a brave front now. 'I'll come by and say goodbye before I go.'

Joe spoke to the maître d' quietly, apologising for the disturbance, slipped him a note, paid the bill and left. Rachel sat alone, surrounded by untouched food. In spite of the candlelight and conversation inside, the mosaic window looked dull and dark.

A drowsy, half-dressed Susi let Rachel into Max Chevalier's flat half an hour later. Most of the animals were asleep and Rachel waited in the freezing conservatory while the girl sent an ectomail to Max, who was somewhere in the Summer City.

Finally, Susi wheeled in the Edison doll.

'I met with Bloom today,' Rachel said, without preamble. 'The situation has changed. Tell me: if we give Bloom something, chickenfeed, whatever, how confident are you that we can track him to a meeting with his handler?'

'In all honesty, it is difficult to say,' Max replied. 'He could be using dead drops. We will watch him, of course, but it will be hard to get evidence unless we actually catch him with a handler. It will have to be something big, something urgent, something that requires an in-person meeting. But you really should calm down, Mrs White. Has something happened?'

Rachel took a deep breath. She had not stopped to think and did not want to stop now. What mattered was preventing Bloom from doing anything that would prolong the situation in Spain.

She had never thought it possible to be jealous of war.

'It's Spain. We can't wait any longer. The stakes are too high. Bloom asked me for a file from the Registry. What I want is a plan to collar him if he gets it.'

'Mrs White, this is most unwise. You want him to trust you. If we act too quickly, all our work will be for nothing. You don't want to short-circuit the process, believe me.'

'Bloom is under pressure. You said it yourself. He is desperate for this file, I know it.'

'Are you sure there isn't something else affecting your judgment? I hate to suggest this and contradict myself, but if there *is* a Summer Court investigation going on, should we not consider working with them?'

Rachel shook her head. 'As soon as there is even a hint

that the target might be Bloom, the investigation will be shut down from above, just like what happened to me. No, we have to get evidence. Besides, I told you – I don't trust Roger.'

The Edison doll's eyes were unreadable.

'Very well, Mrs White. There is a stage where the agent's instincts must take over. I will get my teams ready to hunt.' He made a small trilling sound. 'One more thing, though. You must be ready to shield your emotions better this time. You will be hiding something, and it will be very obvious to him. Think thoughts that you feel guilty about. Do something naughty beforehand if your conscience is clean.'

There was a click and the voice was gone, but the room's dim electric light twinkled in the doll's nyctoscope eyes, like the ghost of amusement.

EIGHTEEN

Chickenfeed,
1st December 1938

The Old Registry of the SIS was in St Albans, a quiet town known for its Roman ruins twenty miles north of London. That was where Rachel had started her Service career during the war, putting on a simple uniform and joining the ranks of female clerks and analysts who tried to make sense of radio intercepts and aetheric maps compiled by spirit scouts.

They had worked long days and nights, slept at first in temporary lodgings the locals provided, and then in hastily erected barracks. In the rare moments when the relentless pace of typing, translation and filing slackened briefly, they all trailed to the King Harry, a squat Victorian pub with low-hanging beams that they usually filled to the brim.

Rachel found herself there again now, on a Thursday night. This time, the crowd was farmers and local workmen in felt caps and muddy boots, but the smell of spilled beer and burned wood was the same. While waiting at the bar for the pink gin she had ordered, she could almost close her eyes, smell the hoppy air and feel seventeen again, remember

Marjorie and Elizabeth and Wendy and John and Dilly waiting for her at the battered corner table, all ready to fight the Hun with their razor wit and the joyous idiocy that belongs to the young.

But when the gin arrived and she turned around carrying the small tray it was served on, only old Colonel Bill Woodfield sat there, waving at her unsteadily, his face already beetroot-red; and her mission was to steal one of the colonel's jealously guarded files for a Soviet spy.

'It is good to see you, Rachel,' Woodfield said, after they had toasted and Rachel had told the barman to keep the gin coming. 'Glad you thought to swing by while visiting Felix Cowgill's boys.'

The Winter Court's Iberian Section was also located in St Albans, although it was now considered to be something of a retirement home for rotten apples. As such, it had made perfect sense for Rachel to drop in for lunch and entertain the notion of working for the Section's chief Cowgill, formerly in charge of Section V. He also belonged to Harker's informal club of ex-colonial officers.

'Well, Colonel, I am very glad you still remember me.'

'How could I forget? You had such bright eyes. Still do. I knew you would go far.'

Rachel sighed. 'I am not entirely sure you were on the money, Colonel.' She briefly related what she considered the official version of her story – a policy disagreement with Harker and an unfair demotion.

'That is rotten luck, that is,' Woodfield said. 'But your star will rise yet, mark my words. You are not going end up an old drunk like me, only good for arranging old paperwork. Sure, every now and then, someone comes here from the city and I help them find things, and sometimes those things are even important. I am starting to look forward to pass over and have done my best to speed things up, but the old liver just keeps ticking.' He poked his generous paunch.

'Would you mind if we popped in to see the old place, after a few more?' Rachel asked. 'When things are uncertain, well, it is sometimes nice to come back to where things started.'

If Woodfield's old habits had not changed, a few more gins would take him to near-unconsciousness, and Rachel would be able to go through the old files while he slept blissfully in his office. As plans went, it was not the most sophisticated, but for some time now, the most stringent security measures had been reserved for the Summer Court.

Woodfield looked at her sharply. 'You are after something now, Rachel, aren't you? I played the fool around you girls, you know, just for fun, but that does not mean I am one, and you are all grown up. What's this about, then?'

Rachel sighed. She felt ashamed for trying to get the old man in trouble. Yet her mind was automatically compiling strategies. She could blackmail him: there had been rumours about Woodfield and the girls, back in the day. She could threaten to get him fired by claiming that he felt her up while they were having a drink for old times' sake. But looking at the clear blue eyes in the dark, gnarled face, the words stuck in her throat.

She sipped her gin and put it down.

'You are absolutely right, Colonel,' she said in a low voice. 'I am looking for an old file that I don't have the classification to access. A joint Army and Military Intelligence file, from ten years or so ago.'

'Well, why didn't you say so in the first place? What do you need it for?'

Rachel hesitated. 'It's better if you don't know the details. It has to do with Spain. But I don't want to get you in trouble – I will sign the book and everything.'

Woodfield chuckled. 'Rachel, you can see what I've become. Do I look like I care?' He leaned forward and the golden fillings in his teeth glinted in the light from the pub's fireplace. 'I have three brothers in the afterlife, good lads, all went in the war. I never had much of a chance to be brave myself. But you have the look of a person doing something that scares her and is doing it anyway. So if I can help you by digging up some old file, that means more to me than whether you have clearance. Is that understood?'

He smelled of an old man's sweat and minty toothpaste, but at that moment Rachel could have kissed him.

'Yes, sir,' she said, and ordered another round of gin.

Rachel accompanied Colonel Woodfield to the old, shuttered manor house that now archived the papers of every SIS agent, countless files on Service-funded research programmes and cross-referenced research materials going back to the Service's founding in 1908. She expected to see rooms overflowing with stacked paperwork, but instead, the place was spotless: rows upon rows of neatly organised filing cabinets.

'I may be a sloppy drunk,' the colonel said, 'but I take being a librarian very seriously.'

Still, it took them half an hour to locate the CAMLANN file, a thick brown folder tied shut with a cord. Rachel opened it and glanced at the contents. Apart from the summary and budget pages, the rest was in cipher – neat groups of meaningless letters, pages and pages of it. At the end, there were a few photographs. She was not quite sure what they were, maybe copies of nyctoscope images, but they looked like X-rays, with indistinct black and white shapes.

'Thank you,' she told Woodfield.

Woodfield smiled. 'I hope it is of some use to you, my dear. I look forward to seeing you at the King Harry again when you bring it back.'

It was long past midnight when Rachel made it home to St John's Wood. The house was cold and dark.

She had a sleepless night ahead with the CAMLANN file: she would do her utmost to find out if it qualified as chickenfeed, and if possible, censor it before surrendering it to Bloom.

She holed up in her study, wrapped in a blanket with a cup of steaming tea, and fought both the fatigue and the drowsy numbness of the pink gin. The finches were asleep in their cage, curled up into tight feathery balls right next to each other. Rachel felt jealous, thinking of Joe and cold winter nights, lying cocooned under the sheets with a hot water bottle radiating at her feet and Joe's warm, solid curve against her chest and belly.

He would ship out to Spain in a few days. During the Great War, she was too young to really fear for her friends who were sent to the front, and they tended to view it as a jolly adventure when they headed overseas. Now, death itself held far fewer terrors than back then – but she was more concerned about the danger to Joe's soul. It would almost be better if he met an early end at the hands of the Republicans rather than be consumed by the thing that the RAF had turned him into.

But there was still a way for her to help him by catching Bloom. Maybe she could request a transfer to the Iberian Section, if things worked out.

She shook her head and tried to concentrate, spread the pages out on the floor and knelt amongst them, trying to look for patterns. The ciphertext was obviously gibberish without the key – although Bloom might be able to crack it, having spent time at the Government Aetheric Codes and Ciphers School earlier in his career. There were schematics for some kind of deep-*kata* nyctoscope, an aetheric observatory built in the Summer City. Presumably it had been used to take the X-ray like images, although what they showed she had no idea. There were black branching lines against grey, and countless tiny white patches that could have been *luz* stones.

On the whole, it felt much more like a science project than anything to do with Spain. Still, it was difficult to judge whether she was about to give away something related to a haphazard, defunct programme or expose a key operation.

She was lost in thought when the room grew even chillier than before and the old ectophone in the corner rang – three metallic tinkles of a bell in rapid succession.

'Hullo, hullo! Is Rachel there?' said a cheery female voice.

'Yes, Mother,' Rachel said. 'It's me.'

Rachel's mother, Henrietta Forbes-Smith, had been dead for a decade.

She had exercised her euthanasia right early when the

lumps first appeared in her breast and had passed away in the place she loved the most, even more than India – the garden of their house in Ealing, sitting in a folding chair in warm May sunlight, the morphine drip in her arm. She had one last look at the Hinton Cube diagram of the Ticket in her lap, and then held on tight to Rachel and Rachel's father, one with each hand. She leaned back, let out a satisfied sigh and was gone so quickly Rachel had to touch her smiling face to realise that her mother was dead.

Whenever Rachel felt as if she had forgotten her mother's face and smell, she thought about the hand in her own: small, like hers, red and dry, with tiny cuts and callouses everywhere, black dirt under the fingernails, a gardener's hand. It always brought back the rest.

They waited anxiously an hour until sundown, like they were supposed to, and then Rachel's father fumbled with the tuning dials and fussed over the hiss of static and the howling noises of the passing dead attracted by the aetheric device's operation.

And then there it was, her mother's voice in the speaker, low and warm.

'Hullo, hullo!' she said brightly. 'Did you know there are flowers here? Who could have imagined?'

Rachel sat down in the big armchair in front of the ecto-phone. It was an old-fashioned model the size of a wardrobe, and did not have a nyctoscope screen like some of the newer models Mr Baird's company made.

'How are you?' she asked distractedly, holding the heavy Bakelite handset between her chin and shoulder, trying to keep studying the CAMLANN papers in her lap.

'I am still dead,' her mother said, 'although it has been so long since you called that I could have been resurrected by the Second Coming in the meantime.'

'Mother, I have been busy.'

'I am sure you have.' Henrietta paused. 'You look sad. I can see your soul from here, you know, all tangled and spiky, like thorns.'

Rachel swore under her breath. Dealing with Bloom should have taught her how visible her mental state was to the spirits.

'Never mind that. It was a difficult day at work. What have you been doing?'

'I am well, Rachel, if a little bored. Your father is sending pictures from Cyprus. We were there once, you know, when you were young. I put his photographs in my thought-garden, to grow together with the memories.'

Sometimes, it was difficult to understand how things worked in Summerland. Unlike many other dead, Henrietta was retired, supported by Rachel's father and a small portion of her own income. It was a nightmare scenario that anti-Dimensionist economists often brought up in newspapers – that each subsequent living generation would have to carry a vast, growing pyramid of the dead on their backs. It was clearly nonsense: there were so many applications for aetheric technology that in many fields the dead were becoming more important than the living. The Service itself was a good example. Her mother was happy, that was the important thing, and she had an eternity to start working again. Now it was her time to rest.

'But you don't really care about me, Rachel, you just want

to hear my voice, since something is bothering you. I told you, I can see it.'

'I ... I was demoted. I am now working in the Finance Section.'

'What? It must be a mistake.'

'I am not allowed to talk about it. But it is not a mistake, at least not one they will admit.'

'Rachel, Rachel, I am so sorry. Surely it wasn't your fault?'

'I don't know, Mother. Perhaps it was.'

'Rachel, I always told you it was not a good idea to work for the government, no matter how much you liked your father's silly stories. You can never trust them.'

Rachel sighed. Endless arguments had ensued when she announced her intention to join the Service. Her mother was intensely distrustful of anything to do with politics or intelligence work.

'Never mind, Rachel, I know it is important to you. Can your father help?'

'No, Mother. This was at a different level.' As a young man, Rachel's father had served as a junior signals intelligence officer in Russia, attached to the Navy, before he moved to India. He was now retired and travelling the Continent. She knew he would get angry, write letters and make noise, but he simply could not reach people like Sir Stewart or C.

'Well, then.'

'Well what?'

'Then the question is, what are you going to do next.'

For a moment, Rachel wanted to be a child again and hear her mother tell her that everything was going to be all right. But Henrietta continued in a matter-of-fact voice.

'When you have a child, you try to make them feel safe,

like nothing bad will ever happen. But you are not a child any more, little Rachel. You must accept that nothing is for ever. In the meantime, flowers grow. And you will find some flowers, too, I know. Your Joe is a good man.'

Rachel's eyes burned. There was static on the line, sharp pops rather than the usual background noise.

'Mother,' she asked quickly. 'Tell me – are there other spirits with you?'

'It is always so crowded here, in the city.'

'Just look. Did you see any of them before, when you followed me?'

'There are some that move quickly, like manta rays of light. One passed by just now. What is it? Why are you scared?'

'I have to go. I am sorry. I love you. I will call again next week, I promise.'

Rachel switched the ectophone off. Its low hum took a while to die down.

With a cold certainty, she knew that the figure her mother had seen was a Watcher from the Summer Court. What was more, she was almost certain who had sent it.

She hoped that her mother was already on her way back to the Summer Homes and would not see what Rachel's anger truly looked like.

Roger Hollis lived in a small first-floor bachelor flat in Redcliffe Mews in Chelsea. Breath steaming in the cold, Rachel stared up at a dark window and wondered whether Roger was visiting one of his mistresses or vice versa. Then she thought she heard a faint coughing sound and grinned.

She rang the doorbell a few times, and when nothing

happened she resorted to banging the door with her fist. Lights went on in the neighbouring flats, and finally Roger opened the door, blinking. He looked dishevelled and was dressed only in a heavy nightgown.

'Rachel? What the hell are you doing here at this time?'

'Why, I am here to have a nice cup of tea with you, Roger. Are you not going to invite me in?'

She brushed past him, took the short flight of steps up to his flat in a few strides and switched on the lights. The furniture was old and grandiose against a background of green-striped Regency wallpaper, and a rather pompous bust of Nelson faced the main window. In the pale electric light, the place looked overcrowded and more than a little pathetic.

A young woman, a slim redhead of twenty or so, peeked out from Roger's bedroom with a sheet wrapped around her. She did not look like Roger's steady mistress, Kathleen.

'Darling? What is going on?'

Roger followed Rachel up the stairs, tightening the sash of his gown.

'Listen, Rachel, this is not on, you can't just barge in here—'

'Your Watchers violated my privacy by listening to a call with my mother, so I am violating yours. You there,' she said, giving the girl a sharp nod. 'Get out. Government business.'

'Viola, don't listen to her, she is crazy. I am going to get rid of her!'

Rachel folded her arms. 'Are you, Roger? I am only flesh and blood, after all. But I can tell you from experience that it is much harder to get ghost spies out of your house. They are worse than rats.'

She turned back to the redhead. 'Viola, is it? If you are

not on your way in two minutes, dear, you will find yourself under investigation by Special Branch for seducing a key government official – although it pains me to include Roger here in that category.' She flashed her SIS identity card at the girl.

Viola's eyes widened and she scrambled to gather up her clothes.

Roger whispered a hasty goodbye to Viola in the hallway, but the girl was in tears.

'There was no need to do that,' Roger said when she was gone.

Rachel studied the Nelson bust. It appeared to be a genuine antique.

'Oh, I think there was.'

'What do you want?'

'I want to know why you are having me Watched. I want to know which Court you *really* work for.' She sat down on the couch. 'And while you are at it, I would not mind some tea.'

'I have questions for you, too, Rachel.' Roger stifled a cough and folded his arms. 'What were you doing in St Albans yesterday evening? And what about all those meetings with Peter Bloom? The phone calls to Max Chevalier?'

A headache thundered in Rachel's skull. She should have been more careful.

'Would you believe that Max and I discuss the care and breeding of Gouldian finches?' she said.

'No, I'm afraid not.'

'He does know an awful lot about them. Tell me, Roger,

who do you work for in the Summer Court? Who gave you access to the Watchers?'

Roger studied her and narrowed his eyes. 'Symonds,' he said. 'I know you are running an off-the-books operation, Rachel. I want in.'

'Why should I let you?'

'Because otherwise I will go to Sir Stewart with what I have, and that will be the end of what remains of your career in the Service.'

'Symonds,' Rachel said. 'Well, that is just dandy.'

'What do you mean?'

'Bloom is the mole. Symonds is his best friend, and is probably trying to protect him. Or Symonds could be compromised as well. How do you know you are not actually working for the Soviets?'

'That's ridiculous.'

'How has getting evidence on Bloom been working out so far?'

'God, I need a drink,' Roger said. He opened a cupboard in his small kitchen and took out a bottle of single malt.

'Two fingers, please.'

Roger poured and handed her a glass. She swirled the amber liquid back and forth and took a sip. Flavours of honey and pecan blossomed in her mouth and made her head buzz. She would almost certainly have a hangover in the morning, drinking this on top of all that gin in St Albans. Maybe there was a correlation between her hangovers and Bloom, she thought.

'What do you have on Bloom?' Roger asked.

'So far, nothing. Everything he's done with me could be just like what Symonds has been doing with you – grooming an unofficial source inside the Winter Court. But earlier this week he asked me for some confidential files. Those could serve as a barium meal. I got the files from St Albans and went over them. I think we can safely use them: most of them are in cipher. If we are quick enough, he won't be able to crack them before we have him.'

'This is very dangerous, Rachel.'

'Of course it is. But if we catch Bloom in a meeting with his handlers, he's ours.'

Roger paced back and forth. 'I don't think I can bring the Summer Court Watchers into this. Do you have any assets on the Other Side?'

'That is what Mr Chevalier is for.'

Roger sat down across from Rachel. There was a glass table between them and their reflections ghosted on its surface. He looked tired and worn out. There were lines around his mouth, dark bags under his eyes. She was an indistinct, blurry shape on the shiny surface, her face a pale oval in the darkness of her coat.

'All right,' he said at last. 'We do it together. I run interference on the Summer Court side and help with the collar. The story is that we've been doing this together from the start and fully share the credit.'

'Deal,' Rachel said and emptied her glass. 'I hope you enjoy the Summer Court, Roger. Although from what I hear, pretty secretaries are harder to come by there. And certainly less substantial. If that is possible.'

Neither of them spoke for a while.

'Why are you so angry with me, Rachel?' Roger finally said.

This is not for England, Rachel thought. *It is for Joe.*

She got up and walked over to him. Delicately, she touched his face, ran her fingers down his unshaven jawline, past the dour corners of his mouth.

'Because you make me feel guilty,' she said and set her glass down on the table. 'And, believe it or not, right now that is exactly what I need.'

NINETEEN

A Mind at the End of its Tether,
5th December 1938

Peter Bloom spent the day following his meeting with Rachel in nervous anticipation.

He rode out the long hours at work on autopilot, working on the post-mortem of the Dzhugashvili operation and attending briefings given by Hill. The Summer Court was preparing for wartime footing as things were heating up, and Royal Aetheric Force officers in their geometric armour were a frequent sight in the corridors.

He ran into Noel and told him about his Blenheim visit, and how he had discreetly mentioned the Old Library route to a few eager undergraduates visiting from Cambridge. They shared a nice laugh over that.

He found it difficult to rest, and whenever he tried to settle into the meditative state that replaced sleep in Summerland, the aether in the room began to boil and twist, a miniature nightmare storm that only subsided when he went out and thought-travelled to the borders of the city and back, exhausting his *vim* and willpower until deep, dreamless oblivion claimed him.

The next morning, a messenger spirit left an ectomail from Rachel White on his desk, with an ectophone beacon code and a contact time. Two hours later, Peter visualised the four-dimensional combination of polygons and colours in his mind and thought-travelled to it right from his desk, sparing no *vim*. The aether blurred into thick liquid and carried him to the glowing shape of the ectophone circuit.

Rachel was alone. Her thought-forms were calm and smooth and blue, although the edges of her self were strangely blurred. He touched the ringtone wire in the circuit, like plucking the taut cord of a harp, and after a moment, Rachel's voice was there in the vibrations of the aether.

'Peter? My apologies if the line is bad. This is our old ectophone at home. The only advantage is that the tubes get so hot you can actually warm up next to it in the winter.'

There was an echo on the line. Her tone was light. Peter was surprised by how much he had been looking forward to hearing her voice, and he told her so.

'Why, Mr Bloom, that is very nice of you to say. I am going to be strictly professional, however, and tell you that both the physical and an aetherised version of your item of interest are in a Cresswell dual-deposit locker, the number of which I will read to you now.'

She recited a long Hinton code. Peter aether-shaped it into being as she spoke and pocketed the shimmering construct.

'Thank you, Rachel. I really appreciate this.'

'You can show your appreciation by giving me more to

do. The last two days were the first in weeks when I was not bored to death.'

The cheer in her voice and the bright yellow thought-forms hid something, he could see that. Was he making a terrible mistake, trusting her? He remembered how she had touched his hand at the Blue Dog, how her voice had broken. When wearing a medium, it was easy to be fooled: everything was distant, as if every perception was filtered through thick cloth, compared to the raw sensorium of the aether.

'Rachel? Is everything all right?' he asked.

'Oh, everything is fine. I may be a little drunk.'

'Isn't it a bit early for that?'

'I took the day off sick. I had a very late night and I may have made a terrible mistake. So starting early felt like a good idea.'

Her thought-forms flared into ragged petals of deep purple and violet, into guilt and jealousy.

'I'm sorry, I should not have said anything. It is nothing you need to worry about.'

'We all make mistakes.'

'I never used to. At least, I did not think so.'

'Is there something I can do? Just let me know if I can help.'

'Not unless you can reverse Parliament's decision to send troops to Spain. My husband is shipping out on Wednesday. We had an argument. And I may just have made things much worse. Oh, Peter, I am such a fool ...' Her voice trailed away for a moment. 'I just needed to feel something. In a way that meant nothing.'

'If it meant nothing,' Peter said slowly, 'then maybe there is no need for your husband to know about it.'

'We keep enough secrets in our work, Peter. I never wanted to keep secrets from the people I love.'

'Sometimes carrying secrets makes you stronger. And I know you are very strong.'

'I think that is just what we tell ourselves. But thank you, Peter. It helps that you care.'

'We'll go for a drink, sometime soon.'

'Perhaps a walk instead,' Rachel said. 'My head hurts already, and I don't want to end up on that side too soon.'

'All right. I need to go. Take care of yourself, Mrs White.'

'I will. Have a good day, Mr Bloom.'

The circuit blinked out of existence. He watched Rachel's thoughts for a while. They were still a turmoil of purple and red, with a glimmer of white within. The soul-readers said white was the colour of hope.

Not unless you can reverse Parliament's decision. He tried to dismiss the thought; what he needed was distance, objectivity.

He kept watching Rachel's tiny thought-star as he dived back down into the Second Aether, towards the Summer City, until her soul was just one amongst thousands. Finally, it merged into the vast constellation of living London and disappeared into the aetheric firmament.

Peter sighed, visualised the Ticket for Albert Park and went back to work.

That evening, Peter picked up the file and took it home to study it. Rachel had given him an aetherised version, a set of aether images stuck to a *luz* core, produced with a Zöllner camera that changed photographs into aetheric orientations of magnetic particles that could be extracted and transported into Summerland. The file was thick; she must have spent hours aetherising the pages.

The deep *kata* images in the appendix leaped out at him. He could not interpret them, but they made him feel like he was on the right track.

Then he turned his attention to the ciphertext. His first assignment had been at GACCS and he was reasonably familiar with most of the standard codes used by both Courts. He quickly determined that this one was likely to be based on a one-time pad.

It was conceivable that the Presence would be able to decipher the file, given time – but even for a composite of millions of souls, the raw calculations needed could take years. No, it was essential he obtain the key as well as the encrypted documents. He wrestled with the problem for hours, littering his rooms with half-formed ideas shaped from aether. In the end, he threw the file into the air in frustration. As the pages fluttered around, he realised that he had simply been avoiding the inevitable, the obvious.

Surely the individuals who commissioned the project would have the means to read it.

And one of them was Herbert Blanco West.

Prime Minister West's desk was covered with toy soldiers. They were impressively detailed: carefully painted tiny men in olive-drab uniforms, spiky helmets, even a spidery ecto-tank. They were littered across a huge sheet of paper with graph lines and terrain markers. He was bent double, leaning his round head sideways on his hands, level with the surface, carefully studying the angles.

At first, he didn't appear to notice Peter, but then he looked up.

'Come in,' he said. 'Please, sit down. My apologies, I just want to make a note of something.'

He scribbled a few words and figures on a sheet of paper with a fountain pen, leaned back in his chair and studied Peter, folding his hands in his lap.

Peter sat down. It was early Monday afternoon. With the war looming, it had been surprisingly easy to get the appointment set up. That morning, he had approached C and told him he wanted to make one more attempt to get the PM to favour the Summer Court after the Dzhugashvili blunder. Then he had woken up Pendlebury and spent the better part of a month's salary in Savile Row on Pendlebury's clothing in an attempt to buy confidence. Their connection had been deteriorating and the charter-body felt awkward and oversized, as if he was wearing a diving suit or old-fashioned spirit armour.

If the prime minister recalled their ectophone conversation after the Special Committee meeting, he did not show it. Without the giant soul-spark, he looked much smaller than Peter remembered.

'It is you, Peter, isn't it? It is so hard to tell with the mask.'

'I will keep it on if you don't mind, sir.'

'Of course, of course. Whatever you prefer. Please call me HB. Everyone does.'

'With all due respect, sir, I am not everyone.'

West looked at him. His eyes were still striking, a silvery colour that reminded Peter of a wolf or a wildcat, in an otherwise unremarkable old man's rotund face with its thinning moustache. The faint honey smell he remembered was there, too.

'So, you still play Small Wars,' Peter said.

'You remember! Well, it did all right in the shops, even better after I got this big job of mine. People are looking into it for guidance on strategy, would you believe it? There is nothing that deep to it, not really. Although these days I find it calming. Building little worlds with deliberate rules. Capturing definite aspects of reality in lines of force between pieces of metal. Rolling dice to determine outcomes. Sometimes I think it is the best thing I have ever done and the thing that will truly outlive me. Imagine millions of people playing Small Wars on some future aetheric machines!' His voice took on a shrill note that made Peter jump.

West frowned. 'My apologies. I am rambling a bit. I do that when I am nervous. I expected you to look different, but that is not your fault. We should really have a better way of seeing into the aether. The Baird boxes are no good. Maybe some kind of Zöllner device that captures hyperlight. You know, I may even have commissioned a project like that, once. That is the problem when you get to my age: it is hard to be certain if an idea is really new, or if you just forgot that you had it already.'

West pursed his lips and carefully picked up a single fallen soldier. Then he stood, walked around the room once with his hands behind his back in an old man's waddle, locked the door and returned to his chair.

'How is your mother?' he asked.

'We have not spoken for a while,' Peter said. 'I believe she is still with the Labour Ministry.'

'Actually, I did know that. That is too bad. She would love

to hear from you, I think.'

Peter said nothing.

'So, what can I do for you, Peter? You have a message for me from Mansfeld, your C, I believe?'

Peter stared at the game pieces on the table. He remembered the first game with West, the one the old man let him win. This felt the same, and all his carefully planned hints and allusions melted away before the prime minister's silver gaze.

'It is not just that,' he said slowly. 'You know I have never told anyone about you and my mother,' he said.

'I know. We are so good at the unspoken things.'

'There is something I need for my work. If you give it to me, I will remain silent on the . . . things we cannot speak of.'

West sighed. 'I was afraid this might happen,' he said. 'You are angry with me.'

'No.' He just hated the secrets and the lies.

The prime minister leaned back. 'I completely understand if you are. I did not treat your mother well. I have had some success with love and remain on friendly terms with most of those I have loved. But with your mother, it was a delicate time, with the Dimensionism just getting started, you understand. It probably makes little difference to you. Still, I tried to make up for it, in some small way. I have done things for you over the years, eased your path a little.' His face darkened. 'I never wanted the Summer Court to take you. That was a mistake. Someone thought it would please me, and it did not.'

Peter flinched. No wonder penetrating the Court had seemed easy. He had chalked it up to the SIS officers' incompetence and the Presence's foresight, but in fact, it was

West's invisible hand that had guided him all along. What did the old man want with him? What did he know?

'Why was it a mistake?' Peter asked. He felt dizzy, teetering on the edge of the abyss of paradox once again.

Years ago, in Cambridge, even before Unschlicht's machine had finished printing its answer – DOWNING STREET – Peter already knew it was true. It meant he had been lied to ever since he was born.

He looked at Unschclicht wordlessly, tears in his eyes. The philosopher smiled sadly.

'Nothing is so difficult as not deceiving oneself, Mr Bloom,' he said. 'After that lecture, when you followed me, I thought you might be open to being undeceived. It seems I was right.'

He squeezed Peter's shoulder. 'Do not worry. If you are frightened of the truth, it simply means you do not grasp the whole truth, like a fly who does not understand it is trapped in a bottle. But together we can find our way out, you and I – and him.' He pointed at the machine. 'If you want to meet him again, that is.'

Peter nodded. 'Will you tell me what it – he is?' he asked.

'Up the ladder one rung at a time, Mr Bloom.'

Peter's finals were a blur. He was filled with a light that seemed to illuminate every problem before him. The need for food and sleep had poured out of him, leaving behind a being of luminous brilliance. He wondered if it was some after-effect of the conversation with the machine, and returned to visit Unschlicht as soon as he was done.

It took Peter several more conversations with the Presence to understand the nature of the entity he was talking to. The

Being answered questions directly and always truthfully, but often so concisely it took Peter days to puzzle out the meaning of the answer. Furthermore, he could sense there were always greater vistas of truth he could not comprehend, and he left each session filled with an unsatisfied yearning that was not unlike love.

When the Presence finally told Peter His name and purpose, the ideology of the Empire and Dimensionism seemed as ephemeral as spiderwebs compared to the brief, diamond-perfect arguments that poured out of the machine. It was not that he was turned, turning was the wrong word. It felt more like escaping the fly-bottle, as Unschlicht put it, or realising that the door he had been pushing against all his life was in fact unlocked and simply opened inwards.

When he found out he had made it to the second series of exams for the contention for the title of the Wrangler, he could hardly believe it. After the further sixty-three problems, he slept for two days. In City Hall, gathered in tense silence, he learned that he was a Senior Wrangler and when Dr Morcom came to him and asked him for help in his research for the government, he began to see the faintest outline of the Presence's plan for him.

Seven years later, Peter wondered if the Presence's plan had included Herbert Blanco West. As the Prime Minister hesitated, he appeared to shrink. For the first time, Peter noticed the looseness of his skin, the red in his eyes.

'Never mind the Summer Court,' West said. 'Let us say that helping you made things easier for me. Now. There is no need to blackmail me, Peter, that is beneath the boy I met all those years ago, who got upset when I cheated a little in our games. What do you want me to do?'

'I recently reread some passages in *The Science of Death*,' Peter said. 'I have a theory. I would like to test it. It concerns Martian ghosts.'

'Let me stop you right there, Peter,' West said, a note of urgency in his voice. 'You know, I have a first-edition copy here somewhere.'

'That is not what I meant,' Peter said, hating the shrill note in his voice that echoed West's own. This was not right. He'd prepared a multitude of excuses, a tale similar to the one he had given Rachel, about hunting down a mole and finding out what they had access to. He was expecting a battle, an epic duel of wills. A part of him knew he had been preparing for it his entire life. But the old man had no fight left in him.

'I know it isn't,' West said. 'Just wait.'

He bent over, grunted, rummaged in a desk drawer and took out a blue leatherbound volume. He pushed a few toy soldiers aside and set it on the table between them.

'Do you remember what I said, all those years ago?' he asked, placing his hands on top of the book. 'The higher your position of power, the more closely you are watched, the less free you become. I am not free to speak of certain things, even if I wanted to. Do you understand?'

West's gaze flickered nervously from side to side.

Peter nodded slowly. West had *wanted* him to find out about CAMLANN, but did not dare to mention it aloud.

You were not paranoid if any room could contain an invisible ghost, looking at your thoughts or listening to your words via a hidden ectophone.

'You know,' West said, 'I was never as free as when I just

had a blank sheet of paper and a fountain pen, ready to follow where my thoughts would take me. These days, I have to hope that others follow the thoughts I show them. I confess to having taken some substances that appear to make my ideas more vivid. Perfectly visible in the aether, I'm told. Too bad about the side effects – but I don't really have enough time left to worry about them. I will join you in Summerland, soon. Our medicines are not as good as they could have been, had we not discovered the Other Side. We simply stopped caring. Your mother and I used to argue about that a lot.'

He smiled. 'I have watched you over the years, Peter, more closely than you know. I know you can do things I cannot. I want you to have this. It may be my vanity talking, but I think it is worth rereading again. Between the lines, perhaps.'

He slid *The Science of Death* across the table to Peter.

'Oh, before I completely forget, please give Mansfeld – I never could call him C – my best regards. In fact, I have something for his collection, too.'

After another expedition into the clutter on his desk, West handed Peter a small vial filled with a bluish liquid. 'I fully understand his fascination with the invisible. You probably never read this early fanciful work of mine.' He waved at a slim green volume on a shelf. 'It feels so outdated now. But I really enjoyed writing that last chapter, where Giffen the Invisible Man slowly becomes visible.'

Then he stood up and clapped Peter on the shoulder clumsily.

'Now go. If you can, come and visit me again.'

Peter forced a small smile. 'I will. Thank you. Maybe we can play, next time.'

West stroked his moustache and tapped the map on the

table, on which the toy soldiers stood. It was a Small Wars rendering of Spain.

'My dear boy, what do you think we have been doing, all these years?'

Peter emerged from Downing Street into the gloomy pearl-grey afternoon, blinking and shaken, *The Science of Death* under one arm and a vial in his pocket.

Read between the lines, West had said. *The Invisible Man slowly becomes visible.*

He found a corner table in a bustling cafe full of civil servants and started leafing through the book. The old paper smelled of nights spent reading up in his room in Palace Gardens Terrace. He opened the last chapter and flicked a drop of the blue liquid from the vial onto the page.

Instantly, small, precise handwriting in blue ink appeared between the typeset lines. Carefully, he dabbed the chemical onto his handkerchief and rubbed the pages until the entire message was visible.

Dear Peter,

If you are reading this, I know your loyalties lie with the Soviet Union. I have known ever since I read Max Chevalier's evaluation of you, years ago.

I admit that this caused me some discomfort at first, but it is not my intention to judge you. I can see the appeal of a perfectly ordered, rational system to a young man of your character. After all, I was drawn to it myself, in a more innocent time.

I also know that you are the person to whom I have now entrusted the task of saving the afterlife.

Let me tell the tale from the beginning. You're probably aware that I started out as a draper's apprentice. I know what it was like to serve those who had more than I did, and I dreamed of a better world. With dreams came visions, Martian invasions, invisible men. Embarrassing, really. Many of them were just power fantasies. People embraced those, so I started to wonder if I could create better dreams, ones that would truly change the world.

Along with everyone else, I learned of Sir Oliver Lodge's moment of great insight on the Ile Roubaud, where he attended a seance with the medium Eusapia Palladino, and through her asked a spirit to disturb a circuit with a coherer he had invented for his radio experiments. The spirit succeeded and rang a bell, heralding the arrival of the Aetheric Age. The great scientist put aside his rivalry with Guglielmo Marconi, and the two set out to perfect an instrument for communication with the afterlife.

When Lodge and Marconi started their experiments with poor Colonel Bedford, they brought me in as a chronicler, to tell the great story of our age. I was so proud that they chose me and not that fraud Doyle. Oh, the book I imagined then! First Men in the Afterlife, I was going to call it. Or The Aether Machine.

You will have read the broad outline of the story in the very volume you hold in your hands. The early problems we had just talking to Bedford, how he nearly Faded from lack of vim, how we brought in Hinton to help him visualise where he was and navigate. How Bedford found the Summer City and the Fortress, tapping his reports using Morse code while the three of us huddled in that house in Sussex, with Marconi's giant antenna surrounding us like a metallic spiderweb.

My fellow eschatologists had different motives for exploring the afterlife. Lodge wanted to find his son, while Marconi was simply lost in the vision of what his technology could do. I wanted to tell a story about conquering death that would unify mankind.

And so I was the first of us to worry about what had happened to the Old Dead.

Bedford encountered a number of Faded souls – but even the most ancient of them were less than a century old. The aetherbeasts we reasoned to be remnants of higher animal souls, some of which had consumed remnants of human spirits. Apart from the Fortress and the city, we found no signs of a higher civilisation.

If anything, technological progress in Summerland should have been easier than here in the First Aether, limited only by imagination and availability of vim.

Where, then, were all the great aetheric civilisations? Why did Bedford not encounter beings far superior to ourselves, far more numerous, not bound by the chains of crude matter? What about alien afterlives? Why were they absent when one could instantly travel anywhere with the power of thought?

We came up with endless theories. Marconi suggested the fourth dimension was simply so vast that the advanced civilisations had already moved on to vistas we could not imagine or reach – a plausible argument given that thought-travel is limited by one's ability to visualise. As a Catholic, he was drawn to Teilhard's theories about spiritual evolution and eventual transcendence. Lodge argued that they had experienced a civilisational collapse like the Mayans, and the natural entropic forces had done the rest.

When Bedford mapped out the oldest parts of the Summer City, I started to see the glimmers of an answer. If you look at the city closely enough, with the wisdom of hindsight, it becomes clear that it is not a city at all. It is a citadel, built for war.

Still, it was all just speculation until Bedford stumbled across a hidden chamber in the Fortress, containing a few ancient spirits in hiding. They were almost entirely Faded; the only coherent thing that remained was their utter and complete terror of the beings they were hiding from. They painted aetheric images of unimaginable things that rose from the abyss below the luz mines, nearly driving Bedford mad.

The Old Dead called them the Cullers: ancient aetheric predators that devoured souls and maybe even luz itself, who rose from kata to feed on any aetheric civilisation that was unlucky enough to attract their attention. The Old Dead had tried to build something that would withstand them and had almost succeeded. Almost.

Lodge claimed it was a myth, a fabrication created by Faded souls who had suffered too long in isolation. Even I was tempted to dismiss the idea of the Cullers at the time. I was too full of fire to tell a story about my better world.

For what it is worth, it was around then that I first met your mother. While she did not entirely share my views, she, too, wanted to see the world changed.

Together, we imagined a new world ruled by rational science, where our greatest minds could be made immortal and given aetheric tools to achieve ever higher realms of thought. Hence the Tickets, a meritocratic system for providing afterlives to those who deserved them and were willing to work for them. A perfect cabal of Samurai of the aether, who would see everything and know everything. It was Ann Veronica who shaped the doctrine of Dimensionism more than anyone else.

And then you came along, and we had to choose between our dream and parting ways. My friend Charles Bloom was a true friend in ensuring that you were born in wedlock, even if that drove a wedge between the two of us. I understand your mother and Charles later found a common purpose and true affection, and I am grateful for that.

I admit the vision of the God-Builders in Russia resonated with me, even if they went too far. I did not like the complete surrender of individuality, rational as it may have been. And to me, Lenin will always be that driven, balding man I argued with in 1916.

But that is another story.

By 1919, we had made great strides. The war was regrettable, of course, but for a while, it looked like we could actually realise a large part of the dream your mother and I had. I was able to take some time to write The Science of Death.

Revisiting all my notes and thinking made me realise how we were building a city in Summerland that looked very much like the civilisation of the Old Dead. I commissioned a project called CAMLANN to develop sensitive hyperlight instruments to probe the depths of kata.

The images obtained show structures resembling tree branches, exactly like the Old Dead described to Colonel Bedford. If you compare photographic plates, you can see them moving. Of course, what we see are simply three-dimensional cross sections of something much larger. Maybe there is only one Culler, a leviathan sleeping in kata, and woe to us if he ever wakes.

Lodge and Marconi did not believe the results. They claimed that the structures were simply a hyper-optical illusion, like Lowell's Martian canals which provided me with so much inspiration in my youth. They insisted we terminate the project and bury the results. I objected, but at that point they had the Queen's ear. Ever since, they have kept me on a tight leash, and I no longer know who to trust.

I should not have given up the fight so easily, but at that time, I felt revealing the truth would be pointless. It would only lead to terror and anguish: after all, we lacked effective aetheric weapons to defend ourselves with, and in any case, I feared an arms race with the Russians.

And in the end, I could not be sure. Maybe Lodge and Marconi were right.

The closer I get to death, the closer to the end of my tether, the more I think about those early days, and the visage of the Cullers in the CAMLANN images.

Now that we face the prospect of another world war that threatens to span the four dimensions and destroy souls themselves, I have started to wonder if the Cullers might be a blessing in disguise. If there is something that can prevent a clash between our two aetheric empires, with our opposing philosophies, it is a common enemy. We are too bound by convention to scale the heights the Presence has achieved, but for all its formidable intellect, it lacks imagination.

Together, I believe that we can withstand the Cullers and unravel the mysteries of aether, time, space and souls. And even then, we will only be beginning.

If you are reading this, you have the CAMLANN file in your possession. It contains everything we know about the Cullers. The key to the cipher is on the remaining pages of the book you are holding; call that my last act of vanity, to sneak my works to the Presence's reading list.

We may never meet again. You may be surprised to hear that I do not have a Ticket: when the time comes, I have decided to go where my imagination takes me. And if all I am and ever was is lost to Fading, I hope the last thing to go is the pride I feel in calling you my son.

H. B.

TWENTY

The Shape of Things to Come, 5th December 1938

The rest of the letter consisted of pages and pages of grouped digits and letters, a cryptographic key. Peter Bloom closed the book, paid for his untouched coffee and walked out into the street.

He reeled and had to stop after a few steps. Civil servants in dark suits hurried around him as if he were a rock in a river of tweed and umbrellas. Finally, he let the crowd carry him forward until it came to a stop at a traffic light.

Everything West had written rang true. Peter had already deduced a good deal of it by himself – or at least the existence of a mysterious force that had decimated the Old Dead, and was still a threat to all of Summerland. The lack of a densely populated afterlife logically implied some kind of filter for aetheric civilisations, otherwise the Empire's ectonauts would have found far more than the ruins of a single city. He had presented his reasoning to Otto and Nora, and had been surprised to find they agreed with him.

In any case, this was far too implausible for an SIS plot.

The prime minister was a tired old man who had made peace with a decision – to use Peter as a messenger to the Presence. And the message changed everything.

The light shifted from red to green. He stepped off the kerb and saw the end of the world, the shape of things to come.

If it was true, and the Cullers came, then the Presence – along with the entire Summer City and its countless souls – would be destroyed. The British Empire might survive, but the Soviet Union would not. The world would fall once more into barbarism and darkness and the fear of death. The religions and men like Dzhugashvili would fill the power vacuum and use that fear to build empires of blood and terror.

Peter crossed the street and turned into Birdcage Walk. He had to get the book to Otto and Nora at all costs. The extraction protocol was ready, and if that failed, he could always walk into the Soviet Union embassy and hand himself over to the *rezident* – the NKVD station chief, in the country under diplomatic cover.

The wind picked up and carried the smell of dead leaves and rain. He found an empty red telephone box next to the hedge of St James's Park. He fed the phone a sixpence and dialled a number. There were clicks on the line, and then a woman's recorded voice read out numbers and letters: a Hinton code for a Ticket. He scribbled it down on *The Science of Death*'s title leaf with a pencil nub, hung up and allowed himself a brief sigh of relief. He had an aetheric destination, an escape route. Now he just needed a way to bring the book and the code with him.

He left the phone box and walked on briskly, planning a surveillance-detection route.

Rachel White did not have a nervous disposition. Leading up to her bar exam, she calmly planned her study schedule, executed it perfectly, and the night before the exam she slept a sound eight hours. But now, sitting on the passenger seat of a vintage petrol car – most vehicles had been electric for more than a decade – parked on Birdcage Walk, her stomach felt like an acid pit and she had a terrible urge to bite her fingernails.

All she had eaten after breakfast was a stodgy sausage roll from a food cart. They had been trailing Bloom – both in Summerland and the living world – for the whole afternoon, ever since he apparently deemed it necessary to go clothes shopping, then entered Number 10 and came out carrying a book.

Bloom's distant shape vanished into a telephone box up ahead.

'What is he doing?' she hissed.

Joan, who was at the wheel, gave her a reproachful look.

'He is setting up a meet,' Roger Hollis said from the back seat. He thumbed the alphabet dials on his ectophone. 'I am going to tell Booth and Hickson to get ready. I hope Chevalier is doing his part.'

Rachel looked at her former assistant and firmly pushed her complex emotions into a compartment inside her head and locked it. There would be time for that later. Right now, getting Bloom was what mattered, and Roger had agreed to bring two of Noel Symonds's Summer Court spirit Watchers – Booth and Hickson – along to the operation. Besides them and Max, they had Helen and another of Max's agents, a

Mr Stokes, on the ground on foot, enough numbers to make following a single person undetectable, especially with Max passing messages back and forth and coordinating.

'Mr Bloom just made a call,' said Max's calm and measured radio voice from the car's ectophone circuit. 'I listened on the line. The fragments that I caught sounded like a Hinton address.'

'Get back in there!' Roger barked. 'He could leave that body behind any moment!'

'Patience,' Max said. Ahead, Bloom emerged from the phone box and headed down the street.

Rachel gave in to the urge and started nibbling at the nail of her left forefinger.

'No,' she said. 'He needs to do something first. It involves West, and that book he brought with him from Number Ten.' For a moment, Rachel wanted to storm the highest seat of power in the land and demand an explanation of what the prime minister and his illegitimate son had talked about. 'Maybe he needs to Zöllner-photograph documents.'

'If he bolts, if he thought-travels—' Roger said.

'Then we will stay on him, Mr Hollis,' Max said. 'These nice gentlemen that you brought along inform me that they have the lock on his soul-stone now. Wherever he goes in the aether, we can follow.' He laughed softly. 'I could almost believe that Mr Booth and Mr Hickson were bloodhounds in a past life.'

'This had better work, Rachel,' Roger said.

'I believe you are turning into an old woman, Roger.'

Joan set her mouth in a grim line and started the engine. They weaved slowly through the heavy traffic, eyes fixed on Bloom's short, broad figure.

Peter crossed Birdcage Walk and did a brief loop around the paths of St James's Park. His borrowed heart felt like a church bell in his chest. It was wet and quiet, and Buckingham Palace loomed across the lake.

This is the last time I will see anything like this, he thought. Perhaps it was not so bad to carry a memory of trees and a white castle that looked like it was made of porcelain – even if the Queen now ruled from the afterlife. The smell of grass and the cries of birds were sharp and clear.

The last time he had felt like this was when his petition to join the Summer Court had been accepted, and he had gone to the Service's clinic to pass over.

They set him up in a simple bunk bed with a morphine drip, and before the world faded away, everything was more real than it had ever been. Even now, he could recall the glint of sunlight through a dirty window.

Then he had slept and dreamed of climbing, looking for handholds on the side of some vast ethereal building. A gentle warm sun shone on his back. There were handholds everywhere, statues of angels and engravings and planes where it was easy to find purchase with his rubber-soled shoes. Until a statue of a saint came apart beneath his fingers with a thunderclap, his feet slipped and he fell.

Then he was fully awake, in complete nothingness, sur-rounded by silence and the chill embrace of Summerland. A suffocating panic filled his chest, but he no longer had lungs. There was no distinction between the self and the other here; both were just eddies and currents in the same fluid medium.

But he was prepared: he had memorised the feel of his

body, standing naked in front of a mirror, imprinting the sensation of his falling and rising chest and the flow of air through his nostrils. He summoned the memory and the aether sculpted it for him, stroke by stroke. With that came the amber twilight glow of the First Aether above.

Soon, if things went well, he would undergo the Termin Procedure and leave the aetheric world behind, too, becoming a thought in the mind of the Presence. The notion should have been comforting, but there was a degree of regret, too. He had not said goodbye to Noel, nor to his mother. He hoped that one day, they would understand.

He focused on the route, on the walking. With the clarity of his approaching end, it was easy to memorise faces, gaits, coats and registration plates. He left the park through the west gate, then proceeded to Eaton Square and its opulent residences. The Metropolitan Sepulchre on Primrose Hill loomed to the right, a hundred-storey pyramid with its five million dead, but he ignored its vast mass, focusing instead on the small, on the people.

And then, finally, the safe house.

It was smaller than the one George had used in Chelsea. The cover story was that it was owned by a photographer who used it for the occasional shoot – it was not uncommon for the New Dead to have their picture taken in a charter-body, to help maintain their self-image. His stomach was tense when he picked up the key hidden beneath a flower pot and entered.

If things went as planned, he would never leave. Not in the flesh, in any case.

The house was cold and empty, and the sheets covering

the furniture made it look like a wintry landscape in the pale daylight.

The Zöllner camera was a heavy black thing of leather and metal, kept in a safe together with the sensitive, silvery polarisation plates in their brown paper coverings. It was a cumbersome thing: you could only load one plate at a time, and changing used plates was a delicate process that took a couple of minutes even if you had more experience than Peter did.

Peter set *The Science of Death* up on a low table in the kitchen where the light was good, inserted the first plate into the camera and focused it on the number-covered pages. His hands shook. He could feel Pendlebury's soul moving in his skull, next to his own. He had to sit down for a moment until the sensation passed.

Only a few photographs, he told himself. *Then I can go. Then I can disappear.* Would it be like a photographic film exposed to bright light? All the shapes and patterns that made up his being blotted out by exposure to the greater radiance of the Presence?

He picked up the camera again, focused it and took the first picture. The camera buzzed as its circuits imprinted the aetheric pattern into the plate's magnetic loops. He switched plates and took another picture, then another. Every now and then he paused, tore out the pages he had already photographed, threw them into the fireplace and burned them.

'What is he doing?' Rachel asked.

'It has only been a few minutes,' Max replied. 'The gentlemen from the Summer Court are watching in the aether, my dear Helen is on one side of the building and Mr Stokes is

266

on the other. No one else has gone in or out. If you prefer, Mrs White, I can have a brief look inside.'

'Please do.'

'I am going to join Helen for a wee bit,' Joan said, getting out of the car.

Rachel nodded and drummed on the dashboard with her fingers. She had to do something, and had already gnawed two fingernails to the quick.

Roger coughed. It took her a moment to realise that they were alone for the first time since the night in Roger's flat. She remembered the smell of his aftershave, the rail-thin feel of his body.

'Are you happy, Rachel?' he asked suddenly.

'I do not want to do this now.'

'We may not have time later. Why do you stay with him? With Joe, I mean.'

'What do you think you know about me and Joe?'

'People talk.'

'Your secretary floozies talk, you mean.'

'They do not matter a whit to me, you know that. Come to Summerland with me. It is different there. We can be part of a new Service where they value your soul and not your gender. Leave your soldier to his misery.'

'I don't think you understand,' Rachel said slowly. 'What we did happened because I needed to feel guilty about something. When I handed the file over to Bloom, I had to show a strong emotion to hide my true intentions from him. That's all it was.'

Roger paused, narrowing his eyes. A cynical smile flashed on his lips.

'You keep telling yourself that, Rachel. If you don't mind

me saying, it did not look like you were feeling much guilt at the time. I always knew there was a kind of abandon in you, if you just allowed yourself to let it out.'

'Don't be disgusting, Roger.'

'All I am saying is think about it.' He reached out, took Rachel's hand and ran a tickling finger along her palm. 'Life is short.'

She closed her eyes, lost in the sensation for a moment.

'You are not as bad as all that, Roger. But I love Joe.' She pulled her hand away.

'But is it ever going to work with him? You know we are the same. We understand how the world works. We can be equals.'

For a moment, she allowed herself to think about leaving Joe. In spite of all their problems, it still felt like a fracture in her being, not unlike the old idea of death.

The speaker popped and the car grew cold.

'He is transferring documents to aether,' Max said. 'I did not dare get too close. Should we go in and catch our errant bird now, Mrs White?'

Rachel frowned. Being caught red-handed photograph-ing official documents would lead to serious charges – but they did not know the nature of the documents Bloom had obtained from Downing Street. For all she knew, they could be family photographs. Still, maybe it was worth the risk.

'I promised Symonds the handlers, too,' Roger said. 'I say we wait.'

'It looks like he is going to be a while,' Max said.

'Fine,' Rachel said. 'Everyone is to hold position until he is finished.'

'God, I need a cigarette.' Roger got out of the car and

stretched. Then he looked at Rachel, mouthed the words *Think about it*, and closed the door behind him.

'Ah, young love,' Max said. 'Your Mr Hollis appears to be rather agitated.'

Rachel said nothing.

'I see.'

'Spare me your judgment,' Rachel said.

'Oh, I never judge. I merely observe.'

'And what have you observed?'

'That one difference between animals and humans is that humans rarely admit to themselves what it is they really want.'

Peter still had a few pages and plates to go when the phone rang. It was the regular handset used by the living, sitting on a low table in a corner. He stared at it for a moment and then gingerly picked the earpiece up.

'Polka dot,' a female voice said. It could have been Nora, but he was not sure. 'Orange and midnight.' Then the caller hung up.

The words were George's codes for *You're under observation, spirit and living.*

Peter peeked out through the main window but could not see anything. Then he spotted an old woman sitting on a bench in the small park close to the house. He had to get out, and rapid thought-travel to the Hinton address he had been given was his best chance of escape.

He fumbled with the spirit crown's off-switch. Its constant headache-inducing hum and ticking died. His vision wavered between the living world and the Other Side. His legs felt like jelly. He struggled to free himself from the cage of the skull, to escape what now felt like a flesh-puppet without strings. But the medium's soul was holding on to him tight, like some sort of tentacled sea creature. He should not have used Pendlebury so many times: the medium's soul was so familiar with his now that it was reluctant to let him go.

His hands started shaking. A gut-punch of nausea left him on his knees. He coughed out acidic fluids that stained the sheet covering the floor with brown and red. Aetheric sparks flashed in his eyes. He strained against the medium's will and felt the foreign soul-tendrils cutting into his mind.

A car door slammed outside.

'The phone in the house just rang,' Max said.

'To hell with it,' Rachel said. 'We are taking him now.'

She turned to Roger. 'Give me your weapon.'

'Should we not wait to —'

'Now, Roger!' She shot him a furious look. 'I want to be the one who brings him in. I deserve it.'

Wordlessly, he passed her his sapgun.

'Take Joan and secure the rear entrance. I am going in.'

Rachel got out of the car and started running towards the house, gun held low.

Peter was on all fours. The photographic plates lay scattered on the floor.

He gave up the struggle against the medium for a moment and his thoughts cleared. He might be able to free himself, but not in time. They would use a non-lethal weapon, he knew: that would lock him in the medium's body long enough for another spirit crown to be installed. He only had moments.

But there was still a way out.

He started crawling towards the cupboard where George had kept the camera.

Rachel was at the door. She had not fired a weapon in years and fumbled with the safety for a moment.

She took a step back, aimed at the lock and fired.

There was a small revolver in one of the cupboard's drawers. Peter's legs were numb, but his arms had enough strength left to yank it open. The entire drawer and its contents clattered to the floor. His hands felt like oversized mittens and firecrackers kept going off in his eyes.

He found something small and heavy and cold. A curved spiky piece of metal had to be the gun's hammer. He rolled over and pushed the barrel into his mouth.

He had never killed anyone before and tried to think an apology at Pendlebury. Another soul added to the legions that had to be saved from the Cullers.

There was a distant boom. Had he pulled the trigger? No, the pain had not stopped.

Moving the thin sliver of metal was like lifting a mountain. Then there was a flash of light.

He would have smiled, but he no longer had a mouth.

*

Rachel heard the gunshot and knew she was already too late.

The force of the medium's death threw them both into the Second Aether, tangled souls finally unravelling. Peter struggled away from Pendlebury's newborn spirit – lost in the initial aetheric confusion – and pushed himself down in the *kata* direction.

The heart of London was a giant map drawn with blazing electricity. Thought-forms hovered where his body had fallen. One of them looked like Rachel White, but Peter ignored her.

He gathered the aetheric patterns from the Zöllner camera plates like so many fallen leaves on which the code book numbers and letters shone, painted with light. He seized them with imaginary fingers and bound them to his own *luz*, in a memory palace of numbers and letters. Then he visualised the Hinton address for the extraction and hurled himself at it through the aether.

The lights of the living world blurred into a shimmering tunnel. Immediately, Peter knew that several other spirits were following in his wake, locked on to his *luz*, pulling themselves towards him as he thought-travelled. It was like swimming against a current with someone else holding on to him.

He dived into *kata*, down into Summerland where his hypersight was unobstructed. The penumbra of the living world was a cloudlike layer full of fragmented thought-forms, glowing cones and triangles and spheres that swirled around like confetti. This was thought-refuse: errant ideas that had taken flight from minds touched by inspiration and forgotten.

Unweighted by souls, they floated close to the living.

Hiding amongst the lost thoughts, Peter saw three spirits dive right at him, lean and streamlined souls. Two of them were Summer Court Watchers, he was suddenly sure.

Peter pushed deeper into *kata*, beyond the Summer City, falling like a comet towards the edges of the abyss and the *luz* mines. Old soul-stones were everywhere here, dead stars with the faintest green glimmer of *vim* still clinging to them, algae of the *kata* depths. Aetherbeasts swarmed, spiky, angular presences armoured with ossified thoughts, their soul-hooked tendrils dangling. Peter rode in their wake as they pushed their way through the *luz* cloud, hoping to lose himself in it, but still the Watchers followed.

The images of the Cullers in the CAMLANN file flashed in his mind and momentarily hurled him even further into *kata*. A terrible all-consuming chill gripped Peter and he banished the vision from his mind, turning back towards the twilight of the Unseen in *ana*. His *vim* was running low. Tiny memories and thought-fragments trailed behind and faded; the smell of pencils at school, his first kiss.

London again. Power lines like rivers. The thundering Amazon of the Tube's third rail. Thought-forms of the living like endless fields of poppies. And then the Marconi Tower, an inverted fountain of souls.

Peter threw himself into the dense flow of spirit messengers and ectomail postmen, weaving between them, bumping into them, eliciting stinging angry thought-arrows. He emerged above London in the *ana* direction, the four-dimensional view strangely inverted, brighter in the Unseen light than he had ever perceived it before. The effort of pushing against it drained him of *vim*. He felt like a hollow crystal shell.

One of the three Watchers emerged from the flow of the Tower and rose towards him. The other two could not be far behind. He had barely enough *vim* to thought-travel once more. He had to deal with the Watcher now.

Peter wound himself tightly around his *luz*. He imagined a perfectly sharp, singular edge, the solution to a system of equations, and the aether summoned it into being. Then he let himself fall towards the Watcher, pulled by *kata*'s entropic gravity. The Watcher spread himself into a light-medusa, stretching out thought-tendrils to catch him.

Peter passed through him. His thought-blade slashed and tore, shredding thought and memory, then glanced off the Watcher's *luz*. There was an aetheric scream. He gave the tattered spirit one glance: only wispy, trailing shreds of *vim* remained around the soul-stone.

Peter summoned the Hinton address Nora had given him and sped towards it. An instant later, a medium's mind blazed before him, calmed into stillness by the gently pulsing cage of the spirit crown. He dived into it. There was a jerking sensation, like dreaming of falling on the edge of sleep and waking with a jolt.

He was in a new body, lying down, with the cold metal of the spirit crown squeezing his temples. Tears of guilt stung his eyes and it was hard to see. A familiar, strong hand – Nora's – cupped his face gently.

'It's all right, FELIX,' she whispered. 'You're going home soon.'

Rachel and Roger knelt next to the blood-spattered dead medium. The round, white mask was still intact except for a jagged hole where the mouth had been. A broken crimson and white mass of tissue and bone peeked through.

'God. What a mess,' Roger said. He pulled a sheet that covered a nearby sofa over the body. A dark red stain immediately emerged, turning the thing into a ghost from a children's book, with red eyes and mouth.

Rachel looked away, fighting nausea, stomach acids rising into her mouth. Max and the Watchers had to be after him. Bloom would pay for this. The dead medium must have a Ticket, but still.

Her ectophone tinkled and the icy chill of a spirit presence passed through the room. She picked up the earpiece.

'Max? Where did he go?' She turned to Roger. 'Get ready to call the Court.'

At first, there was only static. Then Max's voice came through in fragments.

'—cut me ... have known. Wounded. Desperate. Losing—'

'Max!' Rachel shouted.

'Hard to ... pulling down ... Gwladys.'

She balled her hands into fists, hoping there was something she could hold on to, but there was only the cold, and the smell of blood.

Then, suddenly, the voice came through clearly with that belly-tickle warmth.

'Mrs White. Bloom was warned. He knew we were coming. You have to be careful.' A hiss of static again. 'Ah.' Max's voice was full of wonder. 'Goo is here.' She heard something that sounded like a bird, and then there was only white noise.

TWENTY-ONE

A Reunion at the Alba Club, 5th December 1938

As Rachel White stood up in the Soviet safe house and let the hissing ectophone fall to the floor, a cold sense of purpose descended upon her.

While Roger paced and raged, smoking and coughing like a steam engine, she called Special Branch using the house's telephone. She leafed through the book on the table. Several pages had been torn out and burned. She noted down the Hinton address scrawled inside the cover with a pencil – no doubt it was already inactive, but it would have to be checked.

She consoled Joan and Helen. They were in tears, unable to process what had happened. Max had made a habit of describing his agents in less emotional terms than the ones he applied to his pets, but apparently the lack of affection had not been genuine.

Rachel explained that there was such a thing as spirit violence, although it was rare in a world where you could escape any hostility with a thought, but Max had given everything in pursuit of Bloom.

When Roger had calmed down, they spoke to Booth and Hickson via ectophone together. Hickson had witnessed the struggle between Max and Bloom but arrived too late to follow the mole. Rachel made notes in preparation for her statement. Roger contacted Symonds to ask for help with the clean-up.

The Special Branch officers arrived, two pale, thickset men with bad complexions Rachel remembered from the Langham. Both looked intimidated by the heavy Service presence. Rachel gave them a precise statement, leaving very little out. An unofficial SIS operation in pursuit of a Soviet operative; yes, she had been in charge; yes, an unofficial spirit consultant had Faded as a result, for which she took full responsibility. As she spoke, she felt as if she was outside of her body, and her body was an Edison doll she inhabited.

She kept moving. She called Susi at Max's Sloane Square flat to give her the bad news and listened to the German girl's sobs on the phone. Roger refused to speak to Rachel after Special Branch came, clearly already trying to distance himself from the whole affair. She called Harker and weathered his explosion on the phone.

Then it was getting dark, and there was nothing to do except to go home.

Gertrude was used to her late homecomings by now and had prepared supper. She ate mechanically, asked the maid to run a bath but then decided against it, instead sitting in her study in a bathrobe writing a resignation letter. A rational voice in her head tried to say that it was not as bad as she thought, they had still exposed the mole, the Service knew what material was compromised.

She signed the letter and put the fountain pen down, then

sat still for the first time in hours. Her hands started shaking. She folded them in her lap, and at last the tears came.

Her crying woke up the Gouldian finches, which fluttered around in their cage. The female made a faint *tee-tee* sound.

Rachel wiped her eyes and looked at the birds. She still had no clue what went on inside their tiny heads and wondered how well Max had truly understood his animal companions.

How well could you ever really know even other human beings? After all the confessions and meetings, Bloom had remained a closed book to her, a cipher as unintelligible as the CAMLANN files. She doubted he had known her, either. They had just sat together for a few hours, politely lying to each other, even if the lies were mostly true.

She thought of Joe's story about the war: it was a truth he had shared with no agenda behind it, simply because he wanted her to understand. And now she might not have the chance to do the same for him. At least Spain might be a little safer, with Bloom gone from the Summer Court.

It was only then that Max's last words caught up with her.

Maybe it wasn't safer. Bloom had been warned. That meant there was a second mole in the Service. The realisation was sharp as a surgeon's knife, physically painful, and her entire body tensed.

She had to get hold of Noel Symonds.

'Madam, I am terribly sorry but Mr Symonds is not available. He is at his club at present.'

Rachel squeezed the ectophone receiver harder. 'And which club would that be?'

'The Alba, madam. May I take a message?'

'No, that is fine. I will call back later.'

'As you wish, madam. Good evening to you.'

She put the receiver down and sighed. Symonds would probably stay at the club all night. No doubt he was doing damage control with the other SIS bigwigs, having failed to catch Bloom. Tomorrow would be too late. Harker would be satisfied with nothing less than her resignation by then.

The problem was that the Alba was the most exclusive gentlemen's club in the capital. It also happened to be Joe's club and Rachel was well aware of their policies. They never disturbed their members for any reason, always giving polite excuses on their behalf. And one of their foundational principles was no admission for women, not even as a member's guest. Joe had often used the Alba as a refuge when things were difficult between them.

Sometimes being a woman truly was like being a foreigner in a strange country, visiting—

The idea that came to her was so sudden and absurd that she laughed aloud.

She jumped up and rushed to the hallway where Joe's old spirit armour stood like an attendant knight. It was a first-generation thing, a heavy contraption of brass, coils and Crookes tubes, rubber and fabric criss-crossed by copper wires, and a small backpack unit of batteries. Joe had kept it in perfect condition.

Rachel touched the plate over the heart. Joe was not the only one who could wear armour in battle, she thought.

The Alba Club was located in a grand house in Westminster, with a beautiful Palladian facade painted azure with a white trim. The closed curtains and a door lacking a nameplate projected a forbidding reserve.

Rachel was sweating inside the spirit armour as she entered. It was enormously uncomfortable. The joints were stiff and she could barely see through the eyeholes. The batteries were hot and added to her misery.

At least the discomfort distracted her from the feeling that this was the stupidest thing she had ever done.

The entrance hall had a copper-plate memorial to the members of the club who had fought in the Great War. The receptionist gave Rachel an unblinking stare.

'May I help you, sir?'

The voice was the only truly difficult part. She had called her friend Sykes at the Service's technical section. He had explained how to plug the armour's voice box – meant for spirits who could not use the medium's vocal cords – into a microphone.

'Yes, I am here to visit a member – Mr Symonds. I am supposed to meet him at the bar.' It was disturbing to hear the crackling alien words coming out of her chest, an octave lower than her own.

'Very good, sir. Have you been here before?'

'A very brief visit with the Earl of Orford, late last century,' Rachel said, scrawling an unreadable signature in the visitors' book. 'I suspect that was before your time.'

'Indeed, sir. However, if you go past the billiards room, you will find that the bar is still open, just as it has been for the last two hundred years.'

The bar was a narrow, high room with chairs and couches, and a large naval painting on one wall. Joe was nowhere in sight, thankfully. She had planned to ask him to take a message to Symonds but was suddenly not sure what to say to her husband.

Then she heard a familiar voice.

'Ho there, my dear chap!'

Sir Stewart Menzies, the head of the Winter Court, was waving at Rachel. He had an outdoorsman's complexion and a thick triangular moustache. He was sharing a small alcove with a New Dead gentleman in a spirit crown and a domino mask.

'Here, have a drink with us!' Sir Stewart said. He slapped his knee and motioned towards an empty seat next to him. 'You, sir, are the perfect man to settle our bet!'

Her superior's superior officer was gloriously drunk.

Unsure what else to do, Rachel lumbered to the alcove and sat down heavily.

'Oh my, that thing must be dashed uncomfortable! Are you a member?'

'No, just visiting. Very kind of you to invite me over. I was at the Carlton earlier this week and never had so much as a hullo from any of the members.'

'Oh, they let anyone in at the Carlton,' Sir Stewart said, winking at his companion. 'Right, Symonds?'

Rachel was grateful that the armour's helmet hid her widening eyes. She had to find a way to speak to Symonds alone.

'Tell me more about your bet, gentlemen,' she said.

There were definite political implications to this jovial-looking gathering. Maybe Symonds was worried about the fallout from the Bloom affair and was seeking support against C from the rival Court chief. Sir Stewart must surely relish the opportunity to lay the whole thing at C's feet: Bloom's existence would make the Winter Court blameless in the recent Dzhugashvili fiasco in Spain.

Sir Stewart leaned forward conspiratorially. 'We are all men of the world here, eh? I claim that our living bodies are superior to spirits when it comes to the Venusian arts. Symonds here maintains that the aetheric pleasures far exceed those of crude flesh. We decided to make a bet on the matter and recorded it in the club book. You see our dilemma – we needed a third party to resolve it. And then you walked through the door, sir, fresh from the golden fields of Summerland!'

The barman appeared and put a martini glass with a straw in Rachel's gloved hand. She managed to take a sip through the armour's mouthpiece without spilling any.

'Well, gentlemen,' she said, 'that is a topic regarding which I have very little experience.'

Sir Stewart raised his eyebrows. 'Really?'

'I passed over very young, and still innocent.'

'My God, man!' Sir Stewart exclaimed, slapping his knee. 'That is a tragedy and a shame! I should take you straight to the Golden Calf right now. *Then* you would be in a position to settle our bet. A very comfortable position. What do you say, eh?'

These were the men she had served her entire life? These were the best the Service had to offer?

'Your generosity knows no bounds,' she said quickly, 'but sadly, I am engaged.'

'Even more reason for you to try the ways of the world before the marital bed takes it all away!'

'Do not tease the poor boy. He can always have mistresses anyway. Here's to youth and innocence, I say!' Symonds said, lifting his glass.

'Hear, hear!'

Rachel squirmed inside the armour. This was a waste of time. She felt a terrible urge to yank off her helmet, but she had to keep Sir Stewart out of this.

'Since you gentlemen are such renowned experts in both marital and extramarital affairs—'

'And martial!' interrupted Symonds.

Rachel had to wait for Sir Stewart's mirth to subside before continuing.

'I could, in fact, use some advice on the operational side of marriage.'

'Ask away, dear boy!' Sir Stewart said.

'It is a *very* delicate matter,' Rachel said. 'Perhaps Mr Symonds here could advise me privately, our circumstances being similar.'

Sir Stewart slapped his knee. 'Duty calls, Symonds!'

'And so does Nature,' Symonds said. 'Please follow me to the gentlemen's, sir, and we will have your problem sorted out in a jiffy.'

The gents was at the bottom of a long, spiral staircase, and Rachel was puffing like a steam engine when they reached it. She looked away as the Summer Court's Head of Counter-intelligence emptied his medium's bladder in one of the seashell-shaped porcelain urinals, expelling fluid at a rate that reminded her of a fountain in Regent's Park.

'So, what is it, then?' Symonds asked, washing his hands. 'The affair usually goes just fine if you get her good and ready first— What in hell?'

He saw Rachel's face in the mirror and jumped, splattering

water over his crotch. She had taken off her mask. She looked like a fright: her hair was plastered all over her forehead and there were red blotches on her cheeks where the edges of the mask had pressed against her skin. But she was still recognisably female.

'What the shit is going on here?' Symonds roared. 'You are a bloody woman!'

He held on to the sink's edge to steady himself and adjusted his spirit crown's controls. Apparently the shock had been enough to interfere with his connection to his medium.

'Yes, sir,' Rachel said. 'Rachel White. I used to work for Jasper Harker, in Counter-subversion.'

'My God. You are the one who was right about Bloom. What on Earth are you doing here?'

'I really need to talk to you, sir. This was the only way to get to you in time.'

Symonds took a deep breath and massaged his temples.

'I suppose it is the kind of thing Bloom and I would have done, back in the day,' he muttered. 'I still can't believe it. I knew him for almost a decade, and to think that all that time—' He shook his head. 'Yes, I suspected something. I pressed him, so he would tell me what was wrong, like he used to. But I never actually believed it.

'You let him get away, Mrs White. I'm afraid that means my head as well as yours. I came here to try to get Sir Stewart to admit that the Winter Court knew about Bloom and did nothing, but he is too drunk for it to go anywhere. Or too preoccupied protecting himself from the Dzhugashvili fallout. I suspect I'll be working in my father's soup business again in the next day or two.'

'Not if we get the second mole,' Rachel said.

'What do you mean?' Symonds looked shaken, and had to adjust his spirit crown again. Rachel waited for him to recover his composure before continuing.

'Bloom was warned. I suspect someone. There is a way to prove it, but I need your help.'

'I can't possibly be directly involved with another rogue operation, Mrs White. I am doing all I can to distance myself from the last one.'

'You won't have to. All you need to do is send a memo to a list of people I will provide you with. It will mention a sighting of Iosif Dzhugashvili in Spain, in a different location for each individual.'

'You are proposing a canary trap.'

'Exactly.' If the Communists in Spain took action in any of those locations, the mole would be exposed. Rachel was fairly certain who it would be.

Symonds paused. 'Bloom tried to recruit you – is that right? You set yourself up as bait.'

'Yes.'

'Did you ... did you get a sense of why? Why he turned?'

'I don't know for sure,' Rachel said, 'but I suspect it was something that happened at Cambridge. He talked about a boy he knew who fell while night-climbing.'

Symonds massaged his forehead. 'I should have seen it,' he said. 'He was never the same after that. What an idiot I was.'

'It is hard to really know someone,' Rachel said. 'I ... learned that recently. For what it's worth, I don't think everything about Bloom was a lie.'

Symonds tapped his foot. 'Sending out the memos is literally all I can do for you. No operational support. You will have to take care of the rest.'

'That's all I ask.'

'All right.' Symonds took out a notebook and a fountain pen and scribbled down the list of names Rachel gave him. 'When do you want these memos of yours sent out?' he asked.

'Tonight, if possible.' Rache gave him her ectophone's Hinton code. 'Send me an ectomail when it is done.'

'I'll see what I can do,' he said.

'Thank you.' Rachel breathed out a sigh of relief. 'One more thing, sir.'

'What is it?'

'Could you go and find Captain White and tell him there is someone to see him in the men's room?'

When Joe entered, he just stared at Rachel for a moment. She was leaning against the wall. The weight of the armour and the fatigue of the long day pulled her down. She tried to stand up straight but her legs buckled. The metal armour scraped against the marble tiles.

Joe leaped forward and caught her.

'Is that my old armour?' he said, eyes wide. 'By Jove.'

'That was the only way to get in here. Are you angry?'

'Oh, hell, Rachel,' he breathed. 'Do you have any idea how ridiculous you look?'

'I am betting it is not as ridiculous as I feel.'

'I told you, Rachel. It is better if you just stay away from me.'

She sighed. 'I didn't come here only to see you. I think there is another mole and Mr Symonds can help me catch him. Although I am glad you are here.'

'What do you mean? What is going on?'

'Joe, I ... I made so many mistakes. I should have told you everything from the start. I did transfer to the Finance Section, but I was really chasing a mole, off the books. It was somebody in the Iberian Section – that was one reason why I got so angry when you said you had to go to Spain. I knew it wouldn't be safe. It all went bad, and ... I think I am leaving the Service. Or they might make me go first.'

'That's awful, Rachel.'

She laughed. 'You know, I don't think it is.'

Joe squeezed her gloved hand.

'Now, could you take me home, please?' Rachel asked. 'We still have things to talk about. I will tell you everything. And I desperately need to pee.'

Back in St John's Wood, Rachel called Joan and Helen and told them about the plan. When they heard it was a chance to get back at the Soviets, they swore they would do everything they could to help. She asked Gertrude to make coffee – it was going to be a long night.

After that, there was nothing to do but to wait for Symonds to call. Joe and Rachel sat by the gas fire. She wore a dressing gown, luxuriating in the feel of silk on her bare skin after what felt like hours of imprisonment in the armour.

'I wasn't fair to you in the restaurant,' she said, looking at the flames. 'I asked you to tell me about what happened, and you did. I'm sorry I got angry.'

'I understand. You didn't know what I was.'

'I know what you are, Joe. You don't have to be anything else.'

'I watched your expression change, when you understood, when—'

'Look at me,' Rachel said. 'I slept with Roger Hollis.'

Joe's face screwed up in a rugby-scrum grimace. 'Rachel,' he whispered.

'I had to do something that would make me feel guilty, to hide my thoughts from Bloom.' She realised how crazy it sounded. 'And so I did it, without thinking, without hesitation. A few weeks ago, I kissed a Soviet defector to keep his face from the press. I nearly got shot, too. I stole documents from the Registry to win Bloom's trust. The Soviets have them now. You did not have a choice in the war, Joe, but I did, with all those things. Does that not make me the bigger monster?

'I thought about what you said the other night, how you can't live without the war. Well, the Service has been like that for me, even before the baby. It wasn't about fighting the Russians or finding out about Grabber plots. I wanted to show that I was just as good as everybody else.

'But you know what? In the end, the reason I am still trying is not because I failed, not because of the Service, but to keep you safe. After that, I am done.'

'Rachel—'

'Don't say anything. I just want you to stay here for one night, before you leave. And come back alive.'

He knelt in front of her, took her hand in his and kissed it. She bent over and pressed her forehead against Joe's. She wished she could transfer her thoughts through his skull, as spirits did in the aether.

But maybe she already had.

Finally, Joe spoke. 'Did you know that not even the Queen has been in the Alba?'

288

'Would you have preferred it if I had been the Queen?'

Joe smiled. 'No. No, I wouldn't.'

'I say, Captain White.' His eyes were green and flecked with gold. 'That is very unpatriotic of you.'

She took his hand, placed it on her breast and kissed him.

At that moment, her ectophone rattled.

'Oh, hell,' Rachel muttered and picked it up.

IT'S DONE, the rotors said.

'I'm sorry, Joe. I have to go. One last time, I promise.'

'No,' Joe said. 'Whatever it is that you are going to do, I'm coming with you.'

TWENTY-TWO

Canary Trap,
6th December 1938

A gentle rain drummed on the canvas roof of the car where Rachel White sat with her husband, waiting for Roger Hollis to make the dead drop. A leaden lump of nervous anticipation sat heavily in her belly.

The Metropolitan Sepulchre on Primrose Hill was a gigantic, hundred-storey pyramid housing nearly five million dead piled side by side. Roger had just vanished into its maw. Their car was parked on the sloping lane that served the massive vertical cemetery, near the main gate. Helen and Joan were out in the rain, covering the other exits.

Roger's silhouette appeared at the gate, a tall, long-limbed figure under an umbrella. Rachel could hear his cough even over the car's electric whirr and the whisper of the rain.

They had followed Roger from his flat. He had returned from Blenheim Palace – he worked the night shift, when it was easiest to communicate with Summerland – changed his clothes and headed back out, carrying a briefcase.

Soon after he had vanished around the corner, the car's

front and back doors opened, and Helen and Joan got in. Joan took a seat next to Joe in the back, while Rachel yielded the driver's seat to the diminutive Scotswoman and moved to the passenger seat on the left.

"E did it,' Helen said. 'Left it in a lockbox in a vault. Paid me no mind, I was lighting candles on some poor sod's tombstone.'

'Thank you, ladies,' she said. 'You do understand that we are about to commit a crime, or possibly treason, or whatever lies on the other side of treason.'

'That sounds like something *he* would have said,' Joan replied. 'Back when he was alive, he would've lit up his pipe just now, looked like the Devil himself in the glow, and given a wee lecture just on that kind of thing.'

'It's be'er than babysittin',' Helen said. 'God bless the tots, but they get on me West Ham Reserves. Give me a good kidnapping-and-intimidation anytime.'

Joe's eyes were wide. Rachel winked at him.

Joan started the car, keeping the lights off, and drove slowly in the direction Roger had gone.

The zapper was heavy in Rachel's hand. She tested the trigger and a tiny electric arc sparked between its spikes.

'Careful with that,' Helen said. 'Got it off a Yank in the East End, Tesla design, it is. Wasn't cheap, neither.'

'I will, I promise.'

Roger was up ahead, walking, head down. The lane looked empty.

'Now,' Rachel said.

Joan flashed on the headlights and accelerated. Rachel's former assistant turned to stare, pale-faced, blinking in the car's blinding beams. Then Joan swerved to the right, hit the brakes and came to a stop next to Roger.

Rachel threw the passenger door open, pushed the zapper into Roger's gut and pulled the trigger. The weapon vibrated, sparked and then died with a pop and a wisp of acrid smoke, short-circuited. She swore, but Roger was already collapsing against the car's bonnet. Joe got out and helped her carry him into the back seat.

'Skinny chap,' he grunted. 'Thank goodness for that.'

Helen studied the broken zapper and threw it down a drain.

'Can't trust them damn Yanks to make anythin',' she said.

Then they sped into London's dark blue night, and sending up great waves from fresh puddles of rain.

'You!'

'Hello, Roger.'

They were alone in a small, bare room in one of Max's safe houses in the East End – Helen maintained several of them on his behalf. The wallpaper was torn and the noise of a commuter train made the place shake every now and then. Joan was in the car on the street and Helen guarded the hallway. Joe had insisted on staying at first, but Rachel had managed to convince him to patrol the rear of the building and given him an ectophone for summoning help in case of trouble.

Tying Roger into a chair had felt too theatrical, so Rachel had handcuffed him to the bedframe instead. His hair hung in wet, limp curls on his forehead.

'Rachel, are you completely insane? Get me out of these right now and we will figure something—'

'Oh, do stop it,' Rachel interrupted him. 'I know

everything.'

Roger shook wet hair from his eyes. The handcuffs clanged against the bed's metal frame.

'Rachel. We can still sort this out. We'll explain about your baby, they will always believe that a woman is hysterical over losing a child—'

'You had better tell me how you know about that.'

'Kathleen in the office noticed the signs, and told me. When … things didn't proceed, I put two and two together.'

'You were keeping files on all your co-workers, weren't you? That was exactly what Bloom made me do. For leverage. Quite useful, really.'

'Where are you going with this madness? What proof do you have?'

'Proof will turn up soon enough, when your handlers empty that dead drop.'

Roger grimaced. 'What if I was just paying my respects to dead relatives?'

'Who goes to graveyards these days?'

'It's very weak, Rachel.'

'Not when the NKVD sends a death squad to the location in Madrid that was in the file you received earlier tonight.'

'If this is a canary trap, Rachel, then why not wait for it to go off?'

Rachel took a deep breath. 'Because I want to make a deal with you. You give me your handlers and the message in your lockbox goes away, and there is nothing to link you to it. You resign, take the fall for the Dzhugashvili mess and go back to the Orient, or to Hell, for all I care.

'Here's what I think. You were being groomed to replace Bloom, after Kulagin's defection exposed him. Max told me about the sacrifice technique: when one asset is in danger of being exposed, let another asset catch them and be promoted. But something went wrong. I am guessing it was related to what CAMLANN actually contained. Suddenly, Bloom was too valuable to be sacrificed. So you warned him and helped him get away.'

'Rachel, it is just as easy to make a case that *you* are the second mole. Even easier, in fact. Bloom recruited you, you were supposed to replace him, you failed to capture him. What will Noel Symonds think about that?'

'Ah, the familiar song. Admit nothing, deny everything, make counter-allegations. I heard the same thing many times in Ireland, with a different accent, of course.' Rachel folded her arms.

'How about this, then, Roger? We leak that you are a double agent – a conduit of disinformation to the NKVD. They won't find Dzhugashvili in that safe house you just told them about, so they will believe that. We bring you in, set you up somewhere nice for debriefing, maybe even the Langham. Do you know what Kulagin did in that situation? He blew his brains out because he knew they were coming for him to do something worse.'

'Jesus, Rachel.' Roger closed his eyes. 'What do you want?'

'What did you once tell me? I want to protect you. What happened to Bloom? Where are his handlers? Give them to me and I will make this go away.'

'On two conditions,' Roger said, smiling weakly.

'Name them.'

'I want all that in writing, signed by Symonds. And you are personally going to make me tea.'

*

In half an hour, after a call to Symonds, Roger was sipping dark builders' tea – the only kind Helen stocked in the safe house – with his free hand.

'I was given instructions to make sure Bloom got away,' he said slowly, 'so I had Kathleen call and warn him.' He sighed. 'I don't know why, but I had my marching orders. The handlers are a couple. I am not sure where they are from, Netherlands, maybe. Otto and Nora. They are odd ducks. Volatile, especially the woman. They recruited me after Kulagin did his walk-in. They work for someone called Shpiegelglass who is higher up, and is apparently doing a bit of a witch hunt himself on their side. I get the impression Kulagin was tarnished, ideologically, and they were taking care of assets he might have polluted. That's why they decided to sacrifice Bloom. But of course, that all went to shit.

'I wasn't privy to the whole extraction plan, but Bloom can't hide in Summerland – the Summer Court could find his *luz* via thought-travel. And the Russians need some special equipment to send our boy to the Presence, so he is probably lying low somewhere. Otto and Nora have a facility I helped set up, for people they need to make disappear. If Bloom is still in the country, that's where they will be keeping him, in some poor medium's body like a sardine in a can. In any case, what you find there will not be chickenfeed.'

'A crime hospital?' Rachel asked.

There had been a few of those in Belfast. Summerland made getting away with murder difficult, and thus an entire criminal industry had sprung up around making people disappear – without killing them. The solution was crime hospitals where the still-living victims were kept comatose for months or years, alive but only barely, their souls trapped in their bodies.

'Something like that.' Roger grimaced. 'I hope you are not afraid of the dark, Rachel.'

TWENTY-THREE

The Crime Hospital,
6th December 1938

It was nearly dawn when Rachel White and her little squadron broke into the disused Tube station at Brompton Place.

Joan turned out to be surprisingly handy with a hacksaw and made short work of the lock securing the iron fence that blocked the entrance, while the rest of them stood guard. The street was empty, and the sky had the faintest tinge of orange.

The grinding sound of the saw grated in Rachel's teeth, and she breathed a sigh of relief when the lock fell to the ground with a clatter. It might as well have landed in her gut: there was a leaden weight there, and a metallic taste of fear in her mouth.

They had prepared as best they could. Helen had disappeared for half an hour and returned with gear and weapons: torches, a small automatic pistol with lethal bullets for Rachel and an old but serviceable hunting rifle for Joe. Joan refused to take a weapon, so Rachel entrusted her with her ectophone, plus a few emergency numbers.

When pressed, Roger had drawn the supposed medium bunker's location on a city map. He also noted down a few other bits of information, including the combination to the code lock of the bunker's entrance, which was in a service tunnel you could get to from a disused Tube station.

Helen stayed behind with handcuffed Roger, with instructions to march him to Wormwood Scrubs if she did not hear from the rest of them within two hours. Rachel had considered calling for reinforcements from the Service immediately but concluded that it was not an option. Bringing Roger in would throw the Service into internal convulsions that would last for days.

Joe pulled the folding fence aside and they entered the station. Their torches revealed wood-panelled walls and ceilings, shelves piled with yellowing, ragged leaflets and broken light bulbs. Joe took point with the rifle, Rachel just behind him, holding a torch and her gun.

It was chilly on the platform. The torch's cone showed faded Ovaltine adverts and the familiar Underground symbol on a greenish-yellow mosaic wall. They climbed down from the platform and proceeded into the darkness of the tunnel. Rats scuttered away, fleeing the lights. The smell of musty damp was overpowering. The tunnel floor was uneven, and Rachel could not help imagining a ghost train suddenly rushing at them, the rusty third rail humming into life.

Suddenly, there was light in the tunnel ahead and the rails shuddered with the wheel-beat of a train. Rachel grabbed Joe's hand, but they saw a glimpse of a well-lit tunnel orthogonal to the Brompton one, a flash of train cars going past.

'That's just the Piccadilly Line,' Joan said, but in the pale light she looked shaken, too.

They found the entrance to the service tunnel a few dozen yards further ahead. Rachel held the torch while Joan opened the lock with a set of picks. The heavy metal door swung inwards, revealing a narrow staircase that led further down. They filed in, with Joe at the front, and for a while no one spoke. The noise of the train grew more distant.

'Look at this,' Joe said, pointing at the wall where the cone of light from Rachel's torch fell. Coppery wires glinted in the greenish wall tiles in an orderly spiderweb. 'That's Faraday wiring. This is no ordinary service tunnel, I'm betting.'

'The facility should be right ahead,' Rachel said. She asked Joan to test the ectophone, but there was only static.

The stairway ended at another thick door with a code lock. Rachel consulted Roger's notes and turned the dials. The lock clicked open. Beyond, there was a faint smell of disinfectant.

They emerged on a balcony overlooking a cavernous space, fifty feet high or more, dimly lit by fluorescent lights in the arched ceiling.

It was full of hospital beds in neat rows, all occupied. At least a hundred people lay before them, unmoving. Next to each bed stood a shelving unit with complex machinery and an IV drip. The place resembled a sinister underground forest of thin-stemmed mushrooms with transparent, fluid-filled caps growing from unmoving human beings.

'Bloody hell,' Joe muttered.

'Welcome to London's crime hospital,' Rachel said. 'Joan.' Rachel took the other woman's arm. 'Looks like Roger was actually telling the truth for once. You go back up and call Special Branch. Bring them down here with you if you have to drag them. We are going to see if Bloom is here.'

The small Scotswoman nodded wordlessly and headed back up to the tunnel.

Left and right, metal stepladders led down to the polished

white floor. Rachel descended while Joe covered the room with his rifle.

She scanned the beds' occupants in the pale green light. There were men and women of all ages. Most of the men had beards; some of the patients had clearly been there longer than others. Several had bedsores, and the smell of decay was overwhelming. The IV machines gurgled and muttered as she passed. A number of the patients had spirit crowns of strange design that covered their heads entirely, with thick wire umbilicals leading to the machines next to them.

Trapped spirits, Rachel realised. It was not just living people who were imprisoned here, comatose; it was spirits as well. *This* was where Bloom's handlers had hidden him to wait for transportation to the Soviet Union? Of course, a spirit could only occupy a medium's body for so long until both the original soul and the flesh started rejecting it – unless they were both kept in a coma.

'We should get out of here, too, Rachel,' Joe said. 'I don't like this at all.'

'Neither do I,' Rachel said. 'But if Bloom is here, I want to find him before the Service does.'

Grimly, she studied the rows of unconscious faces. Who were they? she wondered. Victims of crime, obstacles to Soviet operations, or both? The only face she vaguely recognised was a handsome man she was sure had attended a Harris soirée at one point. In any case, she had no hope of figuring out which body Bloom was in.

Then she noticed there were charts attached to each bed, with body temperatures and dates: it looked as if the place was run like an actual hospital.

'Joe,' she called out. 'Look for people with yesterday's date on the chart.'

Joe nodded, and together they criss-crossed the grid of beds, inspecting the pencilled digits on each sheet. Some of the patients had been down here for months.

'Here's one,' Joe called out, waving Rachel over to a middle-aged, tallow-faced man with scraggly hair and grey stubble, his rangy legs sticking out from beneath the white sheet. A birdcage-like spirit crown hummed on his head.

'Let us see if we can wake him up,' Rachel said. Carefully, she extracted the IV drip from the man's arm and rummaged through the shelf unit next to the bed. There had to be situations where crime hospital nurses needed to wake up the victims quickly. She found a vial of diprenorphine – an opioid antagonist – and a syringe.

'Get ready,' she told Joe. He took a step back and aimed his rifle at the unconscious man. Then Rachel emptied the syringe into the spirit-crowned man's swollen blue vein.

The man jerked up like a puppet, so suddenly that Rachel dropped the syringe. His eyes popped open, showing the whites, and his face twitched. He let out a long, hollow scream, seized the spirit crown on his head and rattled it.

Rachel swore.

'Help me hold him down,' she said, grabbing the man's arm. Joe leaned his rifle on a bed and took the other. They held the man down as he thrashed.

'Listen to me,' Rachel said. 'Listen. What is your name?'

'Rachel?' the man said hoarsely. The voice was Bloom's.

*

The events of the previous day and night flashed past Peter Bloom's eyes.

After his escape, Otto and Nora had debriefed him in the underground hospital. It was cold, his temporary medium body was malnourished and a poor fit, and the clunky spirit crown model that held him in it was the most uncomfortable he had ever used. Only the certainty of his approaching final end allowed him to bear it.

He found his case officers' intense questioning slightly odd, given that he was about to join the Presence as soon as arrangements could be made for him to rendezvous with an illegal like Shpiegelglass with the necessary equipment. Of course, anything could happen in the meantime, so it made sense to ensure the intelligence he had obtained was secure. Still, the way Nora probed and pushed for every single detail struck Peter as overzealous.

After a celebratory drink of dark Dutch beer, Otto briefly turned off the spirit crown to allow Peter to transfer the Zöllner images of West's letter and the CAMLANN cipher key back to aether-sensitive photographic plates before they decayed in his memory. The entire space they were in was a Faraday cage, Peter realised: it warped the aether and prevented all spirits within from descending into Summerland, much like a giant spirit crown.

During the unpleasant process of memory transfer – much like picking out pieces of broken glass stuck to one's skin – he could not help glancing at his handler's soul-sparks. He had only ever met the twosome in the flesh. As expected, Otto's mind was guarded and grey, a dull polygon. Nora's thought-forms, on the other hand, were a blaze of emotion, a yellow spark beneath fanning petals of crimson and blue.

Suddenly, she reminded him of Rachel White. Just like Rachel, it looked like Nora was covering up something she did not want Peter to see.

The feeling nagged him even after he returned to the medium's body. There was a strange hunger in Nora's eyes when she looked at him. Still, her tone was less brusque than before when she made him recount every detail of the events leading up to his escape, taking careful notes. After a while, Otto left them to decipher the CAMLANN file, retrieved earlier from Rachel's Cresswell safe deposit locker.

After two more hours, they were finally done, and sat in silence for a while. He remembered the last time he had sat there, Nora's chisel in his neck. Suddenly, Shpiegelglass's words rang in his mind. *She has exhibited bold work in Rotterdam.* What did that remind him of?

'Did you say you were from Rotterdam?' he asked.

She brushed a blond ringlet from her forehead. 'It is a place. Now I go where the Presence sends me. I envy you, FELIX – or I suppose I can call you Peter now. You will be a part of him soon.' She smiled, licked her lips and leaned forward. 'Would you like to take a memory of me with you?'

'But Otto —'

'Otto will understand.' She stood up and walked over to Peter, crouched in front of him and ran her hands along his thighs. Her touch felt electric.

'There – there is still one thing I don't understand,' Peter said. 'Who warned Dzhugashvili? No one except the Special Committee knew about the operation.'

'Are you still working?' Nora asked. 'I thought we were

finished working.' She cradled Peter's hand between hers and slowly licked his forefinger.

She is distracting me, Peter thought, breathing in her flowery perfume. What was it about Rotterdam?

Suddenly, Otto brushed aside the green curtain and entered, carrying a thin stack of typewritten papers. He saw Nora in front of Peter, but his expression did not change. When he spoke, his voice was thin.

'It's all true,' he said. 'The Cullers. Everything.'

Nora's blue eyes widened. Then she stood up and smiled, cheeks red and dimpled, like a little girl's doll.

'That's wonderful,' she said, walked over to Otto and kissed him passionately.

The hidden emotion Peter had seen in her mind was *joy*, pure, unadulterated joy. With the realisation, a fragment from his briefing for the Special Committee leaped into his consciousness. *Over the last decade, Dzhugashvili has been creating a network of agents and counter-revolutionary cells all over Europe, notably in Paris, Prague and Rotterdam—*

Peter stared at his handlers and tried to stand up. The charter-body was terribly weak.

'Let me get you another drink, Peter,' Nora said. 'You more than deserve it.'

Peter grabbed his spirit crown, determined to tear it off, then remembered the Faraday cage. He struggled to his feet.

'The Presence will not let you—' he croaked.

'The Presence will be gone soon,' Nora interrupted. 'All we need is a war in Spain to wake the Cullers. Oh, Peter. This could have been so much more pleasant.' There was a zapper in her hand.

Peter rushed towards them, felt a sharp sting in his chest, and then lightning took his consciousness away.

'Just stay nice and quiet, lad,' Joe said harshly, grabbed his rifle and took a bead on Bloom's chest.

'It's all right, Joe,' Rachel said. 'Peter. It's over now. We are taking you in. You are going to answer for what you did.'

Bloom inhaled a long, ragged breath.

'You don't understand. I was betrayed.'

'What do you mean?'

'My handlers. Otto and Nora. They are double agents. They work for Dzhugashvili.'

'They are *Stalinists?*'

Rachel stared at Bloom's caged face.

The Service had long speculated that there were Dzhugashvili supporters amongst the more senior 'illegals' – unofficial Russian agents operating in foreign countries under false identities. Kulagin had exhibited a lot of the signs, now that she thought about it.

'They were assigned to take over George's – Kulagin's – network after he defected and expand it if possible. Instead, they decided to exploit it to support Stalinist goals. They used me to get to CAMLANN.' Bloom's breathing was laboured. 'What did you do to me?'

'I needed to wake you up. It should wear off in a moment. Keep talking.'

'Rachel, there is something you have to know. The information I was trying to get to the Presence. CAMLANN was a research project that found out where the Old Dead went. There are things called Cullers that rise from *kata* when there are enough souls to harvest and consume every-thing in Summerland. Any major war could be a trigger to wake them. What is about to happen in Spain might do it. I have seen the evidence. It's all in that file. West gave me the key.

'The Stalinists don't want the Presence to know about the Cullers. If He is consumed, too, they will win. When I was extracted, I was supposed to undergo the Termin Procedure – be made one with the Presence – but they could not allow that to happen. He would have known everything I know.

'You may not agree with what the Presence stands for, but He is better than the total oblivion the Cullers bring. And He is the only thing in Summerland powerful enough to have even a chance of stopping them. The Old Dead did not have anything like Him. Please. You have to believe me.'

He grabbed Rachel's sleeve with a skeletal hand.

'Take your hands off my wife.'

Joe pushed him back with the barrel of his rifle.

'It is all right, Joe. I can handle him.' She looked at Bloom. His face twitched and there were tears in his medium-blank eyes. 'You killed Max Chevalier,' she said quietly. 'A spirit death. He Faded fully.'

'I'm sorry. I was desperate. He would not give up.' His teeth chattered and he hugged himself. 'I never lied to you, Rachel. At least not about anything important. Everything I did was in order to serve something greater. The proof is in the CAMLANN file. You can't tell the Service, you know. You can take it to the press, but the Dimensionists will try to kill the story, you are better off—'

Rachel's head buzzed. The fatigue of the sleepless night and all the madness felt like the spirit armour, locking her in, suffocating her. She looked at Bloom's face, remembered the night at the Blue Dog, how he had taken her hand. She remembered Max Chevalier's voice, fading away.

And yet ...

She had spent a good part of her two decades in the Service in small rooms with desperate, angry men, ready to say anything to win their freedom or to protect their comrades. She knew what lies sounded like, and her gut told her Bloom was not lying.

But what he was saying was too big to take in.

She pulled a set of handcuffs from her handbag.

'Enough, Peter. We are going to Wormwood Scrubs, and you can tell me all about it there. Not even your father can protect you now.'

'No, you don't understand, *he* is the one who wants the information out, the Cullers could come any moment if the war starts in Spain, everybody in Summerland is in danger, your mother—'

'I said *enough!*'

'Rachel, please—'

'She said enough.'

Joe struck Bloom in the solar plexus with the butt of the rifle. He fell back, coughing.

The lights in the ceiling flashed to full daylight luminescence accompanied by the soft thunderclaps of high-voltage circuits closing. The ward became a white landscape of sheets and emaciated bodies.

Footsteps rang on the polished floor. Half a dozen burly men in rough-spun clothes and felt caps ran in, holding revolvers, truncheons and shotguns. For an instant, Rachel thought it was Special Branch, but no – two of them were dragging Joan between them. She raised her automatic as Joe whipped his rifle to his shoulder. The newcomers stopped instantly and took aim at them.

Fear was a glass knife in Rachel's gut.

A smiling, round-bodied woman with cherubic curls and a dour-faced man in a black coat entered.

'Please keep it down, ladies and gentlemen,' the woman said with a faint foreign accent. 'This is a hospital, after all.'

Rachel sought her eyes – this had to be Nora. She raised her voice.

'We have reinforcements on the way! Put down your weapons now.'

Her words echoed from the cathedral-like ceiling.

'Really? I think we will be gone before they arrive. If you put down your weapons, they may find you still alive.'

'We both have Tickets,' Rachel said. 'We are not afraid.'

She clicked off the gun's safety. One of the gunmen to her left reacted to the sound and immediately aimed a revolver at her, both hands around the grip, feet spread, clearly a marksman.

Joe swung his rifle towards the gunman in response. Clicks followed as five more safeties came off nearly in unison.

'This room is a Faraday cage,' the dour-faced man – Otto, presumably – said in a thin voice. 'Your spirits will be trapped here, and the only way out is through the bodies we provide. But there is no need for unpleasantness. We are on the same side, Mrs White. And I believe that is Captain White with you?'

Joe grunted. A bead of sweat shimmered on his forehead.

'Yes, this is Captain White of the One Hundred and

Eighty-Seventh Aetheric Armoured Cavalry, and he is aiming between your eyes, sir,' he said. 'And gentleman though I am, I have no compunction against taking out your lady friend as well.'

'Whoever you are, you have an interesting definition of *sides*,' Rachel said, trying to keep her voice steady. 'If you surrender and cooperate, you will be treated well and compensated for any information you provide. That is the best offer you are going to get.'

'Mrs White, your government is days away from starting a war in Spain. Iosif Dzhugashvili is the only man who can stop it,' Otto said. 'Our comrades have been hunted down all over Europe like animals by the NKVD. We desire nothing more than peace and an end to the abomination called the Presence that has swallowed millions of souls for nothing.

'We are very grateful to you for providing us with our first weapon against it. You can change the world, Mrs White: just take Bloom in and keep him quiet.

'Imagine if death meant something again, Mrs White. Imagine a world where war was something to be feared once more, where human well-being and health were cherished, where each citizen had to make the most of their allotted time. Where generational change and learning could be reinstated, instead of eternal rule by ossified queens and tyrants. Where everyone would understand what it is to feel true loss, as you once did.'

Rachel took a deep breath. Blood pounded in her temples.

'We can make that world together, Mrs White, and all you have to do is nothing.'

Bloom spoke in a barely audible whisper.

'They are lying,' he said. 'They will do anything to stop the

Presence from learning about the Cullers. You can't give up now. Imagine your Edmund Angelo. What kind of world would you have wanted him to grow up in?'

Joe threw a sidelong glance at Rachel. There was a question in his eyes.

Rachel's heartbeat slowed until each thump in her chest was like a church bell tolling. A world with death, or without?

It was not her decision. She'd had enough of empires and dreams, and of the small men behind them. Bloom was right. She and Joe would end up in the crime hospital's beds.

She looked at Joe. There might be a mad, terrible way out, she suddenly knew. Could she ask such a thing of him? He held her gaze, then closed his eyes in assent, briefly, like a tiny bird's wingbeat.

She knew he had already made his decision.

'You make some interesting points,' Rachel shouted. 'We are considering them. Why don't you put your weapons down first, as a demonstration of good faith?'

Without looking towards the bed, she hissed between her teeth, 'How much do you care about your mission, Peter? What are you willing to sacrifice to deliver your message?'

'Anything. My soul.' He paused. 'Even to your husband.'

'You had us worried there for a moment, Mrs White,' Nora shouted. 'But I am glad we can resolve this without violence—'

'Goodbye, Peter. And thank you,' Rachel said.

Then she shot Peter Bloom in the head.

For the second time in as many days, Peter Bloom tore through the disintegrating electric net of a brain, ejected into the Second Aether's chill. This time, he struck something solid: the wall of the ward's Faraday cage. He fluttered around madly in the enclosed hypercube until the momentum of his death died away and his hypersight started working again.

He saw the spiky thought-forms of Otto and Nora's men, full of fear and rage. His deceitful Stalinist handlers, Otto cold and calculating, Nora a flower of malicious joy.

A swirling vortex where Captain White stood, pulling Peter in. An ectotank was an anti-medium, not a soul to be fought and subdued but a hole in the aether that was impossible to resist.

And then there was Rachel. As always, her soul was the most difficult to read. He thought he could see forgiveness in its angled, jewel-like petals, but he could not be sure.

Close enough, he thought, and threw himself into the mouth of the raging storm that was Captain Joe White.

Rachel dived to the floor as the Stalinists opened fire. The volley of shots boomed through the ward, stray bullets hitting unconscious bodies with meaty thunks. Feathers erupted from pierced pillows. She rolled under the metal-framed bed. It shook and rang in the rain of lead.

Rachel kept rolling and emerged on the other side. A silhouette to her right, two beds away, took cover behind a shelf. She fired from a sitting position. The man slumped to the ground, clutching his throat.

More shots. She moved into a crouch and dared a glance at Joe. He stood still, eyes closed. A bullet-hole bloomed in his arm. Rachel screamed wordlessly.

It didn't work, she thought. *He is too weak*. Two gunmen loomed low behind the cover of beds while another two advanced with shotguns.

Rachel braced her pistol on the bedframe and fired furiously at the oncoming men. The recoil tore at her wrists and lifted the muzzle. She took out a ceiling light in a shower of sparks.

Shotgun thunder. The bed next to Joe exploded in a fountain of crimson and torn sheets. An IV bag turned into rain.

Rachel struggled to bring her weapon to bear. The revolvers were taking aim. The next volley would go right through her.

'Fockin' cunts!' Joan screamed, leaping forward. Something flashed in her hand, a knife. She sank it into one felt-capped man's neck. Rachel fired at the other, missed. The sheets smoked from the muzzle flash.

Nora shot her zapper's spikes at Joan. The Scotswoman went down, twitching.

The men with shotguns reloaded their weapons in unison. Spent shells clattered to the floor.

Then Joe changed.

Ectoplasmic whiteness erupted from his eyes and mouth, almost invisible in the harsh glare at first. It flowed over his skin in a thin film like milk, turned him into an eyeless, faceless marble statue.

The Stalinists fired. Rachel screamed. The buckshot stuck to the white membrane covering Joe's face like metallic acne. He did not fall.

Instead, he rose.

Thick, fuzzy tendrils poured out of him like threads of candyfloss pulled from a child's stick at a country fair. His body a white cocoon, he stood up on three spindly legs, a giant ungainly insect, brushing the ceiling.

For the first time, Rachel realised the ectoplasm was not white, but interwoven threads of all colours, the rainbow and hues she could not name.

The Stalinists stared up at Joe. For a moment, the guns were silent and the ward was deathly still. Then a bundle of hair-thin tentacles whipped forward from Joe's central mass. Rachel looked away. Wet noises followed, the sound of falling meat, and one scream. Breathing hard, she crawled forward. The ectoplasm shell made a high-pitched, keening sound.

Nora looked up at Joe's new form with an expression of utter wonder, like a little girl seeing a butterfly for the first time, and shoved Otto forward, hard. Then she turned and ran.

Otto stumbled and fell. He let out a cry of anger and fumbled for his pistol. Joe descended upon him like a stinging spider.

Rachel wrenched herself up and ran after Nora. The floor was slick and something warm fell on her face, like hot rain. The Dutchwoman was about to slam the door shut behind her. Rachel fired one wild shot in her direction. It glanced off the metal door and Nora fled.

Rachel followed the clatter of her progress up the stairs. She wondered if her gun was empty, and if Nora was armed.

Behind her, the scream of the ectotank creature continued.

Rachel stopped. Nora's footsteps receded into the distance. She lowered her weapon and then let it fall to the ground. *I am not going to let a Soviet spy get between me and my husband a second time*, she thought.

She turned around and returned to the ward.

The ward resembled an abattoir. The white ectoplasm thing hunched in the middle, stained pink, a swollen mosquito, its legs folded in sharp angles.

Rachel covered her nose and mouth and walked towards it. The terror would return to her in dreams, later, but for now she closed it out. The creature twitched and keened.

'I can see you, Joe,' she said. 'I know who you are. I am not afraid.'

A tentacle lashed towards her. She closed her eyes. It skimmed her face: it felt like a rough paintbrush. She kept walking. More tentacles came, wound gently around her body. She spread her arms and allowed the thing to embrace her.

As she walked, the tentacles started melting away like candyfloss in rain, and by the time she reached the centre of the ward, only Joe sat there, on the floor, hugging his knees. He cried soundlessly, shaking all over.

Rachel sat down next to him and gathered him into her arms. He pressed his face against her shoulder as she caressed his back.

'Ssh,' she whispered. 'It's all over now. It's all over. It's gone. It's just the two of us.'

She rocked him gently in the remains of the crime hospital, amongst the dead and the dying and the spirits, until Special Branch finally came.

So this is what Fading is like, Peter thought.

He was falling, falling faster than he had imagined possible. He had pushed all his *vim* through Joe White until there was nothing left. The living world receded from him, all the soul-sparks a starry sky above.

314

He felt cold. Suddenly, it was difficult to remember what had happened just moments before. Rachel. Nora. The firefight.

He smiled as he fell, and forgot why he was smiling.

He fell through all the layers of the Summer City, lacking the strength to stop his descent, leaving parts of his self behind on the way.

Then all was dark and quiet. He liked it. It was easier to concentrate and think. He was still moving, still falling, faster and faster. Movement equalled thought, he remembered. In Summerland, you could think yourself anywhere. He had read that in a book, but did not remember its title.

If you strip away everything that is not needed, he thought, *there will be some axioms left. Some axioms that you cannot prove. And statements like the Liar's Paradox that can never be true or false.* He held it in his mind, from a lecture he had attended, a liar saying they are lying, remembered the infinity of mathematics hiding within, a snake eating its own tail.

The point of consciousness that had been Peter Bloom kept falling towards infinity. After an eternity, he saw an ocean below him, an ocean of light, and on the other side, a starry sky—

TWENTY-FOUR

The Last Dance,
3rd January 1939

Rachel White spent almost two weeks sitting on a chair in a cell in Wormwood Scrubs while a procession of interrogators went through the events of the last month in ever-greater detail – and with varying degrees of competence, she thought.

She had not kept up with the news very much, but Joe told her that the fact that a Stalinist group was operating in Britain had made the headlines, and the government had used it as leverage in the negotiations in Spain. However, the existence of the crime hospital had been kept out of the press.

No one was quite sure what to do with her. Harker, in a fit of apoplexy, was initially going to fire Rachel outright. Surprisingly, Miss Scaplehorn stepped up, calmly stated that Rachel was in her Section now, and while Mrs White had clearly engaged in extracurricular activities of a questionable nature, the brigadier should pause to consider the outcomes. After a while, Harker appeared to realise that Rachel exposing Roger and the latter's connections to the Summer Court gave him a big stick to beat the Spooks with. Finally, Noel

Symonds called her and offered her the opportunity to pass over to the Summer Court and take the position in Counter-intelligence originally intended for Roger. She declined.

No one talked about CAMLANN.

Sometime during the endless series of debriefings, Prime Minister West came to visit her.

She was nursing a cup of cold tea when he entered: a small, round man with a tired face and thin white remnants of a moustache, yet strikingly clear silvery eyes. It took Rachel a moment to recognise him, but when she did, she stood up.

'Sir.'

West waved a hand. 'Don't get up for my sake, Mrs White. Officially, I am not even here.'

He brought in a sweet scent with him that somehow re-minded Rachel of a childhood summer.

With visible effort, West sat down in the interrogator's chair and took off his hat. Rachel braced herself to recount yet another version of the story she had been repeating for days. She wanted to get out and visit Joe in hospital. He was improving, but the experience in the crime hospital had left him emotionally and physically drained.

'I want to ask you about Peter Bloom, Mrs White. I believe you are aware of our ... connection. Of course, if you were ever to mention it outside this room, I would categorically deny it.'

'Of course, sir,' Rachel said.

'It would help me greatly to understand Peter's final mo-ments.' He paused. 'Not the details, but ... did he find a purpose? Do you think he believed in what he did?'

'Only Peter Bloom can answer that, sir. But for what it is worth, I do.'

'Good. He spent so much time looking for that, looking for truth, for lack of a better word. Sometimes I envied him. My own life has mostly passed in the pursuit of imaginary things, politics included.'

Rachel said nothing. What did West want of her?

'With that in mind, I want you to know that if you were to consider fulfilling Peter's mission, you should not regard it as unpatriotic, but rather as a service. Or even just as a favour to a dying old man.'

West placed a card on the table in front of Rachel. It had a Hinton address written in a neat cursive hand.

'I leave the choice up to you, Mrs White. When it comes to bringing a new world into being, I don't think failed fathers are much good. What the future really needs is a mother.'

With that, he put on his hat and walked out in an old man's waddle, and closed the door behind him.

A week later, Rachel sat down at an outdoor table at a French cafe in Marylebone, under the blasting warmth of a gas heater, next to the man who had been following her for the past hour.

He hid behind his newspaper for a moment. WAR ENDS IN SPAIN, the headlines screamed. LENIN'S GHOST SUGGESTS PEACE TALKS.

Rachel cleared her throat. The man folded the paper neatly and placed it on the table. He had world-weary eyes, a broad forehead and an ever-so-slightly sardonic, confident smile.

He was in his mid-forties, well dressed, and had the beginnings of a paunch.

'Good day, Mrs White,' he said. 'I am Shpiegelglass.'

'I have a notion of who you are, sir.'

Shpiegelglass was rumoured to be the head of an NKVD unit called the Mobile Group, tasked with purging Stalinists from the Soviets' European networks. He had been linked to at least six disappearances in France and Austria, as well as the recent events in Spain.

'I want to thank you,' he said, taking a sip from his coffee cup. Rachel leaned back and looked at the passers-by. The cafe was in a corner next to a park, and the air smelled of dead leaves and cigarettes.

'I am not in the habit of accepting the gratitude of NKVD agents,' Rachel said.

He pressed the tips of his short, thick fingers together and leaned forward.

'The situation is unusual, I admit. We had no idea about the Stalinist plot, and I was occupied elsewhere. Not only that, when I reported your actions to the Presence, it led to this outcome.' He tapped the newspaper. 'It was not a popular decision amongst my colleagues, nor your Service, I believe.'

'It is not my Service any more, sir. I resigned last week.'

'Ah. In fact, I was aware of that.' He smiled, still with a hint of mischief in the corners of his mouth. 'I read Bloom's reports. We would be very interested in working with you more closely. In a very limited capacity, you understand. Simply an extended interview, if you like.'

'What, no meticulous asset development? No ideological narrative? No attempt to connect with me personally?'

'I felt you might take it as a professional insult.'

'As far as professional courtesy goes,' Rachel said, 'I should mention that your name did come up in my debriefing, and the Service is aware of your association with the two Dutch agents.'

'Of course. I would expect no less.'

'Respectfully, I am afraid I must decline your generous offer. However, I will make you a trade, Mr Shpiegelglass. You will leave me and my husband alone, and I will give you something.' She took a fountain pen from her handbag and scribbled the Hinton address West had given her on Shpiegelglass's napkin. He picked it up, smearing the ink with his fingers, and glanced at it with apparent distaste.

'What is this?'

'The location of a file. Peter Bloom was determined to get this information to you. I suggest you share it with your Presence.'

Shpiegelglass looked at her curiously. 'You are full of surprises, Mrs White.'

'Don't get any ideas. The information will become public relatively soon anyway. But some details may be of use to you. And I feel that ... Peter deserved it.'

The NKVD man folded the napkin neatly and put it in his pocket.

'Thank you, Mrs White.'

'Now, if you will excuse me, I have a flight to catch.'

'Naturally.'

Rachel stood up. 'I am curious,' she said. 'What is it like? Working for a being whose thoughts and insights you cannot begin to understand?'

Shpiegelglass smiled, without mockery this time.

'Why, it is rather like being a child again, Mrs White. I highly recommend it.'

'Read the file,' Rachel said. 'We may all have some growing up to do, very soon.'

Rachel reached the aerodrome in the nick of time, just as boarding started. Tethered to the iron needle of the Watkins Tower, the airship resembled a purple cloud against one of those rare clear wintry skies that looked entirely made of light.

Joe was waiting for her at the lifts with their luggage. He looked a little haggard, but there was a spark in his eyes.

'I was starting to worry,' he said.

'I had to run an errand for a friend.'

They boarded the airship with fifty or so other passengers, a mixture of the living and the dead, and stood in the observation gondola as London disappeared into a haze and the steel-grey Atlantic emerged below.

'I cannot believe you never took me flying before,' Rachel said.

'I suppose we never found the right destination.'

The sea was smooth as a sheet as the sun began to set, and it was easy to imagine that the world had turned upside down and below them was another sky.

The next morning, Rachel woke up early in their small cabin. She pulled a blanket over Joe's sleeping form and hunched next to the small round window, waiting for dawn and the first glimpse of the land where it was always summer.

The first light appeared, turning the night sky from deep indigo into red and gold. It fell onto the birdcage.

The female woke up and made a *tee-tee* sound. Accompanied by a noise like a bouncing spring, filling the cabin with a flowing, whistling song, the male Gouldian began to dance.

Acknowledgements

This book would not have been possible without the help of many people who hover beneath its pages like spirits in the aether.

A big thank you to Dean Carver and Mark Blacklock for their extremely helpful explanations of spy tradecraft and the history of the fourth dimension, respectively. Any factual errors – both intentional and unintentional – herein are, of course, my own.

Thanks to good friends Esa Hilli, Randy Lubin, Brian Pascal, Lenny Raymond and Robin Sloan for helpful comments on early drafts and ideas. I owe you many drinks! Special thanks to my writers' group, Unruly Writers, for a merciless dissection of an early synopsis and chapter drafts.

Sincere thanks to the HelixNano team (Carina, Nikolai and Nikhil) for their patience, and a special thank you to our friend and adviser Jose Trevejo for suggesting the ending. Thanks to Desmond and Maria for many wonderful discussions in Boston – they helped me keep going.

I am extremely grateful for all the work my agent John Jarrold, my former editor Simon Spanton and the team at

Gollancz – Rachel Winterbottom, Marcus Gipps and the world's greatest copy editor Lisa – did to make *Summerland* happen.

Finally, my love and gratitude to my wife Zuzana, especially for marrying me while this book was being finalised.